Men Like Gods

DOVER THRIFT EDITIONS

H. G. Wells

DOVER PUBLICATIONS, INC.
MINEOLA, NEW YORK

DOVER THRIFT EDITIONS

GENERAL EDITOR: SUSAN L. RATTINER
EDITOR OF THIS VOLUME: JIM MILLER

Bibliographical Note

This Dover edition, first published in 2016, is an unabridged republication of the work originally published in 1923 by The Macmillan Company, New York.

International Standard Book Number

ISBN-13: 978-0-486-80836-9
ISBN-10: 0-486-80836-X

Manufactured in the United States by LSC Communications
80836X03   2017
www.doverpublications.com

CONTENTS

BOOK THE FIRST
THE IRRUPTION OF THE EARTHLINGS

BOOK THE SECOND
QUARANTINE CRAG

BOOK THE THIRD
A NEOPHYTE IN UTOPIA

CONTENTS

BOOK THE FIRST

THE IRRUPTION OF THE EARTHLINGS

MEN LIKE GODS

CHAPTER THE FIRST

MR. BARNSTAPLE TAKES A HOLIDAY

§ 1

Mr. Barnstaple found himself in urgent need of a holiday, and he had no one to go with and nowhere to go. He was overworked. And he was tired of home.

He was a man of strong natural affections; he loved his family extremely so that he knew it by heart, and when he was in these jaded moods it bored him acutely. His three sons, who were all growing up, seemed to get leggier and larger every day; they sat down in the chairs he was just going to sit down in; they played him off his own pianola; they filled the house with hoarse, vast laughter at jokes that one couldn't demand to be told; they cut in on the elderly harmless flirtations that had hitherto been one of his chief consolations in this vale; they beat him at tennis; they fought playfully on the landings, and fell downstairs by twos and threes with an enormous racket. Their hats were everywhere. They were late for breakfast. They went to bed every night in a storm of uproar: "Haw,

Haw, Haw—*bump!*" and their mother seemed to
like it. They all cost money, with a cheerful disregard of the fact that everything had gone up except Mr. Barnstaple's earning power. And when
he said a few plain truths about Mr. Lloyd George
at meal-times, or made the slightest attempt to
raise the tone of the table-talk above the level of
the silliest persiflage, their attention wandered ostentatiously. . . . At any rate it *seemed* ostentatiously.

He wanted badly to get away from his family to
some place where he could think of its various members with quiet pride and affection, and otherwise
not be disturbed by them. . . .

And also he wanted to get away for a time from
Mr. Peeve. The very streets were becoming a torment to him, he wanted never to see a newspaper or
a newspaper placard again. He was obsessed by
apprehensions of some sort of financial and economic smash that would make the great war seem a
mere incidental catastrophe. This was because he
was sub-editor and general factotum of the *Liberal,*
that well-known organ of the more depressing aspects of advanced thought, and the unvarying pes-
simism of Mr. Peeve, his chief, was infecting him
more and more. Formerly it had been possible to
put up a sort of resistance to Mr. Peeve by joking
furtively about his gloom with the other members
of the staff, but now there were no other members
of the staff: they had all been retrenched by Mr.
Peeve in a mood of financial despondency. Practically, now, nobody wrote regularly for the *Liberal*
except Mr. Barnstaple and Mr. Peeve. So Mr.
Peeve had it all his own way with Mr. Barnstaple.

He would sit hunched up in the editorial chair, with his hands deep in his trouser pockets, taking a gloomy view of everything, sometimes for two hours together. Mr. Barnstaple's natural tendency was towards a modest hopefulness and a belief in progress, but Mr. Peeve held very strongly that a belief in progress was at least six years out of date, and that the brightest hope that remained to Liberalism was for a good Day of Judgment soon. And having finished the copy of what the staff, when there was a staff, used to call his weekly indigest, Mr. Peeve would depart and leave Mr. Barnstaple to get the rest of the paper together for the next week.

Even in ordinary times Mr. Peeve would have been hard enough to live with; but the times were not ordinary, they were full of disagreeable occurrences that made his melancholy anticipations all too plausible. The great coal lock-out had been going on for a month and seemed to foreshadow the commercial ruin of England; every morning brought intelligence of fresh outrages from Ireland, unforgivable and unforgettable outrages; a prolonged drought threatened the harvests of the world; the League of Nations, of which Mr. Barnstaple had hoped enormous things in the great days of President Wilson, was a melancholy and self-satisfied futility; everywhere there was conflict, everywhere unreason; seven-eighths of the world seemed to be sinking down towards chronic disorder and social dissolution. Even without Mr. Peeve it would have been difficult enough to have made headway against the facts.

Mr. Barnstaple was, indeed, ceasing to secrete hope, and for such types as he, hope is the essential

solvent without which there is no digesting life. His
hope had always been in liberalism and generous
liberal effort, but he was beginning to think that
liberalism would never do anything more for ever
than sit hunched up with its hands in its pockets
grumbling and peeving at the activities of baser but
more energetic men. Whose scrambling activities
would inevitably wreck the world.

Night and day now, Mr. Barnstaple was worrying
about the world at large. By night even more
than by day, for sleep was leaving him. And he was
haunted by a dreadful craving to bring out a number of the *Liberal* of his very own—to alter it all
after Mr. Peeve had gone away, to cut out all the
dyspeptic stuff, the miserable, empty girding at this
wrong and that, the gloating on cruel and unhappy
things, the exaggeration of the simple, natural, human misdeeds of Mr. Lloyd George, the appeals to
Lord Grey, Lord Robert Cecil, Lord Lansdowne,
the Pope, Queen Anne, or the Emperor Frederick
Barbarossa (it varied from week to week), to arise
and give voice and form to the young aspirations of
a world reborn, and, instead, to fill the number with
—Utopia! to say to the amazed readers of the
Liberal: Here are things that have to be done!
Here are the things we are going to do! What a
blow it would be for Mr. Peeve at his Sunday breakfast! For once, too astonished to secrete abnor-
mally, he might even digest that meal!

But this was the most foolish of dreaming. There
were the three young Barnstaples at home and their
need for a decent start in life to consider. And
beautiful as the thing was as a dream, Mr. Barnstaple had a very unpleasant conviction that he was

not really clever enough to pull such a thing off. He would make a mess of it somehow. . . .

One might jump from the frying-pan into the fire. The *Liberal* was a dreary, discouraging, ungenerous paper, but anyhow it was not a base and wicked paper.

Still, if there was to be no such disastrous outbreak it was imperative that Mr. Barnstaple should rest from Mr. Peeve for a time. Once or twice already he had contradicted him. A row might occur anywhen. And the first step towards resting from Mr. Peeve was evidently to see a doctor. So Mr. Barnstaple went to a doctor.

"My nerves are getting out of control," said Mr. Barnstaple. "I feel horribly neurasthenic."

"You are suffering from neurasthenia," said the doctor.

"I dread my daily work."

"You want a holiday."

"You think I need a change?"

"As complete a change as you can manage."

"Can you recommend any place where I could go?"

"Where do you want to go?"

"Nowhere definite. I thought you could recommend——"

"Let some place attract you—and go there. Do nothing to force your inclinations at the present time."

Mr. Barnstaple paid the doctor the sum of one guinea, and armed with these instructions prepared to break the news of his illness and his necessary absence to Mr. Peeve whenever the occasion seemed ripe for doing so.

§ 2

For a time this prospective holiday was merely
a fresh addition to Mr. Barnstaple's already excessive burthen of worries. To decide to get away was
to find oneself face to face at once with three apparently insurmountable problems: How to get
away? Whither? And since Mr. Barnstaple was
one of those people who tire very quickly of their
own company: With whom? A sharp gleam of fur-
tive scheming crept into the candid misery that
had recently become Mr. Barnstaple's habitual expression. But then, no one took much notice of
Mr. Barnstaple's expressions.

One thing was very clear in his mind. Not a
word of this holiday must be breathed at home. If
once Mrs. Barnstaple got wind of it, he knew
exactly what would happen. She would, with an
air of competent devotion, take charge of the entire
business. "You must have a *good* holiday," she
would say. She would select some rather distant
and expensive resort in Cornwall or Scotland or
Brittany, she would buy a lot of outfit, she would
have afterthoughts to swell the luggage with inconvenient parcels at the last moment, and she
would bring the boys. Probably she would arrange
for one or two groups of acquaintances to come
to the same place to "liven things up." If they
did they were certain to bring the worst sides of
their natures with them and to develop into the
most indefatigable of bores. There would be no
conversation. There would be much unreal laughter. There would be endless games. . . . *No!*

But how is a man to go away for a holiday without his wife getting wind of it? Somehow a bag must be packed and smuggled out of the house. . . .

The most hopeful thing about Mr. Barnstaple's position from Mr. Barnstaple's point of view was that he owned a small automobile of his very own. It was natural that this car should play a large part in his secret plannings. It seemed to offer the easiest means of getting away; it converted the possible answer to Whither? from a fixed and definite place into what mathematicians call, I believe, a locus; and there was something so companionable about the little beast that it did to a slight but quite perceptible extent answer the question, With whom? It was a two-seater. It was known in the family as the Foot Bath, Colman's Mustard, and the Yellow Peril. As these names suggest, it was a low, open car of a clear yellow colour. Mr. Barnstaple used it to come up to the office from Sydenham because it did thirty-three miles to the gallon and was ever so much cheaper than a season ticket. It stood up in the court under the office window during the day. At Sydenham it lived in a shed of which Mr. Barnstaple carried the only key. So far he had managed to prevent the boys from either driving it or taking it to pieces. At times Mrs. Barnstaple made him drive her about Sydenham for her shopping, but she did not really like the little car because it exposed her to the elements too much and made her dusty and dishevelled. Both by reason of all that it made possible and by reason of all that it debarred, the little car was clearly indicated as the medium for the needed holiday. And

Mr. Barnstaple really liked driving it. He drove
very badly, but he drove very carefully; and though
it sometimes stopped and refused to proceed, it did
not do, or at any rate it had not so far done, as
most other things did in Mr. Barnstaple's life, which
was to go due east when he turned the steering
wheel west. So that it gave him an agreeable sense
of mastery.

In the end Mr. Barnstaple made his decisions with
great rapidity. Opportunity suddenly opened in
front of him. Thursday was his day at the
printer's, and he came home on Thursday evening
feeling horribly jaded. The weather kept obstinately hot and dry. It made it none the less distressing that this drought presaged famine and
misery for half the world. And London was in
full season, smart and grinning: if anything it was
a sillier year than 1913, the great tango year, which,
in the light of subsequent events, Mr. Barnstaple
had hitherto regarded as the silliest year in the
world's history. The *Star* had the usual batch of
bad news along the margin of the sporting and
fashionable intelligence that got the displayed
space. Fighting was going on between the Russians and Poles, and also in Ireland, Asia Minor,
the India frontier, and Eastern Siberia. There
had been three new horrible murders. The miners
were still out, and a big engineering strike was
threatened. There had been only standing room in
the down train and it had started twenty minutes
late.

He found a note from his wife explaining that
her cousins at Wimbledon had telegraphed that

there was an unexpected chance of seeing the tennis there with Mademoiselle Lenglen and all the rest of the champions, and that she had gone over with the boys and would not be back until late. It would do their game no end of good, she said, to see some really first-class tennis. Also it was the servants' social that night. Would he mind being left alone in the house for once? The servants would put him out some cold supper before they went.

Mr. Barnstaple read this note with resignation. While he ate his supper he ran his eye over a pamphlet a Chinese friend had sent him to show how the Japanese were deliberately breaking up what was left of the civilization and education of China.

It was only as he was sitting and smoking a pipe in his little back garden after supper that he realized all that being left alone in the house meant for him.

Then suddenly he became very active. He rang up Mr. Peeve, told him of the doctor's verdict, explained that the affairs of the *Liberal* were just then in a particularly leavable state, and got his holiday. Then he went to his bedroom and packed up a hasty selection of things to take with him in an old Gladstone bag that was not likely to be immediately missed, and put this in the dickey of his car. After which he spent some time upon a letter which he addressed to his wife and put away very carefully in his breast pocket.

Then he locked up the car-shed and composed himself in a deck-chair in the garden with his pipe

and a nice thoughtful book on the Bankruptcy of
Europe, so as to look and feel as innocent as possible
before his family came home.

When his wife returned he told her casually that
he believed he was suffering from neurasthenia, and
that he had arranged to run up to London on the
morrow and consult a doctor in the matter.

Mrs. Barnstaple wanted to choose him a doctor,
but he got out of that by saying that he had to consider Peeve in the matter and that Peeve was very
strongly set on the man he had already in fact con-
sulted. And when Mrs. Barnstaple said that she
believed they *all* wanted a good holiday, he just
grunted in a non-committal manner.

In this way Mr. Barnstaple was able to get right
away from his house with all the necessary luggage
for some weeks' holiday, without arousing any insurmountable opposition. He started next morning
Londonward. The traffic on the way was gay and
plentiful, but by no means troublesome, and the
Yellow Peril was running so sweetly that she might
almost have been named the Golden Hope. In
Camberwell he turned into the Camberwell New
Road and made his way to the post-office at the top
of Vauxhall Bridge Road. There he drew up. He
was scared but elated by what he was doing. He
went into the post-office and sent his wife a telegram. "Dr. Pagan," he wrote, "says solitude and
rest urgently needed so am going off Lake District
recuperate have got bag and things expecting this
letter follows."

Then he came outside and fumbled in his pocket
and produced and posted the letter he had written

so carefully overnight. It was deliberately scrawled
to suggest neurasthenia at an acute phase. Dr.
Pagan, it explained, had ordered an immediate holiday and suggested that Mr. Barnstaple should
"wander north." It would be better to cut off all
letters for a few days, or even a week or so. He
would not trouble to write unless something went
wrong. No news would be good news. Res⁴ assured
all would be well. As soon as he had a ɔertain
address for letters he would wire it, but only very
urgent things were to be sent on.

After this he resumed his seat in his car with such
a sense of freedom as he had never felt since his first
holidays from his first school. He made for the
Great North Road, but at the traffic jam at Hyde
Park Corner he allowed the policeman to turn him
down towards Knightsbridge, and afterwards at the
corner where the Bath Road forks away from the
Oxford Road an obstructive van put him into the
former. But it did not matter very much. Any
way led to Elswhere and he could work northward
later.

§ 3

The day was one of those days of gay sunshine
that were characteristic of the great drought of 1921.
It was not in the least sultry. Indeed there was a
freshness about it that blended with Mr. Barnstaple's mood to convince him that there were quite
agreeable adventures before him. Hope had already
returned to him. He knew he was on the way out
of things, though as yet he had not the slightest

suspicion how completely out of things the way was
going to take him. It would be quite a little adventure presently to stop at an inn and get some lunch,
and if he felt lonely as he went on he would give
somebody a lift and talk. It would be quite easy
to give people lifts because so long as his back was
generally towards Sydenham and the *Liberal* office,
it did not matter at all now in which direction he
went.

A little way out of Slough he was passed by an
enormous grey touring car. It made him start and
swerve. It came up alongside him without a sound,
and though according to his only very slightly inaccurate speedometer, he was doing a good twenty-
seven miles an hour, it had passed him in a moment.
Its occupants, he noted, were three gentlemen and
a lady. They were all sitting up and looking backward as though they were interested in something
that was following them. They went by too quickly
for him to note more than that the lady was radiantly lovely in an immediate and indisputable way,
and that the gentleman nearest to him had a peculiarly elfin yet elderly face.

Before he could recover from the *éclat* of this passage a car with the voice of a prehistoric saurian
warned him that he was again being overtaken.
This was how Mr. Barnstaple liked being passed.
By negotiation. He slowed down, abandoned any
claim to the crown of the road and made encouraging gestures with his hand. A large, smooth, swift
Limousine availed itself of his permission to use
the thirty odd feet or so of road to the right of him.
It was carrying a fair load of luggage, but except

for a young gentleman with an eye-glass who was sitting beside the driver, he saw nothing of its passengers. It swept round a corner ahead in the wake of the touring car.

Now even a mechanical foot-bath does not like being passed in this lordly fashion on a bright morning on the open road. Mr. Barnstaple's accelerator went down and he came round that corner a good ten miles per hour faster than his usual cautious practice. He found the road quite clear ahead of him.

Indeed he found the road much too clear ahead of him. It stretched straight in front of him for perhaps a third of a mile. On the left were a low, well-trimmed hedge, scattered trees, level fields, some small cottages lying back, remote poplars, and a distant view of Windsor Castle. On the right were level fields, a small inn, and a background of low, wooded hills. A conspicuous feature in this tranquil landscape was the board advertisement of a riverside hotel at Maidenhead. Before him was a sort of heat flicker in the air and two or three little dust whirls spinning along the road. And there was not a sign of the grey touring car and not a sign of the Limousine.

It took Mr. Barnstaple the better part of two seconds to realize the full astonishment of this fact. Neither to right nor left was there any possible side road down which either car could have vanished. And if they had already got round the further bend, then they must be travelling at the rate of two or three hundred miles per hour!

It was Mr. Barnstaple's excellent custom when-

ever he was in doubt to slow down. He slowed
down now. He went on at a pace of perhaps fifteen
miles an hour, staring open-mouthed about the
empty landscape for some clue to this mysterious
disappearance. Curiously enough he had no feeling
that he himself was in any sort of danger.

Then his car seemed to strike something and
skidded. It skidded round so violently that for a
moment or so Mr. Barnstaple lost his head. He
could not remember what ought to be done when a
car skids. He recalled something vaguely about
steering in the direction in which the car is skidding,
but he could not make out in the excitement of the
moment in what direction the car was skidding.

Afterwards he remembered that at this point he
heard a sound. It was exactly the same sound,
coming as the climax of an accumulating pressure,
sharp like the snapping of a lute string, which one
hears at the end—or beginning—of insensibility under anaesthetics.

He had seemed to twist round towards the hedge
on the right, but now he found the road ahead of
him again. He touched his accelerator and then
slowed down and stopped. He stopped in the pro-
foundest astonishment.

This was an entirely different road from the one
he had been upon half a minute before. The hedges
had changed, the trees had altered, Windsor Castle
had vanished, and—a small compensation—the big
Limousine was in sight again. It was standing by
the roadside about two hundred yards away.

CHAPTER THE SECOND

THE WONDERFUL ROAD

§ 1

For a time Mr. Barnstaple's attention was very unequally divided between the Limousine, whose passengers were now descending, and the scenery about him. This latter was indeed so strange and beautiful that it was only as people who must be sharing his admiration and amazement and who therefore might conceivably help to elucidate and relieve his growing and quite overwhelming perplexity, that the little group ahead presently arose to any importance in his consciousness.

The road itself, instead of being the packed together pebbles and dirt smeared with tar with a surface of grit, dust, and animal excrement, of a normal English high road, was apparently made of glass, clear in places as still water and in places milky or opalescent, shot with streaks of soft colour or glittering richly with clouds of embedded golden flakes. It was perhaps twelve or fifteen yards wide. On either side was a band of greensward, of a finer grass than Mr. Barnstaple had ever seen before— and he was an expert and observant mower of lawns —and beyond this a wide border of flowers. Where

Mr. Barnstaple sat agape in his car and perhaps for thirty yards in either direction this border was a mass of some unfamiliar blossom of forget-me-not blue. Then the colour was broken by an increasing number of tall, pure white spikes that finally ousted the blue altogether from the bed. On the opposite side of the way these same spikes were mingled with masses of plants bearing seed-pods equally strange to Mr. Barnstaple, which varied through a series of blues and mauves and purples to an intense crimson. Beyond this gloriously coloured foam of flowers spread flat meadows on which creamy cattle were grazing. Three close at hand, a little startled perhaps by Mr. Barnstaple's sudden apparition, chewed the cud and regarded him with benevolently speculative eyes. They had long horns and dewlaps like the cattle of South Europe and India. From these benign creatures Mr. Barnstaple's eyes went to a long line of flame-shaped trees, to a colonnade of white and gold, and to a background of snow-clad mountains. A few tall, white clouds were sailing across a sky of dazzling blue. The air impressed Mr. Barnstaple as being astonishingly clear and sweet.

Except for the cows and the little group of people standing by the Limousine, Mr. Barnstaple could not see no other living creatures at all. The motorists were standing still and staring about them. A sound of querulous voices came to him.

A sharp crepitation at his back turned Mr. Barnstaple's attention round. By the side of the road in the direction from which conceivably he had come were the ruins of what appeared to be a very re-

cently demolished stone house. Beside it were two
large apple trees freshly twisted and riven, as if by
some explosion, and out of the centre of it came a
column of smoke and this sound of things catching
fire. And the contorted lines of these shattered
apple trees helped Mr. Barnstaple to realize that
some of the flowers by the wayside near at hand
were also bent down to one side as if by the passage
of a recent violent gust of wind. Yet he had heard
no explosion nor felt any wind.

He stared for a time and then turned as if for an
explanation to the Limousine. Three of these people were now coming along the road towards him,
led by a tall, slender, grey-headed gentleman in a
felt hat and a long motoring dust-coat. He had a
small upturned face with a little nose that scarce
sufficed for the springs of his gilt glasses. Mr. Barnstaple restarted his engine and drove slowly to meet
them.

As soon as he judged himself within hearing distance he stopped and put his head over the side of
the Yellow Peril with a question. At the same
moment the tall, grey-headed gentleman asked practically the same question:

"Can you tell me at all, sir, where we *are?*"

§ 2

"Five minutes ago," said Mr. Barnstaple, "I
should have said we were on the Maidenhead Road.
Near Slough."

"Exactly!" said the tall gentleman in earnest,
argumentative tones. "Exactly! And I maintain

that there is not the slightest reason for supposing that we are not still on the Maidenhead Road."

The challenge of the dialectician rang in his voice.

"It doesn't *look* like the Maidenhead Road," said Mr. Barnstaple.

"Agreed! But are we to judge by appearances or are we to judge by the direct continuity of our experience? The Maidenhead Road led to this, was in continuity with this, and therefore I hold that this is the Maidenhead Road."

"Those mountains?" considered Mr. Barnstaple.

"Windsor Castle ought to be there," said the tall gentleman brightly as if he gave a point in a gambit.

"*Was* there five minutes ago," said Mr. Barnstaple.

"Then obviously those mountains are some sort of a camouflage," said the tall gentleman triumphantly, "and the whole of this business is, as they say nowadays, a put-up thing."

"It seems to be remarkably well put up," said Mr. Barnstaple.

Came a pause during which Mr. Barnstaple surveyed the tall gentleman's companions. The tall gentleman he knew perfectly well. He had seen him a score of times at public meetings and public dinners. He was Mr. Cecil Burleigh, the great conservative leader. He was not only distinguished as a politician; he was eminent as a private gentleman, a philosopher and a man of universal intelligence. Behind him stood a short, thick-set, middle-aged young man, unknown to Mr. Barnstaple, the natural hostility of whose appearance was greatly enhanced by an eye-glass. The third mem-

ber of the little group was also a familiar form,
but for a time Mr. Barnstaple could not place him.
He had a clean-shaven, round, plump face and a
well-nourished person and his costume suggested
either a high church clergyman or a prosperous
Roman Catholic priest.

The young man with the eye-glass now spoke in
a kind of impotent falsetto. "I came down to Taplow Court by road not a month ago and there was
certainly nothing of this sort on the way then."

"I admit there are difficulties," said Mr. Burleigh
with gusto. "I admit there are considerable difficulties. Still, I venture to think my main proposition holds."

"*You* don't think this is the Maidenhead Road?"
said the gentleman with the eye-glass flatly to Mr.
Barnstaple.

"It seems too perfect for a put-up thing," said Mr.
Barnstaple with a mild obstinacy.

"But, my dear Sir!" protested Mr. Burleigh, "this
road is *notorious* for nursery seedsmen and sometimes they arrange the most astonishing displays.
As an advertisement."

"Then why don't we go straight on to Taplow
Court now?" asked the gentleman with the eye-
glass.

"Because," said Mr. Burleigh, with the touch of
asperity natural when one has to insist on a fact
already clearly known, and obstinately overlooked,
"Rupert insists that we are in some other world.
And won't go on. That is why. He has always had
too much imagination. He thinks that things that
don't exist *can* exist. And now he imagines himself

in some sort of scientific romance and out of our
world altogether. In another dimension. I sometimes think it would have been better for all of us
if Rupert had taken to writing romances—instead
of living them. If you, as his secretary, think that
you will be able to get him on to Taplow in time
for lunch with the Windsor people——"

Mr. Burleigh indicated by a gesture ideas for
which he found words inadequate.

Mr. Barnstaple had already noted a slow-moving,
intent, sandy-complexioned figure in a grey top hat
with a black band that the caricaturists had made
familiar, exploring the flowery tangle beside the
Limousine. This then must be no less well-known
person than Rupert Catskill, the Secretary of State
for War. For once, Mr. Barnstaple found himself
in entire agreement with this all too adventurous
politician. This *was* another world. Mr. Barnstaple got out of his car and addressed himself to
Mr. Burleigh. "I think we may get a lot of light
upon just where we are, Sir, if we explore this building which is burning here close at hand. I thought
just now that I saw a figure lying on the slope close
behind it. If we could catch one of the hoaxers——"

He left his sentence unfinished because he did
not believe for a moment that they were being
hoaxed. Mr. Burleigh had fallen very much in his
opinion in the last five minutes.

All four men turned their faces to the smoking
ruin.

"It's a very extraordinary thing that there isn't a
soul in sight," remarked the eye-glass gentleman,
searching the horizon.

"Well, I see no harm whatever in finding out what is burning," said Mr. Burleigh and led the way, upholding an intelligent, anticipatory face, towards the wrecked house between the broken trees.

But before he had gone a dozen paces the attention of the little group was recalled to the Limousine by a loud scream of terror from the lady who had remained seated therein.

§ 3

"Really this is too much!" cried Mr. Burleigh with a note of genuine exasperation. "There must surely be police regulations to prevent this kind of thing."

"It's out of some travelling menagerie," said the gentleman with the eye-glass. "What ought we to do?"

"It looks tame," said Mr. Barnstaple, but without any impulse to put his theory to the test.

"It might easily frighten people very seriously," said Mr. Burleigh. And lifting up a bland voice he shouted: "Don't be alarmed, Stella! It's probably quite tame and harmless. Don't *irritate* it with that sunshade. It might fly at you. Stel-*la!*"

"It" was a big and beautifully marked leopard which had come very softly out of the flowers and sat down like a great cat in the middle of the glass road at the side of the big car. It was blinking and moving its head from side to side rhythmically, with an expression of puzzled interest, as the lady, in accordance with the best traditions of such cases, opened and shut her parasol at it as rapidly as she

could. The chauffeur had taken cover behind the
car. Mr. Rupert Catskill stood staring, knee-deep
in flowers, apparently only made aware of the
creature's existence by the same scream that had
attracted the attention of Mr. Burleigh and his
companions.

Mr. Catskill was the first to act, and his act
showed his mettle. It was at once discreet and
bold. "Stop flopping that sunshade, Lady Stella,"
he said. "Let me—I will—catch its eye."

He made a detour round the car so as to come face
to face with the animal. Then for a moment he
stood, as it were displaying himself, a resolute little
figure in a grey frock coat and a black-banded top
hat. He held out a cautious hand, not too suddenly
for fear of startling the creature. *"Poossy!"* he
said.

The leopard, relieved by the cessation of Lady
Stella's sunshade, regarded him with interest and
curiosity. He drew closer. The leopard extended
its muzzle and sniffed.

"If it will only let me stroke it," said Mr. Catskill,
and came within arm's length.

The beast sniffed the extended hand with an expression of incredulity. Then with a suddenness
that sent Mr. Catskill back several paces, it sneezed.
It sneezed again much more violently, regarded Mr.
Catskill reproachfully for a moment and then leapt
lightly over the flower-bed and made off in the direction of the white and golden colonnade. The grazing cattle in the field, Mr. Barnstaple noted,
watched its passage without the slightest sign of
dismay.

Mr. Catskill remained in a slightly expanded state in the middle of the road. "No animal," he remarked, "can stand up to the steadfast gaze of the human eye. Not one. It is a riddle for your materialist. . . . Shall we join Mr. Cecil, Lady Stella? He seems to have found something to look at down there. The man in the little yellow car may know where he is. Hm?"

He assisted the lady to get out of the car and the two came on after Mr. Barnstaple's party, which was now again approaching the burning house. The chauffeur, evidently not wishing to be left alone with the Limousine in this world of incredible possibilities, followed as closely as respect permitted.

MEN LIKE GODS

CHAPTER THE THIRD

THE BEAUTIFUL PEOPLE

§ 1

The fire in the little house did not seem to be making headway. The smoke that came from it was much less now than when Mr. Barnstaple had first observed it. As they came close they found a quantity of twisted bits of bright metal and fragments of broken glass among the shattered masonry. The suggestion of exploded scientific apparatus was very strong. Then almost simultaneously the entire party became aware of a body lying on the grassy slope behind the ruins. It was the body of a man in the prime of life, naked except for a couple of bracelets and a necklace and girdle, and blood was oozing from his mouth and nostrils. With a kind of awe Mr. Barnstaple knelt down beside this prostrate figure and felt its still heart. He had never seen so beautiful a face and body before.

"*Dead,*" he whispered.

"Look!" cried the shrill voice of the man with the eye-glass. "Another!"

He was pointing to something that was hidden from Mr. Barnstaple by a piece of wall. Mr. Barnstaple had to get up and climb over a heap of rub-

ble before he could see this second find. It was a
slender girl, clothed as little as the man. She had
evidently been flung with enormous violence against
the wall and killed instantaneously. Her face was
quite undistorted although her skull had been
crushed in from behind; her perfect mouth and
green-grey eyes were a little open and her expression was that of one who is still thinking out some
difficult but interesting problem. She did not seem
in the least dead but merely disregardful. One hand
still grasped a copper implement with a handle of
glass. The other lay limp and prone.

For some seconds nobody spoke. It was as if
they all feared to interrupt the current of her
thoughts.

Then Mr. Barnstaple heard the voice of the
priestly gentleman speaking very softly behind
him. "What a *perfect* form!" he said.

"I admit I was wrong," said Mr. Burleigh with
deliberation. "I have been wrong. . . . These
are no earthly people. Manifestly. And *ergo*, we
are not on earth. I cannot imagine what has happened nor where we are. In the face of sufficient
evidence I have never hesitated to retract an opinion. This world we are in is not our world. It is
something——"

He paused. "It is something very wonderful
indeed."

"And the Windsor party," said Mr. Catskill without any apparent regret, "must have its lunch without us."

"But then," said the clerical gentleman, "what
world *are* we in, and how did we get here?"

"Ah! *there*," said Mr. Burleigh blandly, "you go altogether beyond my poor powers of guessing. We are here in some world that is singularly like our world and singularly unlike it. It must be in some way related to our world or we could not be here. But how it can be related, is, I confess, a hopeless mystery to me. Maybe we are in some other dimension of space than those we wot of. But my poor head whirls at the thought of these dimensions. I am—— I am *mazed—mazed.*"

"Einstein," injected the gentleman with the eyeglass compactly and with evident self-satisfaction.

"Exactly!" said Mr. Burleigh. "Einstein might make it clear to us. Or dear old Haldane might undertake to explain it and fog us up with that adipose Hegelianism of his. But I am neither Haldane nor Einstein. Here we are in some world which is, for all practical purposes, including the purposes of our week-end engagements, Nowhere. Or if you prefer the Greek of it, we are in Utopia. And as I do not see that there is any manifest way out of it again, I suppose the thing we have to do as rational creatures is to make the best of it. And watch our opportunities. It is certainly a very lovely world. The loveliness is even greater than the wonder. And there are human beings here— with minds. I judge from all this material lying about, it is a world in which experimental chemistry is pursued—pursued indeed to the bitter end— under almost idyllic conditions. Chemistry—and nakedness. I feel bound to confess that whether we are to regard these two people who have apparently just blown themselves up here as Greek gods or as naked savages, seems to me to be altogether a question of individual taste. I admit a bias for the Greek god—and goddess."

"Except that it is a little difficult to think of two dead immortals," squeaked the gentleman of the eye-glass in the tone of one who scores a point.

Mr. Burleigh was about to reply, and to judge from his ruffled expression his reply would have been of a disciplinary nature. But instead he exclaimed sharply and turned round to face two newcomers. The whole party had become aware of them at the same moment. Two stark Apollos stood over the ruin and were regarding our Earthlings with an astonishment at least as great as that they created.

One spoke, and Mr. Barnstaple was astonished beyond measure to find understandable words reverberating in his mind.

"Red Gods!" cried the Utopian. "What things are you? And how did you get into the world?"

(English! It would have been far less astounding if they had spoken Greek. But that they should speak any known language was a matter for incredulous amazement.)

§ 2

Mr. Cecil Burleigh was the least disconcerted of the party. "Now," he said, " we may hope to learn something definite—face to face with rational and articulate creatures."

He cleared his throat, grasped the lapels of his long dust-coat with two long nervous hands and assumed the duties of spokesman. "We are quite unable, gentlemen, to account for our presence here," he said. "We are as puzzled as you are. We have discovered ourselves suddenly in your world instead of our own."

"You come from another world?"

"Exactly. A quite different world. In which we have all our natural and proper places. We were travelling in that world of ours in—Ah!—certain vehicles, when suddenly we discovered ourselves here. Intruders, I admit, but, I can assure you, innocent and unpremeditated intruders."

"You do not know how it is that Arden and Greenlake have failed in their experiment and how it is that they are dead?"

"If Arden and Greenlake are the names of these two beautiful young people here, we know nothing about them except that we found them lying as you see them when we came from the road hither to find out or, in fact, to inquire——"

He cleared his throat and left his sentence with a floating end.

The Utopian, if we may for convenience call him that, who had first spoken, looked now at his companion and seemed to question him mutely. Then he turned to the Earthlings again. He spoke and again those clear tones rang, not—so it seemed to Mr. Barnstaple—in his ears but within his head.

"It will be well if you and your friends do not trample this wreckage. It will be well if you all return to the road. Come with me. My brother here will put an end to this burning and do what needs to be done to our brother and sister. And afterwards this place will be examined by those who understand the work that was going on here."

"We must throw ourselves entirely upon your hospitality," said Mr. Burleigh. "We are entirely at your disposal. This encounter, let me repeat, was not of our seeking."

"Though we should certainly have sought it if we had known of its possibility," said Mr. Catskill, addressing the world at large and glancing at Mr. Barnstaple as if for confirmation. "We find this world of yours—*most* attractive."

"At the first encounter," the gentleman with the eye-glass endorsed, "a *most* attractive world."

As they returned through the thick-growing flowers to the road, in the wake of the Utopian and Mr. Burleigh, Mr. Barnstaple found Lady Stella rustling up beside him. Her words, in this setting of pure wonder, filled him with amazement at their serene and invincible ordinariness. "Haven't we met before somewhere—at lunch or something— Mr.—Mr.——?"

Was all this no more than a show? He stared at her blankly for a moment before supplying her with:

"Barnstaple."

"Mr. Barnstaple?"

His mind came into line with hers.

"I've never had that pleasure, Lady Stella. Though, of course, I know you—I know you very well from your photographs in the weekly illustrated papers."

"Did you hear what it was that Mr. Cecil was saying just now? About this being Utopia?"

"He said we might *call* it Utopia."

"So like Mr. Cecil. But is it Utopia?—*really*
Utopia?

"I've always longed so to be in Utopia," the lady
went on without waiting for Mr. Barnstaple's reply
to her question. "What splendid young men these
two Utopians appear to be! They must, I am sure,
belong to its aristocracy—in spite of their—informal
—costume. Or even because of it." . . .

Mr. Barnstaple had a happy thought. "I have
also recognized Mr. Burleigh and Mr. Rupert Catskill, Lady Stella, but I should be so glad if you
would tell me who the young gentleman with the
eye-glass is, and the clerical gentleman. They are
close behind us."

Lady Stella imparted her information in a charm-
ingly confidential undertone. "The eye-glass," she
murmured, "is—I am going to spell it—F.R.E.D.D.Y.
M.U.S.H. Taste. Good taste. He is awfully clever
at finding out young poets and all that sort of
literary thing. And he's Rupert's secretary. If
there is a literary Academy, they say, he's certain
to be in it. He's dreadfully critical and sarcastic.
We were going to Taplow for a perfectly intellectual
week-end, quite like the old times. So soon as the
Windsor people had gone again, that is. . . .
Mr. Gosse was coming and Max Beerbohm—and
everyone like that. But nowadays something always happens. Always. . . . The unexpected
—almost excessively. . . . The clerical collar"
—she glanced back to judge whether she was within
earshot of the gentleman under discussion—"is
Father Amerton, who is so dreadfully outspoken

about the sins of society and all *that* sort of thing.
It's odd, but out of the pulpit he's inclined to be
shy and quiet and a little awkward with the forks
and spoons. Paradoxical, isn't it?"

"Of *course!*" cried Mr. Barnstaple. "I remember
him now. I knew his face but I couldn't place it.
Thank you so much, Lady Stella."

§ 3

There was something very reassuring to Mr.
Barnstaple in the company of these famous and
conspicuous people and particularly in the company
of Lady Stella. She was indeed heartening; she
brought so much of the dear old world with her, and
she was so manifestly prepared to subjugate this
new world to its standards at the earliest possible
opportunity. She fended off much of the wonder
and beauty that had threatened to submerge Mr.
Barnstaple altogether. Meeting her and her company was in itself for a man in his position a
minor but considerable adventure that helped to
bridge the gulf of astonishment between the hum-
drum of his normal experiences and this all too
bracing Utopian air. It solidified, it—if one may
use the word in such a connexion—it *degraded* the
luminous splendour about him towards complete
credibility that it should also be seen and com-
mented on by her and by Mr. Burleigh, and viewed
through the appraising monocle of Mr. Freddy
Mush. It brought it within range of the things that
get into the newspapers. Mr. Barnstaple alone in

Utopia might have been so completely overawed
as to have been mentally overthrown. This easy-
mannered-brown-skinned divinity who was now ex-
changing questions with Mr. Burleigh was made
mentally accessible by that great man's intervention.

Yet it was with something very like a catching of
the breath that Mr. Barnstaple's attention reverted
from the Limousine people to this noble-seeming
world into which he and they had fallen. What
sort of beings really were these men and women of
a world where ill-bred weeds, it seemed, had ceased
to thrust and fight amidst the flowers, and where
leopards void of feline malice looked out with
friendly eyes upon the passer-by?

It was astounding that the first two inhabitants
they had found in this world of subjugated nature
should be lying dead, victims, it would seem, of
some hazardous experiment. It was still more
astonishing that this other pair who called themselves the brothers of the dead man and woman
should betray so little grief or dismay at the tragedy. There had been no emotional scene at all, Mr.
Barnstaple realized, no consternation or weeping.
They were evidently much more puzzled and interested than either horrified or distressed.

The Utopian who had remained in the ruin had
carried out the body of the girl to lay it beside her
companion's, and he had now, Mr. Barnstaple saw,
returned to a close scrutiny of the wreckage of the
experiment.

But now more of these people were coming upon
the scene. They had aeroplanes in this world, for

two small ones, noiseless and swift in their flight as
swallows, had landed in the fields near by. A man
had come up along the road on a machine like a
small two-wheeled two-seater with its wheels in
series, bicycle fashion; lighter and neater it was
than any earthly automobile and mysteriously able
to stand up on its two wheels while standing still.
A burst of laughter from down the road called Mr.
Barnstaple's attention to a group of these Utopians
who had apparently found something exquisitely
ridiculous in the engine of the Limousine. Most
of these people were as scantily clothed and as
beautifully built as the two dead experimentalists,
but one or two were wearing big hats of straw, and
one who seemed to be an older woman of thirty or
more wore a robe of white bordered by an intense
red line. She was speaking now to Mr. Burleigh.

Although she was a score of yards away, her
speech presented itself in Mr. Barnstaple's mind
with great distinctness.

"We do not even know as yet what connexion
your coming into our world may have with the
explosion that has just happened here or whether,
indeed, it has any connexion. We want to inquire
into both these things. It will be reasonable, we
think, to take you and all the possessions you have
brought with you to a convenient place for a conference not very far from here. We are arranging
for machines to take you thither. There perhaps
you will eat. I do not know when you are
accustomed to eat?"

"Refreshment," said Mr. Burleigh, rather catching at the idea. "Some refreshment would cer-

tainly be acceptable before very long. In fact, had we not fallen so sharply out of our own world into yours, by this time we should have been lunching— lunching in the best of company."

"Wonder and lunch," thought Mr. Barnstaple. Man is a creature who must eat by necessity whether he wonder or no. Mr. Barnstaple perceived indeed that he was already hungry and that the air he was breathing was a keen and appetizing air.

The Utopian seemed struck by a novel idea. "Do you eat several times a day? What sort of things do you eat?"

"Oh! Surely! They're *not* vegetarians!" cried Mr. Mush sharply in a protesting parenthesis, dropping his eye-glass from its socket.

They were all hungry. It showed upon their faces.

"We are all accustomed to eat several times a day," said Mr. Burleigh. "Perhaps it would be well if I were to give you a brief résumé of our dietary. There may be differences. We begin, as a rule, with a simple cup of tea and the thinnest slice of bread-and-butter brought to the bedside. Then comes breakfast." . . . He proceeded to a masterly summary of his gastronomic day, giving clearly and attractively the particulars of an English breakfast, eggs to be boiled four and a half minutes, neither more nor less, lunch with any light wine, tea rather a social rally than a serious meal, dinner, in some detail, the occasional resort to supper. It was one of those clear statements which would have rejoiced the House of Commons, light, even gay, and yet with a trace of earnestness. The

Utopian woman regarded him with deepening interest as he proceeded. "Do you all eat in this fashion?" she asked.

Mr. Burleigh ran his eye over his party. "I cannot answer for Mr.—Mr.——?"

"Barnstaple. . . . Yes, I eat in much the same fashion."

For some reason the Utopian woman smiled at him. She had very pretty brown eyes, and though he liked her to smile he wished that she had not smiled in the way she did.

"And you sleep?" she asked.

"From six to ten hours, according to circumstances," said Mr. Burleigh.

"And you make love?"

The question perplexed and to a certain extent shocked our Earthlings. What exactly did she mean? For some moments no one framed a reply. Mr. Barnstaple's mind was filled with a hurrying rush of strange possibilities.

Then Mr. Burleigh, with his fine intelligence and the quick evasiveness of a modern leader of men, stepped into the breach. "Not habitually, I can assure you," he said. "Not habitually."

The woman with the red-bordered robe seemed to think this over for a swift moment. Then she smiled faintly.

"We must take you somewhere where we can talk of all these things," she said. "Manifestly you come from some strange other world. Our men of knowledge must get together with you and exchange ideas."

§ 4

At half-past ten that morning Mr. Barnstaple
had been motoring along the main road through
Slough, and now at half-past one he was soaring
through wonderland with his own world half forgotten. "Marvellous," he repeated. "Marvellous.
I knew that I should have a good holiday. But
this, this——! "

He was extraordinarily happy with the bright,
unclouded happiness of a perfect dream. Never
before had he enjoyed the delights of an explorer in
new lands, never before had he hoped to experience
these delights. Only a few weeks before he had
written an article for the *Liberal* lamenting the "End
of the Age of Exploration," an article so thoroughly
and aimlessly depressing that it had pleased Mr.
Peeve extremely. He recalled that exploit now with
but the faintest twinge of remorse.

The Earthling party had been distributed among
four small aeroplanes, and as Mr. Barnstaple and
his companion, Father Amerton, rose in the air, he
looked back to see the automobiles and luggage
being lifted with astonishing ease into two lightly
built lorries. Each lorry put out a pair of glittering
arms and lifted up its automobile as a nurse might
lift up a baby.

By contemporary earthly standards of safety Mr.
Barnstaple's aviator flew very low. There were
times when he passed between trees rather than
over them, and this, even if at first it was a little
alarming, permitted a fairly close inspection of the
landscape. For the earlier part of the journey it

was garden pasture with grazing creamy cattle and patches of brilliantly coloured vegetation of a nature unknown to Mr. Barnstaple. Amidst this cultivation narrow tracks, which may have been foot or cycle tracks, threaded their way. Here and there ran a road bordered with flowers and shaded by fruit trees.

There were few houses and no towns or villages at all. The houses varied very greatly in size, from little isolated buildings which Mr. Barnstaple thought might be elegant summer-houses or little temples, to clusters of roofs and turrets which reminded him of country châteaux or suggested extensive farming or dairying establishments. Here and there people were working in the fields or going to and fro on foot or on machines, but the effect of the whole was of an extremely underpopulated land.

It became evident that they were going to cross the range of snowy mountains that had so suddenly blotted the distant view of Windsor Castle from the landscape.

As they approached these mountains, broad stretches of golden corn-land replaced the green of the pastures and then the cultivation became more diversified. He noted unmistakable vineyards on sunny slopes, and the number of workers visible and the habitations multiplied. The little squadron of aeroplanes flew up a broad valley towards a pass so that Mr. Barnstaple was able to scrutinize the mountain scenery. Came chestnut woods and at last pines. There were Cyclopean turbines athwart the mountain torrents and long, low, many win-

dowed buildings that might serve some industrial
purpose. A skilfully graded road with exceedingly
bold, light and beautiful viaducts mounted towards
the pass. There were more people, he thought, in
the highland country than in the levels below,
though still far fewer than he would have seen upon
any comparable countryside on earth.

Ten minutes of craggy desolation with the snow-
fields of a great glacier on one side intervened before
he descended into the upland valley on the Conference Place where presently he alighted. This was
a sort of lap in the mountain, terraced by masonry
so boldly designed that it seemed a part of the geo-
logical substance of the mountain itself. It faced
towards a wide artificial lake retained by a stupendous dam from the lower reaches of the valley. At
intervals along this dam there were great stone
pillars dimly suggestive of seated figures. He
glimpsed a wide plain beyond, which reminded him
of the valley of the Po, and then as he descended
the straight line of the dam came up to hide this
further vision.

Upon these terraces, and particularly upon the
lower ones, were groups and clusters of flowerlike
buildings, and he distinguished paths and steps and
pools of water as if the whole place were a garden.

The aeroplanes made an easy landing on a turfy
expanse. Close at hand was a graceful chalet that
ran out from the shores of the lake over the water,
and afforded mooring to a flotilla of gaily coloured
boats. . . .

It was Father Amerton who had drawn Mr. Barnstaple's attention to the absence of villages. He now

remarked that there was no church in sight and that
nowhere had they seen any spires or belfries. But
Mr. Barnstaple thought that some of the smaller
buildings might be temples or shrines. "Religion
may take different forms here," he said.

"And how few babies or little children are visible!" Father Amerton remarked. "Nowhere have I
seen a mother with her child."

"On the other side of the mountains there was a
place like the playing field of a big school. There
were children there and one or two older people
dressed in white."

"I saw that. But I was thinking of babes. Compare this with what one would see in Italy.

"The most beautiful and desirable young
women," added the reverend gentleman; "*most
desirable*—and not a sign of maternity!"

Their aviator, a sun-tanned blond with very blue
eyes, helped them out of his machine, and they
stood watching the descent of the other members
of their party. Mr. Barnstaple was astonished to
note how rapidly he was becoming familiarized with
the colour and harmony of this new world; the
strangest things in the whole spectacle now were
the figures and clothing of his associates. Mr.
Rupert Catskill in his celebrated grey top hat, Mr.
Mush with his preposterous eye-glass, the peculiar
long slenderness of Mr. Burleigh, and the square
leather-clad lines of Mr. Burleigh's chauffeur, struck
him as being far more incredible than the graceful
Utopian forms about him.

The aviator's interest and amusement enhanced
Mr. Barnstaple's perception of his companions'

oddity. And then came a wave of profound doubt.

"I suppose this is *really* real," he said to Father Amerton.

"Really real! What else can it be?"

"I suppose we are not dreaming all this."

"Are your dreams and my dreams likely to coincide?"

"Yes; but there are quite impossible things—absolutely impossible things."

"As, for instance?"

"Well, how is it that these people are speaking to us in English—modern English?"

"I never thought of that. It is rather incredible. They don't talk in English to one another."

Mr. Barnstaple stared in round-eyed amazement at Father Amerton, struck for the first time by a still more incredible fact. "They don't talk in *anything* to one another," he said. "And we haven't noticed it until this moment!"

CHAPTER THE FOURTH

THE SHADOW OF EINSTEIN FALLS ACROSS THE STORY BUT PASSES LIGHTLY BY

§ 1

Except for that one perplexing fact that all these Utopians had apparently a complete command of idiomatic English, Mr. Barnstaple found his vision of this new world developing with a congruity that no dream in his experience had ever possessed. It was so coherent, so orderly, that less and less was it like a strange world at all and more and more like an arrival in some foreign but very highly civilized country.

Under the direction of the brown-eyed woman in the scarlet-edged robe, the Earthlings were established in their quarters near the Conference Place in the most hospitable and comfortable fashion conceivable. Five or six youths and girls made it their business to initiate the strangers in the little details of Utopian domesticity. The separate buildings in which they were lodged had each an agreeable little dressing-room, and the bed, which had sheets of the finest linen and a very light puffy coverlet, stood in an open loggia—too open Lady Stella thought, but then as she said, "One feels so safe here." The lug-

gage appeared and the valises were identified as if
they were in some hospitable earthly mansion.

But Lady Stella had to turn two rather too
friendly youths out of her apartment before she
could open her dressing-bag and administer refreshment to her complexion.

A few minutes later some excitement was caused
by an outbreak of wild laughter and the sounds of
an amiable but hysterical struggle that came from
Lady Stella's retreat. The girl who had remained
with her had displayed a quite feminine interest in
her equipment and had come upon a particularly
charming and diaphanous sleeping suit. For some
obscure reason this secret daintiness amused the
young Utopian extremely, and it was with some
difficulty that Lady Stella restrained her from putting the garment on and dancing out in it for a
public display. "Then *you* put it on," the girl
insisted.

"But you don't understand," cried Lady Stella.
"It's almost—*sacred!* It's for nobody to see—*ever.*"

"But *why?*" the Utopian asked, puzzled beyond
measure.

Lady Stella found an answer impossible.

The light meal that followed was by terrestrial
standards an entirely satisfactory one. The anxiety
of Mr. Freddy Mush was completely allayed; there
were cold chicken and ham and a very pleasant meat
paté. There were also rather coarse-grained but
most palatable bread, pure butter, an exquisite
salad, fruit, cheese of the Gruyère type, and a light
white wine which won from Mr. Burleigh the tribute
that "Moselle never did anything better."

"You find our food very like your own?" asked the woman in the red-trimmed robe.

"Eckquithit quality," said Mr. Mush with his mouth rather full.

"Food has changed very little in the last three thousand years. People had found out all the best things to eat long before the last Age of Confusion."

"It's too real to be real," Mr. Barnstaple repeated to himself. "Too real to be real."

He looked at his companions, elated, interested and eating with appreciation.

If it wasn't for the absurdity of these Utopians speaking English with a clearness that tapped like a hammer inside his head Mr. Barnstaple would have had no doubt whatever of its reality.

No servants waited at the clothless stone table; the woman in the white and scarlet robe and the two aviators shared the meal and the guests attended to each other's requirements. Mr. Burleigh's chauffeur was for modestly shrinking to another table until the great statesman reassured him with: "Sit down there, Penk. Next to Mr. Mush." Other Utopians with friendly but keenly observant eyes upon the Earthlings came into the great pillared veranda in which the meal had been set, and smiled and stood about or sat down. There were no introductions and few social formalities.

"All this is most reassuring," said Mr. Burleigh. "Most reassuring. I'm bound to say these beat the Chatsworth peaches. Is that cream, my dear Rupert, in the little brown jar in front of you? . . . I guessed as much. If you are sure you can spare it, Rupert. . . . Thank you."

§ 2

Several of the Utopians made themselves known
by name to the Earthlings. All their voices sounded
singularly alike to Mr. Barnstaple and the words
were as clear as print. The brown-eyed woman's
name was Lychnis. A man with a beard who might
perhaps, Mr. Barnstaple thought, have been as old
as forty, was either Urthred or Adam or Edom, the
name for all its sharpness of enunciation had been
very difficult to catch. It was as if large print
hesitated. Urthred conveyed that he was an eth-
nologist and historian and that he desired to learn all
that he possibly could about the ways of our world.
He impressed Mr. Barnstaple as having the easy
carriage of some earthly financier or great newspaper
proprietor rather than the diffidence natural in our
own everyday world to a merely learned man. Another of their hosts, Serpentine, was also, Mr. Barnstaple learnt with surprise, for his bearing too was
almost masterful, a scientific man. He called himself something that Mr. Barnstaple could not catch.
First it sounded like "atomic mechanician," and
then oddly enough it sounded like "molecular chemist." And then Mr. Barnstaple heard Mr. Burleigh say to Mr. Mush, "He said 'physio-chemist,'
didn't he?"

"*I* thought he just called himself a materialist,"
said Mr. Mush.

"I thought he said he weighed things," said Lady
Stella.

"Their intonation is peculiar," said Mr. Burleigh.

"Sometimes they are almost too loud for comfort and then there is a kind of gap in the sounds." . . .

When the meal was at an end the whole party removed to another little building that was evidently planned for classes and discussions. It had a semicircular apse round which ran a series of white tablets which evidently functioned at times as a lecturer's blackboard, since there were black and coloured pencils and cloths for erasure lying on a marble ledge at a convenient height below the tablets. The lecturer could walk from point to point of this semicircle as he talked. Lychnis, Urthred, Serpentine and the Earthlings seated themselves on a semicircular bench below this lecturer's track, and there was accommodation for about eighty or a hundred people upon the seats before them. All these were occupied, and beyond stood a number of graceful groups against a background of rhododendron-like bushes, between which Mr. Barnstable caught glimpses of grassy vistas leading down to the shining waters of the lake.

They were going to talk over this extraordinary irruption into their world. Could anything be more reasonable than to talk it over? Could anything be more fantastically impossible?

"Odd that there are no swallows," said Mr. Mush suddenly in Mr. Barnstaple's ear. "I wonder why there are no swallows."

Mr. Barnstaple's attention went to the empty sky. "No gnats nor flies perhaps," he suggested. It was odd that he had not missed the swallows before.

"Sssh!" said Lady Stella. "He's beginning."

§ 3

This incredible conference began. It was opened by the man named Serpentine, and he stood before his audience and seemed to make a speech. His lips moved, his hands assisted his statements; his expression followed his utterance. And yet Mr. Barnstaple had the most subtle and indefensible doubt whether indeed Serpentine was speaking. There was something odd about the whole thing. Sometimes the thing said sounded with a peculiar resonance in his head; sometimes it was indistinct and elusive like an object seen through troubled waters; sometimes, though Serpentine still moved his fine hands and looked towards his hearers, there were gaps of absolute silence—as if for brief intervals Mr. Barnstaple had gone deaf. . . . Yet it was a discourse; it held together and it held Mr. Barnstaple's attention.

Serpentine had the manner of one who is taking great pains to be as simple as possible with a rather intricate question. He spoke, as it were, in propositions with a pause between each. "It had long been known," he began, "that the possible number of dimensions, like the possible number of anything else that could be enumerated, was unlimited!"

Yes, Mr. Barnstaple had got that, but it proved too much for Mr. Freddy Mush.

"Oh, Lord!" he said. "Dimensions!" and dropped his eye-glass and became despondently inattentive.

"For most practical purposes," Serpentine continued, "the particular universe, the particular system of events, in which we found ourselves and of which we formed part, could be regarded as occurring in a space of three rectilinear dimensions and as undergoing translation, which translation was in fact duration, through a fourth dimension, *time*. Such a system of events was necessarily a gravitational system."

"Er!" said Mr. Burleigh sharply. "Excuse me! I don't see that."

So he, at any rate, was following it too.

"Any universe that endures must necessarily gravitate," Serpentine repeated, as if he were asserting some self-evident fact.

"For the life of me I can't see that," said Mr. Burleigh after a moment's reflection.

Serpentine considered him for a moment. "It *is* so," he said, and went on with his discourse. Our minds, he continued, had been evolved in the form of this practical conception of things, they accepted it as true, and it was only by great efforts of sustained analysis that we were able to realize that this universe in which we lived not only extended but was, as it were, slightly bent and contorted, into a number of other long unsuspected spatial dimensions. It extended beyond its three chief spatial dimensions into these others just as a thin sheet of paper, which is practically two dimensional, extended not only by virtue of its thickness but also of its crinkles and curvature into a third dimension.

"Am I going deaf?" asked Lady Stella in a stage whisper. "I can't catch a word of all this."

"Nor I," said Father Amerton.

Mr. Burleigh made a pacifying gesture towards these unfortunates without taking his eyes off Serpentine's face. Mr. Barnstaple knitted his brows, clasped his knees, knotted his fingers, held on desperately.

He *must* be hearing—of course he was hearing!

Serpentine proceeded to explain that just as it would be possible for any number of practically two-dimensional universes to lie side by side, like sheets of paper, in a three-dimensional space, so in the many-dimensional space about which the ill-equipped human mind is still slowly and painfully acquiring knowledge, it is possible for an innumerable quantity of practically three-dimensional universes to lie, as it were, side by side and to undergo a roughly parallel movement through time. The speculative work of Lonestone and Cephalus had long since given the soundest basis for the belief that there actually were a very great number of such space-and-time universes, parallel to one another and resembling each other, nearly but not exactly, much as the leaves of a book might resemble one another. All of them would have duration, all of them would be gravitating systems——

(Mr. Burleigh shook his head to show that still he didn't see it.)

——And those lying closest together would most nearly resemble each other. How closely they now had an opportunity of learning. For the daring attempts of those two great geniuses, Arden and Greenlake, to use the—(*inaudible*)—thrust of the atom to rotate a portion of the Utopian material universe in that dimension, the F dimension, into which it had long been known to extend for perhaps the length of a man's arm, to rotate this fragment of Utopian matter, much as a gate is swung on its hinges, had manifestly been altogether successful. The gate had swung back again bringing with it a breath of close air, a storm of dust and, to the immense amazement of Utopia, three sets of visitors from an unknown world.

⎯"*Three?*" whispered Mr. Barnstaple doubtfully. "Did he say *three?*"

[Serpentine disregarded him.]

"Our brother and sister have been killed by some unexpected release of force, but their experiment has opened a way that now need never be closed again, out of the present spatial limitations of Utopia into a whole vast folio of hitherto unimagined worlds. Close at hand to us, even as Lonestone guessed ages ago, nearer to us, as he put it, than the blood in our hearts⎯⎯"

("Nearer to us than breathing and closer than hands and feet," Father Amerton misquoted, waking up suddenly. "But what is he talking about? I don't catch it.")

"⎯⎯we discover another planet, much the same size as ours to judge by the scale of its inhabitants, circulating, we may certainly assume, round a sun like that in our skies, a planet bearing life and being slowly subjugated, even as our own is being subjugated, by intelligent life which has evidently evolved under almost exactly parallel conditions to those of our own evolution. This sister universe to ours is, so far as we may judge by appearances, a little retarded in time in relation to our own. Our visitors wear something very like the clothing and display physical characteristics resembling those of our ancestors during the last Age of Confusion. . . .

"We are not yet justified in supposing that their history has been strictly parallel to ours. No two particles of matter are alike; no two vibrations. In all the dimensions of being, in all the universes of God, there has never been and there can never be an exact repetition. That we have come to realize is the one impossible thing. Nevertheless, this world you call Earth is manifestly very near and like to this universe of ours. . . .

"We are eager to learn from you Earthlings, to check our history, which is still very imperfectly known, by your experiences, to show you what we know, to make out what may be possible and desirable in intercourse and help between the people of your planet and ours. We, here, are the merest beginners in knowledge; we have learnt as yet scarcely anything more than the immensity of the things that we have yet to learn and do. In a million kindred things our two worlds may perhaps teach each other and help each other. . . .

"Possibly there are streaks of heredity in your planet that have failed to develop or that have died out in ours. Possibly there are elements or minerals in one world that are rare or wanting in the other. . . . The structure of your atoms (?) . . . our worlds may intermarry (?) . . . to their common invigoration. . . ."

He passed into the inaudible just when Mr. Barnstaple was most moved and most eager to follow what he was saying. Yet a deaf man would have judged he was still speaking.

Mr. Barnstaple met the eye of Mr. Rupert Catskill, as distressed and puzzled as his own. Father
Amerton's face was buried in his hands. Lady Stella
and Mr. Mush were whispering softly together;
they had long since given up any pretence of
listening.

"Such," said Serpentine, abruptly becoming audible again, "is our first rough interpretation of your
apparition in our world and of the possibilities of
our interaction. I have put our ideas before you
as plainly as I can. I would suggest that now one
of you tell us simply and plainly what *you* conceive
to be the truth about your world in relation to ours."

CHAPTER THE FIFTH

THE GOVERNANCE AND HISTORY OF UTOPIA

§ 1

Came a pause. The Earthlings looked at one another and their gaze seemed to converge upon Mr. Cecil Burleigh. That statesman feigned to be unaware of the general expectation. "Rupert," he said. "Won't *you?*"

"I reserve my comments," said Mr. Catskill.

"Father Amerton, you are accustomed to treat of other worlds."

"Not in your presence, Mr. Cecil., No."

"But what am I to tell them?"

"What you think of it," said Mr. Barnstaple.

"Exactly," said Mr. Catskill. "Tell them what you think of it."

No one else appeared to be worthy of consideration. Mr. Burleigh rose slowly and walked thoughtfully to the centre of the semicircle. He grasped his coat lapels and remained for some moments with face downcast as if considering what he was about to say. "Mr. Serpentine," he began at last, raising a candid countenance and regarding the blue sky above the distant lake through his glasses. "Ladies and Gentlemen——"

54

He was going to make a speech!—as though he
was at a Primrose League garden party—or Geneva.
It was preposterous and yet, what else was there to
be done?

"I must confess, Sir, that although I am by no
means a novice at public speaking, I find myself on
this occasion somewhat at a loss. Your admirable
discourse, Sir, simple, direct, lucid, compact, and
rising at times to passages of unaffected eloquence,
has set me a pattern that I would fain follow—and
before which, in all modesty, I quail. You ask me
to tell you as plainly and clearly as possible the
outline facts as we conceive them about this kindred
world out of which with so little premeditation we
have come to you. So far as my poor powers of
understanding or discussing such recondite matters
go, I do not think I can better or indeed supplement
in any way your marvellous exposition of the mathematical aspects of the case. What you have told
us embodies the latest, finest thoughts of terrestrial
science and goes, indeed, far beyond our current
ideas. On certain matters, in, for example, the relationship of time and gravitation, I feel bound to
admit that I do not go with you, but that is rather
a failure to understand your position than any posi-
tive dissent. Upon the broader aspects of the case
there need be no difficulties between us. We accept
your main proposition unreservedly; namely, that
we conceive ourselves to be living in a parallel universe to yours, on a planet the very brother of your
own, indeed quite amazingly like yours, having
regard to all the possible contrasts we might have
found here. We are attracted by and strongly dis-

posed to accept your view that our system is, in all
probability, a little less seasoned and mellowed by
the touch of time than yours, short perhaps by some
hundreds or some thousands of years of your experiences. Assuming this, it is inevitable, Sir, that a
certain humility should mingle in our attitude
towards you. As your juniors it becomes us not to
instruct but to learn. It is for us to ask: What have
you done? To what have you reached? rather than
to display to you with an artless arrogance all that
still remains for us to learn and do. . . ."

"No!" said Mr. Barnstaple to himself but half
audibly. "This is a dream. . . . If it were anyone
else. . . ."

He rubbed his knuckles into his eyes and opened
them again, and there he was still, sitting next to
Mr. Mush in the midst of these Olympian divinities.
And Mr. Burleigh, that polished sceptic, who never
believed, who was never astonished, was leaning forward on his toes and speaking, speaking, with the
assurance of a man who has made ten thousand
speeches. He could not have been more sure of
himself and his audience in the Guildhall in London.
And they were understanding him! Which was
absurd!

There was nothing to do but to fall in with this
stupendous absurdity—and sit and listen. Sometimes Mr. Barnstaple's mind wandered altogether
from what Mr. Burleigh was saying. Then it
returned and hung desperately to his discourse. In
his halting, parliamentary way, his hands trifling
with his glasses or clinging to the lapels of his coat,
Mr. Burleigh was giving Utopia a brief account of

the world of men, seeking to be elementary and
lucid and reasonable, telling them of states and
empires, of wars and the Great War, of economic
organization and disorganization, of revolutions and
Bolshevism, of the terrible Russian famine that was
beginning, of the difficulties of finding honest statesmen and officials, and of the unhelpfulness of newspapers, of all the dark and troubled spectacle of
human life.   Serpentine had used the term "the
Last Age of Confusion," and Mr. Burleigh had
seized upon the phrase and was making much
of it. . . .

It was a great oratorical impromptu.   It must
have gone on for an hour, and the Utopians listened
with keen, attentive faces, now and then nodding
their acceptance and recognition of this statement
or that.   "Very like," would come tapping into Mr.
Barnstaple's brain.   "With us also—in the Age of
Confusion."

At last Mr. Burleigh, with the steady deliberation
of an old parliamentary hand, drew to his end.
Compliments.

He bowed.   He had done.   Mr. Mush startled
everyone by a vigorous hand-clapping in which no
one else joined.

The tension in Mr. Barnstaple's mind had become
intolerable.   He leapt to his feet.

§ 2

He stood making those weak propitiatory gestures
that come so naturally to the inexperienced speaker.
"Ladies and Gentlemen," he said.   "Utopians, Mr.

Burleigh! I crave your pardon for a moment. There is a little matter. Urgent."

For a brief interval he was speechless.

Then he found attention and encouragement in the eye of Urthred.

"Something I don't understand. Something incredible—I mean, incompatible. The little rift. Turns everything into a fantastic phantasmagoria."

The intelligence in Urthred's eye was very encouraging. Mr. Barnstaple abandoned any attempt to address the company as a whole, and spoke directly to Urthred.

"You live in Utopia, hundreds of thousands of years in advance of us. How is it that you are able to talk contemporary English—to use exactly the same language that we do? I ask you, how is that? It is incredible. It jars. It makes a dream of you. And yet you are not a dream? It makes me feel— almost—insane."

Urthred smiled pleasantly. "We *don't* speak English," he said.

Mr. Barnstaple felt the ground slipping from under his feet. "But I *hear* you speaking English," he said.

"Nevertheless we do not speak it," said Urthred. He smiled still more broadly. "We don't—for ordinary purposes—speak anything."

Mr. Barnstaple, with his brain resigning its functions, maintained his pose of deferential attention.

"Ages ago," Urthred continued, "we certainly used to speak languages. We made sounds and we heard sounds. People used to think, and then chose and arranged words and uttered them. The hearer

heard, noted, and retranslated the sounds into ideas.
Then, in some manner which we still do not understand perfectly, people began to *get* the idea before
it was clothed in words and uttered in sounds. They
began to hear in their minds, as soon as the speaker
had arranged his ideas and before he put them into
word symbols even in his own mind. They knew
what he was going to say before he said it. This
direct transmission presently became common; it
was found out that with a little effort most people
could get over to each other in this fashion to some
extent, and the new mode of communication was
developed systematically.

"That is what we do now habitually in this world.
We think directly *to* each other. We determine to
convey the thought and it is conveyed at once—
provided the distance is not too great. We use
sounds in this world now only for poetry and pleasure and in moments of emotion or to shout at a
distance, or with animals, not for the transmission
of ideas from human mind to kindred human mind
any more. When I think to you, the thought, *so far
as it finds corresponding ideas and suitable words
in your mind,* is reflected in your mind. My thought
clothes itself in words in your mind, which words
you seem to hear—and naturally enough in your
own language and your own habitual phrases. Very
probably the members of your party are hearing
what I am saying to you, each with his own individual difference of vocabulary and phrasing."

Mr. Barnstaple had been punctuating this discourse with sharp, intelligent nods, coming now and
then to the verge of interruption. Now he broke

out with: "And that is why occasionally—as for
instance when Mr. Serpentine made his wonderful
explanation just now—when you soar into ideas of
which we haven't even a shadow in our minds, we
just hear nothing at all."

"Are there such gaps?" asked Urthred.

"Many, I fear—for all of us," said Mr. Burleigh.

"It's like being deaf in spots," said Lady Stella.
"Large spots."

Father Amerton nodded agreement.

"And that is why we cannot be clear whether you
are called Urthred or Adam, and why I have found
myself confusing Arden and Greentrees and Forest
in my mind."

"I hope that now you are mentally more at your
ease?" said Urthred.

"Oh, quite," said Mr. Barnstaple. "Quite. And
all things considered, it is really very convenient
for us that there should be this method of transmission. For otherwise I do not see how we could
have avoided weeks of linguistic bother, first principles of our respective grammars, logic, significs,
and so forth, boring stuff for the most part, before
we could have got to anything like our present
understanding."

"A very good point indeed," said Mr. Burleigh,
turning round to Mr. Barnstaple in a very friendly
way. "A very good point indeed. I should never
have noted it if you had not called my attention
to it. It is quite extraordinary; I had not noted
anything of this—this difference. I was occupied,
I am bound to confess, by my own thoughts. I sup-

posed they were speaking English. Took it for granted."

§ 3

It seemed to Mr. Barnstaple that this wonderful experience was now so complete that there remained nothing more to wonder at except its absolute credibility. He sat in this beautiful little building looking out upon dreamland flowers and the sunlit lake amidst this strange mingling of week-end English costumes and this more than Olympian nudity that had already ceased to startle him, he listened and occasionally participated in the long informal conversation that now ensued. It was a discussion that brought to light the most amazing and fundamental differences of moral and social outlook. Yet everything had now assumed a reality that made it altogether natural to suppose that he would presently go home to write about it in the *Liberal* and tell his wife, as much as might seem advisable at the time, about the manners and costumes of this hitherto undiscovered world. He had not even a sense of intervening distances. Sydenham might have been just round the corner.

Presently two pretty young girls made tea at an equipage among the rhododendra and brought it round to people. Tea! It was what we should call China tea, very delicate, and served in little cups without handles, Chinese fashion, but it was real and very refreshing tea.

The earlier curiosities of the Earthlings turned upon methods of government. This was perhaps

natural in the presence of two such statesmen as
Mr. Burleigh and Mr. Catskill.

"What form of government do you have?" asked
Mr. Burleigh. "Is it a monarchy or an autocracy
or a pure democracy? Do you separate the executive and the legislative? And is there one central
government for all your planet, or are there several
governing centres?"

It was conveyed to Mr. Burleigh and his companions with some difficulty that there was no cen-
tral government in Utopia at |all.

"But surely," said Mr. Burleigh, "there is someone or something, some council or bureau or what
not, somewhere, with which the final decision rests
in cases of collective action for the common welfare,
Some ultimate seat and organ of sovereignty, it
seems to me, there *must* be." . . .

No, the Utopians declared, there was no such con-
centration of authority in their world. In the past
there had been, but it had long since diffused back
into the general body of the community. Decisions
in regard to any particular matter were made by the
people who knew most about that matter.

"But suppose it is a decision that has to be generally observed? A rule affecting the public health,
for example? 'Who would enforce it?"

"It would not need to be enforced. Why should
it?"

"But suppose someone refused to obey your
regulation?"

"We should inquire why he or she did not con-
form. There might be some exceptional reason."

"But failing that?"

"We should make an inquiry into his mental and moral health."

"The mind doctor takes the place of the policeman," said Mr. Burleigh.

"I should prefer the policeman," said Mr. Rupert Catskill.

"You *would*, Rupert," said Mr. Burleigh as who should say: "*Got* you that time."

"Then do you mean to say," he continued, addressing the Utopians with an expression of great intelligence, "that your affairs are all managed by special bodies or organizations—one scarcely knows what to call them—without any co-ordination of their activities?"

"The activities of our world," said Urthred, "are all co-ordinated to secure the general freedom. We have a number of intelligences directed to the general psychology of the race and to the interaction of one collective function upon another."

"Well, isn't that group of intelligences a governing class?" said Mr. Burleigh.

"Not in the sense that they exercise any arbitrary will," said Urthred. "They deal with general relations, that is all. But they rank no higher, they have no more precedence on that account than a philosopher has over a scientific specialist."

"This is a republic indeed!" said Mr. Burleigh. "But how it works and how it came about I cannot imagine. Your state is probably a highly socialistic one?"

"You still live in a world in which nearly everything except the air, the high roads, the high seas and the wilderness is privately owned?"

"We do," said Mr. Catskill. "Owned—and competed for."

"We have been through that stage. We found at last that private property in all but very personal things was an intolerable nuisance to mankind. We got rid of it. An artist or a scientific man has complete control of all the material he needs, we all own our tools and appliances and have rooms and places of our own, but there is no property for trade or speculation. All this militant property, this property of manœuvre, has been quite got rid of. But how we got rid of it is a long story. It was not done in a few years. The exaggeration of private property was an entirely natural and necessary stage in the development of human nature. It led at last to monstrous results, but it was only through these monstrous and catastrophic results that men learnt the need and nature of the limitations of private property."

Mr. Burleigh had assumed an attitude which was obviously habitual to him. He sat very low in his chair with his long legs crossed in front of him and the thumb and fingers of one hand placed with meticulous exactness against those of the other.

"I must confess," he said, "that I am most interested in the peculiar form of Anarchism which seems to prevail here. Unless I misunderstand you completely every man attends to his own business as the servant of the state. I take it you have—you must correct me if I am wrong—a great number of people concerned in the production and distribution and preparation of food; they inquire, I assume, into the needs of the world, they satisfy them and

they are a law unto themselves in their way of doing
it. They conduct researches, they make experiments. Nobody compels, obliges, restrains or prevents them. ("People talk to them about it," said
Urthred with a faint smile.) And again others produce and manufacture and study metals for all mankind and are also a law unto themselves. Others
again see to the habitability of your world, plan and
arrange these delightful habitations, say who shall
use them and how they shall be used. Others pur-
sue pure science. Others experiment with sensory
and imaginative possibilities and are artists. Others
again teach."

"They are very important," said Lychnis.

"And they all do it in harmony—and due proportion. Without either a central legislature or
executive. I will admit that all this seems admirable—but impossible. Nothing of the sort has ever
been even suggested yet in the world from which
we come."

"Something of the sort was suggested long ago
by the Guild Socialists," said Mr. Barnstaple.

"Dear me!" said Mr. Burleigh. "I know very
little about the Guild Socialists. Who were they?
Tell me."

Mr. Barnstaple tacitly declined that task. "The
idea is quite familiar to our younger people," he
said. "Laski calls it the pluralistic state, as distinguished from the monistic state in which sovereignty is concentrated. Even the Chinese have
it. A Pekin professor, Mr. S. C. Chang, has written
a pamphlet on what he calls 'Professionalism.' I
read it only a few weeks ago. He sent it to the

office of the *Liberal*. He points out how undesirable it is and how unnecessary for China to pass through a phase of democratic politics on the western model. He wants China to go right straight on to a collateral independence of functional classes, mandarins, industrials, agricultural workers and so forth, much as we seem to find it here. Though that of course involves an educational revolution. Decidedly the germ of what you call Anarchism here is also in the air we come from."

"Dear me!" said Mr. Burleigh, looking more intelligent and appreciative than ever. "And is that so? I had *no* idea——!"

§ 4

The conversation continued desultory in form and yet the exchange of ideas was rapid and effective. Quite soon, as it seemed to Mr. Barnstaple, an outline of the history of Utopia from the Last Age of Confusion onward shaped itself in his mind.

The more he learnt of that Last Age of Confusion the more it seemed to resemble the present time on earth. In those days the Utopians had worn abundant clothing and lived in towns quite after the earthly fashion. A fortunate conspiracy of accidents rather than any set design had opened for them some centuries of opportunity and expansion. Climatic phases and political chances had smiled upon the race after a long period of recurrent shortage, pestilence and destructive warfare. For the first time the Utopians had been able to explore the whole planet on which they lived, and these explorations had brought great virgin areas under the axe, the spade and the plough. There had been an enormous increase in real wealth and in leisure and liberty. Many thousands of people were lifted out of the normal squalor of human life to positions in which they could, if they chose, think and act with unprecedented freedom. A few, a sufficient few, did. A vigorous development of scientific inquiry began and, trailing after it a multitude of ingenious inventions, produced a great enlargement of practical human power.

There had been previous outbreaks of the scientific intelligence in Utopia, but none before had ever occurred in such favourable circumstances or lasted long enough to come to abundant practical fruition. Now in a couple of brief centuries the Utopians, who had hitherto crawled about their planet like sluggish ants or travelled parasitically on larger and swifter animals, found themselves able to fly rapidly or speak instantaneously to any other point on the planet. They found themselves, too, in possession of mechanical power on a scale beyond all previous experience, and not simply of mechanical power; physiological and then psychological science followed in the wake of physics and chemistry, and extraordinary possibilities of control over his own body and over his social life dawned upon the Utopian. But these things came, when at last they did come, so rapidly and confusingly that it was only a small minority of people who realized the possibilities, as distinguished from the concrete achievements, of this tremendous expansion of knowledge. The rest took the novel inventions as they came, haphazard, with as little adjustment as possible of their thoughts and ways of living to the new necessities these novelties implied.

The first response of the general population of Utopia to the prospect of power, leisure and freedom thus opened out to it was proliferation. It behaved just as senselessly and mechanically as any other animal or vegetable species would have done. It bred until it had completely swamped the ampler opportunity that had opened before it. It spent the great gifts of science as rapidly as it got them in a mere insensate multiplication of the common life. At one time in the Last Age of Confusion the population of Utopia had mounted to over two thousand million. . . .

"But what is it now?" asked Mr. Burleigh.

About two hundred and fifty million, the Utopians told him. That had been the maximum population that could live a fully developed life upon the surface of Utopia. But now with increasing resources the population was being increased.

A gasp of horror came from Father Amerton. He had been dreading this realization for some time. It struck at his moral foundations. "And you dare to *regulate* increase! You control it! Your women consent to bear children as they are needed—or refrain!"

"Of course," said Urthred. "Why not?"

"I feared as much," said Father Amerton, and leaning forward he covered his face with his hands, murmuring, "I felt this in the atmosphere! The

human stud farm! Refusing to create souls! The
wickedness of it! Oh, my God!"

Mr. Burleigh regarded the emotion of the reverend gentleman through his glasses with a slightly
shocked expression. He detested catchwords. But
Father Amerton stood for very valuable conservative elements in the community. Mr. Burleigh
turned to the Utopian again. "That is extremely
interesting," he said. "Even at present our earth
contrives to carry a population of at least five times
that amount."

"But twenty millions or so will starve this winter,
you told us a little while ago—in a place called Russia. And only a very small proportion of the rest
are leading what even you would call full and spa-
cious lives?"

"Nevertheless the contrast is very striking," said
Mr. Burleigh.

"It is terrible!" said Father Amerton.

The overcrowding of the planet in the Last Age of
Confusion was, these Utopians insisted, the fundamental evil out of which all the others that afflicted
the race arose. An overwhelming flood of newcomers poured into the world and swamped every
effort the intelligent minority could make to educate a sufficient proportion of them to meet the
demands of the new and still rapidly changing conditions of life. And the intelligent minority was
not itself in any position to control the racial destiny. These great masses of population that had
been blundered into existence, swayed by damaged
and decaying traditions and amenable to the crudest
suggestions, were the natural prey and support of

every adventurer with a mind blatant enough and
a conception of success coarse enough to appeal to
them. The economic system, clumsily and convul-
sively reconstructed to meet the new conditions of
mechanical production and distribution, became
more and more a cruel and impudent exploitation
of the multitudinous congestion of the common man
by the predatory and acquisitive few. That all too
common common man was hustled through misery
and subjection from his cradle to his grave; he was
cajoled and lied to, he was bought, sold and dominated by an impudent minority, bolder and no doubt
more energetic, but in all other respects no more
intelligent than himself. It was difficult, Urthred
said, for a Utopian nowadays to convey the
monstrous stupidity, wastefulness and vulgarity to
which these rich and powerful men of the Last Age
of Confusion attained.

("We will not trouble you," said Mr. Burleigh.
"Unhappily—we know. . . . We know. Only too
well do we know.")

Upon this festering, excessive mass of population
disasters descended at last like wasps upon a heap
of rotting fruit. It was its natural, inevitable destiny. A war that affected nearly the whole planet
dislocated its flimsy financial system and most of its
economic machinery beyond any possibility of re-
pair. Civil wars and clumsily conceived attempts
at social revolution continued the disorganization.
A series of years of bad weather accentuated the
general shortage. The exploiting adventurers, too
stupid to realize what had happened, continued to
cheat and hoodwink the commonalty and burke any

rally of honest men, as wasps will continue to eat even after their bodies have been cut away. The effort to make passed out of Utopian life, triumphantly superseded by the effort to get. Production dwindled down towards the vanishing point. Accumulated wealth vanished. An overwhelming system of debt, a swarm of creditors, morally incapable of helpful renunciation, crushed out all fresh initiative.

The long diastole in Utopian affairs that had begun with the great discoveries, passed into a phase of rapid systole. What plenty and pleasure was still possible in the world was filched all the more greedily by the adventurers of finance and speculative business. Organized science had long since been commercialized, and was "applied" now chiefly to a hunt for profitable patents and the forestalling of necessary supplies. The neglected lamp of pure science waned, flickered and seemed likely to go out again altogether, leaving Utopia in the beginning of a new series of Dark Ages like those before the age of discovery began. . . .

"It is really *very* like a gloomy diagnosis of our own outlook," said Mr. Burleigh. "Extraordinarily like. How Dean Inge would have enjoyed all this!"

"To an infidel of his stamp, no doubt, it would seem most enjoyable," said Father Amerton a little incoherently.

These comments annoyed Mr. Barnstaple, who was urgent to hear more.

"And then," he said to Urthred, "what happened?"

§ 5

What happened, Mr. Barnstaple gathered, was a deliberate change in Utopian thought. A growing number of people were coming to understand that amidst the powerful and easily released forces that science and organization had brought within reach of man, the old conception of social life in the state, as a limited and legalized struggle of men and women to get the better of one another, was becoming too dangerous to endure, just as the increased dreadfulness of modern weapons was making the separate sovereignty of nations too dangerous to endure. There had to be new ideas and new conventions of human association if history was not to end in disaster and collapse.

All societies were based on the limitation by laws and taboos and treaties of the primordial fierce combativeness of the ancestral man-ape; that ancient spirit of self-assertion had now to undergo new restrictions commensurate with the new powers and dangers of the race. The idea of competition to possess, as the ruling idea of intercourse, was, like some ill-controlled furnace, threatening to consume the machine it had formerly driven. The idea of creative service had to replace it. To that idea the human mind and will had to be turned if social life was to be saved. Propositions that had seemed, in former ages, to be inspired and exalted idealism began now to be recognized not simply as sober psychological truth but as practical and urgently necessary truth. In explaining this Urthred expressed himself in a manner that recalled to Mr.

Barnstaple's mind certain very familiar phrases; he seemed to be saying that whosoever would save his life should lose it, and that whosoever would give his life should thereby gain the whole world.

Father Amerton's thoughts, it seemed, were also responding in the same manner. For he suddenly interrupted with: "But what you are saying is a quotation!"

Urthred admitted that he had a quotation in mind, a passage from the teachings of a man of great poetic power who had lived long ago in the days of spoken words.

He would have proceeded, but Father Amerton was too excited to let him do so. "But who was this teacher?" he asked. "Where did he live? How was he born? How did he die?"

A picture was flashed upon Mr. Barnstaple's consciousness of a solitary-looking, pale-faced figure, beaten and bleeding, surrounded by armoured guards, in the midst of a thrusting, jostling, sun-bit crowd which filled a narrow, high-walled street. Behind, some huge, ugly implement was borne along, dipping and swaying with the swaying of the multitude. . . .

"Did he die upon the Cross in *this* world also?" cried Father Amerton. "Did he die upon the Cross?"

This prophet in Utopia they learnt had died very painfully, but not upon the Cross. He had been tortured in some way, but neither the Utopians nor these particular Earthlings had sufficient knowledge of the technicalities of torture to get any idea over about that, and then apparently he had been fast-

ened upon a slowly turning wheel and exposed until
he died. It was the abominable punishment of a
cruel and conquering race, and it had been inflicted
upon him because his doctrine of universal service
had alarmed the rich and dominant who did not
serve. Mr. Barnstaple had a momentary vision of
a twisted figure upon that wheel of torture in the
blazing sun. And, marvellous triumph over death!
out of a world that could do such a deed had come
this great peace and universal beauty about him!

But Father Amerton was pressing his questions.
"But did you not realize who he was? Did not
this world suspect?"

A great many people thought that this man was
a God. But he had been accustomed to call himself
merely a son of God or a son of Man.

Father Amerton stuck to his point. "But you
worship him now?"

"We follow his teaching because it was wonderful
and true," said Urthred.

"But worship?"

"No."

"But does nobody worship? There *were* those
who worshipped him?"

There were those who worshipped him. There
were those who quailed before the stern magnificence of his teaching and yet who had a tormenting
sense that he was right in some profound way. So
they played a trick upon their own uneasy con-
sciences by treating him as a magical god instead
of as a light to their souls. They interwove with
his execution ancient traditions of sacrificial kings.
Instead of receiving him frankly and clearly and

making him a part of their understandings and wills they pretended to eat him mystically and make him a part of their bodies. They turned his wheel into a miraculous symbol, and they confused it with the equator and the sun and the ecliptic and indeed with anything else that was round. In cases of ill-luck, ill-health or bad weather it was believed to be very helpful for the believer to describe a circle in the air with the forefinger.

And since this teacher's memory was very dear to the ignorant multitude because of his gentleness and charity, it was seized upon by cunning and aggressive types who constituted themselves champions and exponents of the wheel, who grew rich and powerful in its name, led people into great wars for its sake and used it as a cover and justification for envy, hatred, tyranny and dark desires. Until at last men said that had that ancient prophet come again to Utopia, his own triumphant wheel would have crushed and destroyed him afresh. . . .

. Father Amerton seemed inattentive to this communication. He was seeing it from another angle. "But surely," he said, "there is a remnant of believers still! Despised perhaps—but a remnant?"

There was no remnant. The whole world followed that Teacher of Teachers, but no one worshipped him. On some old treasured buildings the wheel was still to be seen carved, often with the most fantastic decorative elaborations. And in museums and collections there were multitudes of pictures, images, charms and the like.

"I don't understand this," said Father Amerton.

"It is too terrible.   I am at a loss.   I do not understand."

§ 6

A fair and rather slender man with a delicately beautiful face whose name, Mr. Barnstaple was to learn later, was Lion, presently took over from Urthred the burthen of explaining and answering the questions of the Earthlings.

He was one of the educational co-ordinators in Utopia. He made it clear that the change over in Utopian affairs had been no sudden revolution. No new system of laws and customs, no new method of economic co-operation based on the idea of universal service to the common good, had sprung abruptly into being complete and finished. Throughout a long period, before and during the Last Age of Confusion, the foundations of the new state were laid by a growing multitude of inquirers and workers, having no set plan or preconceived method, but brought into unconscious co-operation by a common impulse to service and a common lucidity and veracity of mind. It was only towards the climax of the Last Age of Confusion in Utopia that psychological science began to develop with any vigour, comparable to the vigour of the development of geographical and physical science during the preceding centuries. And the social and economic disorder which was checking experimental science and crippling the organized work of the universities was stimulating inquiry into the processes of human association and making it desperate and fearless.

The impression given Mr. Barnstaple was not of one of those violent changes which our world has learnt to call revolutions, but of an increase of light, a dawn of new ideas, in which the things of the old order went on for a time with diminishing vigour until people began as a matter of common sense to do the new things in the place of the old.

The beginnings of the new order were in discussions, books and psychological laboratories; the soil in which it grew was found in schools and colleges. The old order gave small rewards to the schoolmaster, but its dominant types were too busy with the struggle for wealth and power to take much heed of teaching: it was left to any man or woman who would give thought and labour without much hope of tangible rewards, to shape the world anew in the minds of the young. And they did so shape it. In a world ruled ostensibly by adventurer politicians, in a world where men came to power through floundering business enterprises and financial cunning, it was presently being taught and understood that extensive private property was socially a nuisance, and that the state could not do its work properly nor education produce its proper results, side by side with a class of irresponsible rich people. For, by their very nature, they assailed, they corrupted, they undermined every state undertaking; their flaunting existences distorted and disguised all the values of life. They had to go, for the good of the race.

"Didn't they fight?" asked Mr. Catskill pugnaciously.

They had fought irregularly but fiercely. The

fight to delay or arrest the coming of the universal scientific state, the educational state, in Utopia, had gone on as a conscious struggle for nearly five centuries. The fight against it was the fight of greedy, passionate, prejudiced and self-seeking men against the crystallization into concrete realities of this new idea of association for service. It was fought wherever ideas were spread; it was fought with dismissals and threats and boycotts and storms of violence, with lies and false accusations, with prosecutions and imprisonments, with lynching-rope, tar and feathers, paraffin, bludgeon and rifle, bomb and gun.

But the service of the new idea that had been launched into the world never failed; it seized upon the men and women it needed with compelling power. Before the scientific state was established in Utopia more than a million martyrs had been killed for it, and those who had suffered lesser wrongs were beyond all reckoning. Point after point was won in education, in social laws, in economic method. No date could be fixed for the change. A time came when Utopia perceived that it was day and that a new order of things had replaced the old. . . .

"So it must be," said Mr. Barnstaple, as though Utopia were not already present about him. "So it must be."

A question was being answered. Every Utopian child is taught to the full measure of its possibilities and directed to the work that is indicated by its desires and capacity. It is born well. It is born of perfectly healthy parents; its mother has chosen to bear it after due thought and preparation. It grows

up under perfectly healthy conditions; its natural
impulses to play and learn are gratified by the
subtlest educational methods; hands, eyes and limbs
are given every opportunity of training and growth;
it learns to draw, write, express itself, use a great
variety of symbols to assist and extend its thought.
Kindness and civility become ingrained habits, for
all about it are kind and civil. And in particular
the growth of its imagination is watched and en-
couraged. It learns the wonderful history of its
world and its race, how man has struggled and still
struggles out of his earlier animal narrowness and
egotism towards an empire over being that is still
but faintly apprehended through dense veils of
ignorance. All its desires are made fine; it learns
from poetry, from example and the love of those
about it to lose its solicitude for itself in love; its
sexual passions are turned against its selfishness,
its curiosity flowers into scientific passion, its combativeness is set to fight disorder, its inherent pride
and ambition are directed towards an honourable
share in the common achievement. It goes to the
work that attracts it and chooses what it will do.

If the individual is indolent there is no great loss,
there is plenty for all in Utopia, but then it will find
no lovers, nor will it ever bear children, because no
one in Utopia loves those who have neither energy
nor distinction. There is much pride of the mate in
Utopian love. And there is no idle rich "society"
in Utopia, nor games and shows for the mere looker-
on. There is nothing for the mere looker-on. It is
a pleasant world indeed for holidays, but not for
those who would continuously do nothing.

For centuries now Utopian science has been able to discriminate among births, and nearly every Utopian alive would have ranked as an energetic creative spirit in former days. There are few dull and no really defective people in Utopia; the idle strains, the people of lethargic dispositions or weak imaginations, have mostly died out; the melancholic type has taken its dismissal and gone; spiteful and malignant characters are disappearing. The vast majority of Utopians are active, sanguine, inventive, receptive and good-tempered.

"And you have not even a parliament?" asked Mr. Burleigh, still incredulous.

Utopia has no parliament, no politics, no private wealth, no business competition, no police nor prisons, no lunatics, no defectives nor cripples, and it has none of these things because it has schools and teachers who are all that schools and teachers can be. Politics, trade and competition are the methods of adjustment of a crude society. Such methods of adjustment have been laid aside in Utopia for more than a thousand years. There is no rule nor government needed by adult Utopians because all the rule and government they need they have had in childhood and youth.

Said Lion: *"Our education is our government."*

CHAPTER THE SIXTH

SOME EARTHLY CRITICISMS

§ 1

At times during that memorable afternoon and evening it seemed to Mr. Barnstaple that he was involved in nothing more remarkable than an extraordinary dialogue about government and history, a dialogue that had in some inexplicable way become spectacular; it was as if all this was happening only in his mind; and then the absolute reality of his adventure would return to him with overwhelming power and his intellectual interest fade to inattention in the astounding strangeness of his position. In these latter phases he would find his gaze wandering from face to face of the Utopians who surrounded him, resting for a time on some exquisite detail of the architecture of the building and then coming back to these divinely graceful forms.

Then incredulously he would revert to his fellow Earthlings.

Not one of these Utopian faces but was as candid, earnest and beautiful as the angelic faces of an Italian painting. One woman was strangely like Michael Angelo's Delphic Sibyl. They sat in easy attitudes, men and women together, for the most

81

part concentrated on the discussion, but every now and then Mr. Barnstaple would meet the direct scrutiny of a pair of friendly eyes or find some Utopian face intent upon the costume of Lady Stella or the eye-glass of Mr. Mush.

Mr. Barnstaple's first impression of the Utopians had been that they were all young people; now he perceived that many of these faces had a quality of vigorous maturity. None showed any of the distinctive marks of age as this world notes them, but both Urthred and Lion had lines of experience about eyes and lips and brow.

The effect of these people upon Mr. Barnstaple mingled stupefaction with familiarity in the strangest way. He had a feeling that he had always known that such a race could exist and that this knowledge had supplied the implicit standard of a thousand judgments upon human affairs, and at the same time he was astonished to the pitch of incredulity to find himself in the same world with them. They were at once normal and wonderful in comparison with himself and his companions who were, on their part, at the same time queer and perfectly matter of fact.

And together with a strong desire to become friendly and intimate with these fine and gracious persons, to give himself to them and to associate them with himself by service and reciprocal acts, there was an awe and fear of them that made him shrink from contact with them and quiver at their touch. He desired their personal recognition of himself as a fellow and companion so greatly that his sense of his own ungraciousness and unworth-

iness overwhelmed him. He wanted to bow down
before them. Beneath all the light and loveliness
of things about him lurked the intolerable premoni-
tion of his ultimate rejection from this new world.

So great was the impression made by the Utopians
upon Mr. Barnstaple, so entirely did he yield himself up to his joyful acceptance of their grace and
physical splendour, that for a time he had no attention left over to note how different from his own
were the reactions of several of his Earthling companions. The aloofness of the Utopians from the
queerness, grotesqueness and cruelty of normal
earthly life made him ready for the most uncritical
approval of their institutions and ways of life.

It was the behaviour of Father Amerton which
first awakened him to the fact that it was possible
to disapprove of these wonderful people very highly
and to display a very considerable hostility to them.
At first Father Amerton had kept a round-faced,
round-eyed wonder above his round collar; he had
shown a disposition to give the lead to anyone who
chose to take it, and he had said not a word until
the naked beauty of dead Greenlake had surprised
him into an expression of unclerical appreciation.
But during the journey to the lakeside and the meal
and the opening arrangements of the conference
there was a reaction, and this first naïve and deferential astonishment gave place to an attitude of
resistance and hostility. It was as if this new
world which had begun by being a spectacle had
taken on the quality of a proposition which he felt
he had either to accept or confute. Perhaps it was
that the habit of mind of a public censor was too

strong for him and that he could not feel normal
again until he began to condemn. Perhaps he was
really shocked and distressed by the virtual nudity
of these lovely bodies about him. But he began
presently to make queer grunts and coughs, to mutter to himself, and to betray an increasing inca-
pacity to keep still.

He broke out first into an interruption when the
question of population was raised. For a little
while his intelligence prevailed over this emotional
stir when the prophet of the wheel was discussed,
but then his gathering preoccupations resumed their
sway.

"I must speak out," Mr. Barnstaple heard him
mutter. "I must speak out."

Now suddenly he began to ask questions. "There
are some things I want to have clear," he said. "I
want to know what moral state this so-called Utopia
is in. Excuse me!"

He got up. He stood with wavering hands, unable for a moment to begin. Then he went to the
end of the row of seats and placed himself so that
his hands could rest on the back of a seat. He
passed his fingers through his hair and he seemed
to be inhaling deeply. An unwonted animation
came into his face, which reddened and began to
shine. A horrible suspicion crossed the mind of
Mr. Barnstaple that so it was he must stand when
he began those weekly sermons of his, those fearless
denunciations of almost everything, in the church of
St. Barnabas in the West. The suspicion deep-
ened to a still more horrible certainty.

"Friends, Brothers of this new world—I have

certain things to say to you that I cannot delay
saying. I want to ask you some soul-searching
questions. I want to deal plainly with you about
some plain and simple but very fundamental matters. I want to put things to you frankly and as
man to man, not being mealy-mouthed about urgent if delicate things. Let me come without parley
to what I have to say. I want to ask you if, in
this so-called state of Utopia, you still have and
respect and honour the most sacred thing in social
life. Do you still respect the marriage bond?"

He paused, and in the pause the Utopian reply
came through to Mr. Barnstaple: "In Utopia there
are no bonds."

But Father Amerton was not asking questions
with any desire for answers; he was asking questions pulpit-fashion.

"I want to know," he was booming out, "if that
holy union revealed to our first parents in the
Garden of Eden holds good here, if that sanctified
lifelong association of one man and one woman, in
good fortune and ill fortune, excluding every other
sort of intimacy, is the rule of your lives. I want
to know——"

"But he *doesn't* want to know," came a Utopian
intervention.

"——if that shielded and guarded dual purity
——"

Mr. Burleigh raised a long white hand. "Father
Amerton," he protested, *"please."*

The hand of Mr. Burleigh was a potent hand that
might still wave towards preferment. Few things
under heaven could stop Father Amerton when

he was once launched upon one of his soul storms, but the hand of Mr. Burleigh was among such things.

"——has followed another still more precious gift and been cast aside here and utterly rejected of men? What is it, Mr. Burleigh?"

"I wish you would not press this matter further just at present, Father Amerton. Until we have learnt a little more. Institutions are, manifestly, very different here. Even the institution of marriage may be different."

The preacher's face lowered. "Mr. Burleigh," he said, "I *must*. If my suspicions are right, I want to strip this world forthwith of its hectic pretence to a sort of health and virtue."

"Not much stripping required," said Mr. Burleigh's chauffeur, in a very audible aside.

A certain testiness became evident in Mr. Burleigh's voice.

"Then ask questions," he said. "Ask questions. Don't orate, please. They don't want us to orate."

"I've asked my question," said Father Amerton sulkily with a rhetorical glare at Urthred, and remained standing.

The answer came clear and explicit. In Utopia there was no compulsion for men and women to go about in indissoluble pairs. For most Utopians that would be inconvenient. Very often men and women, whose work brought them closely together, were lovers and kept very much together, as Arden and Greenlake had done. But they were not obliged to do that.

There had not always been this freedom. In the

old crowded days of conflict, and especially among
the agricultural workers and employed people of
Utopia, men and women who had been lovers were
bound together under severe penalties for life. They
lived together in a small home which the woman
kept in order for the man, she was his servant and
bore him as many children as possible, while he got
food for them. The children were desired because
they were soon helpful on the land or as wage
earners. But the necessities that had subjugated
women to that sort of pairing had passed away.

People paired indeed with their chosen mates, but
they did so by an inner necessity and not by any
outward compulsion.

Father Amerton had listened with ill-concealed
impatience. Now he jumped with: "Then I was
right, and you have abolished the family?" His
finger pointed at Urthred made it almost a personal
accusation.

No. Utopia had not abolished the family. It
had enlarged and glorified the family until it em-
braced the whole world. Long ago that prophet of
the wheel, whom Father Amerton seemed to respect,
had preached that very enlargement of the ancient
narrowness of home. They had told him while he
preached that his mother and his brethren stood
without and claimed his attention. But he would
not go to them. He had turned to the crowd that
listened to his words: "Behold my mother and my
brethren!"

Father Amerton slapped the seat-back in front of
him loudly and startlingly. "A quibble," he cried,
"a quibble! Satan too can quote the scriptures."

It was clear to Mr. Barnstaple that Father Amerton was not in complete control of himself. He was frightened by what he was doing and yet impelled to do it. He was too excited to think clearly or control his voice properly, so that he shouted and boomed in the wildest way. He was "letting himself go" and trusting to the habits of the pulpit of St. Barnabas to bring him through.

"I perceive now how you stand. Only too well do I perceive how you stand. From the outset I guessed how things were with you. I waited—I waited to be perfectly sure, before I bore my testimony. But it speaks for itself—the shamelessness of your costume, the licentious freedom of your manners! Young men and women, smiling, joining hands, near to caressing, when averted eyes, averted eyes, are the least tribute you could pay to modesty! And this vile talk—of lovers loving—without bonds or blessings, without rules or restraint. What does it mean? Whither does it lead? Do not imagine because I am a priest, a man pure and virginal in spite of great temptations, do not imagine that I do not understand! Have I no vision of the secret places of the heart? Do not the wounded sinners, the broken potsherds, creep to me with their pitiful confessions? And I will tell you plainly whither you go and how you stand? This so-called freedom of yours is nothing but licence. Your so-called Utopia, I see plainly, is nothing but a hell of unbridled indulgence! Unbridled indulgence!"

Mr. Burleigh held up a protesting hand, but Father Amerton's eloquence soared over the obstruction.

He beat upon the back of the seat before him. "I will bear my witness," he shouted. "I will bear my witness. I will make no bones about it. I refuse to mince matters, I tell you. You are all living —in promiscuity! That is the word for it. In animal promiscuity! In *bestial* promiscuity!"

Mr. Burleigh had sprung to his feet. He was holding up his two hands and motioning the London Boanerges to sit down. "No, no!" he cried. "You must *stop*, Mr. Amerton. Really, you must stop. You are being insulting. You do not understand. Sit *down*, please. I insist."

"*Sit down and hold your peace*," said a very clear voice. "Or you will be taken away."

Something made Father Amerton aware of a still figure at his elbow. He met the eyes of a lithe young man who was scrutinizing his build as a portrait painter might scrutinize a new sitter. There was no threat in his bearing, he stood quite still, and yet his appearance threw an extraordinary quality of evanescence about Father Amerton. The great preacher's voice died in his throat.

Mr. Burleigh's bland voice was lifted to avert a conflict. "Mr. Serpentine, Sir, I appeal to you and apologize. He is not fully responsible. We others regret the interruption—the incident. I pray you, please do not take him away, whatever taking away may mean. I will answer personally for his good behaviour. . . . *Do* sit down, Mr. Amerton, *please; now;* or I shall wash my hands of the whole business."

Father Amerton hesitated.

"My time will come," he said and looked the

young man in the eyes for a moment and then went back to his seat.

Urthred spoke quietly and clearly. "You Earthlings are difficult guests to entertain. This is not all. . . . Manifestly this man's mind is very unclean. His sexual imagination is evidently inflamed and diseased. He is angry and anxious to insult and wound. And his noises are terrific. Tomorrow he must be examined and dealth with."

"How?" said Father Amerton, his round face suddenly grey. "How do you mean—*dealt* with?"

"*Please* do not talk," said Mr. Burleigh. "*Please* do not talk any more. You have done quite enough mischief. . . ."

For the time the incident seemed at an end, but it had left a queer little twinge of fear in Mr. Barnstaple's heart. These Utopians were very gentlemannered and gracious people indeed, but just for a moment the hand of power had seemed to hover over the Earthling party. Sunlight and beauty were all about the visitors, nevertheless they were strangers and quite helpless strangers in an unknown world. The Utopian faces were kindly and their eyes curious and in a manner friendly, but much more observant than friendly. It was as if they looked across some impassable gulf of difference.

And then Mr. Barnstaple in the midst of his distress met the brown eyes of Lychnis, and they were kindlier than the eyes of the other Utopians. She, at least, understood the fear that had come to him, he felt, and she was willing to reassure him and be his friend. Mr. Barnstaple looked at her, feeling

for the moment much as a stray dog might do who
approaches a doubtfully amiable group and gets
a friendly glance and a greeting.

§ 2

Another mind that was also in active resistance to
Utopia was that of Mr. Freddy Mush. He had no
quarrel indeed with the religion or morals or social
organization of Utopia. He had long since learnt
that no gentleman of serious aesthetic pretensions
betrays any interest whatever in such matters. His
perceptions were by hypothesis too fine for them.
But presently he made it clear that there had been
something very ancient and beautiful called the
"Balance of Nature" which the scientific methods of
Utopia had destroyed. What this Balance of Nature of his was, and how it worked on Earth, neither
the Utopians nor Mr. Barnstaple were able to understand very clearly. Under cross-examination
Mr. Mush grew pink and restive and his eye-glass
flashed defensively. "I hold by the swallows," he
repeated. "If you can't see my point about that
I don't know what else I can say."

He began with the fact and reverted to the fact
that there were no swallows to be seen in Utopia,
and there were no swallows to be seen in Utopia
because there were no gnats nor midges. There had
been an enormous deliberate reduction of insect life
in Utopia, and that had seriously affected every
sort of creature that was directly or indirectly
dependent upon insect life. So soon as the new
state of affairs was securely established in Utopia

and the educational state working, the attention of
the Utopian community had been given to the
long-cherished idea of a systematic extermination of
tiresome and mischievous species. A careful inquiry was made into the harmfulness and the possibility of eliminating the house-fly for example,
wasps and hornets, various species of mice and rats,
rabbits, stinging nettles. Ten thousand species,
from disease-germ to rhinoceros and hyena, were
put upon their trial. Every species found was
given an advocate. Of each it was asked: What
good is it? What harm does it do? How can it
be extirpated? What else may go with it if it
goes? Is it worth while wiping it out of existence?
Or can it be mitigated and retained? And even
when the verdict was death final and complete,
Utopia set about the business of extermination with
great caution. A reserve would be kept and was in
many cases still being kept, in some secure isolation,
of every species condemned.

Most infectious and contagious fevers had been
completely stamped out; some had gone very
easily; some had only been driven out of human life
by proclaiming a war and subjecting the whole
population to discipline. Many internal and ex-
ternal parasites of man and animals had also been
got rid of completely. And further, there had been
a great cleansing of the world from noxious insects,
from weeds and vermin and hostile beasts. The
mosquito had gone, the house-fly, the blow-fly, and
indeed a great multitude of flies had gone; they had
been driven out of life by campaigns involving an
immense effort and extending over many genera-

tions. It had been infinitely more easy to get rid of such big annoyances as the hyena and the wolf than to abolish these smaller pests. The attack upon the flies had involved the virtual rebuilding of a large proportion of Utopian houses and a minute cleansing of them all throughout the planet.

The question of what else would go if a certain species went was one of the most subtle that Utopia had to face. Certain insects, for example, were destructive and offensive grubs in the opening stage of their lives, were evil as caterpillar or pupa and then became either beautiful in themselves or necessary to the fertilization of some useful or exquisite flowers. Others offensive in themselves were a necessary irreplaceable food to pleasant and desirable creatures. It was not true that swallows had gone from Utopia, but they had become extremely rare; and rare too were a number of little insectivorous birds, the fly-catcher for example, that harlequin of the air. But they had not died out altogether; the extermination of insects had not gone to that length; sufficient species had remained to make some districts still habitable for these delightful birds.

Many otherwise obnoxious plants were a convenient source of chemically complex substances that were still costly or tedious to make synthetically, and so had kept a restricted place in life. Plants and flowers, always simpler and more plastic in the hands of the breeder and hybridizer than animals, had been enormously changed in Utopia. Our Earthlings were to find a hundred sorts of foliage and of graceful and scented blossoms that were

altogether strange to them. Plants, Mr. Barnstaple
learnt, had been trained and bred to make new and
unprecedented secretions, waxes, gums, essential oils
and the like, of the most desirable quality.

There had been much befriending and taming of
big animals; the larger carnivora, combed and
cleaned, reduced to a milk dietary, emasculated in
spirit and altogether be-catted, were pets and orna-
ments in Utopia. The almost extinct elephant had
increased again and Utopia had saved her giraffes.
The brown bear had always been disposed to sweets
and vegetarianism and had greatly improved in
intelligence. The dog had given up barking and
was comparatively rare. Sporting dogs were not
used nor small pet animals.

Horses Mr. Barnstaple did not see, but as he was
a very modern urban type he did not miss them very
much and he did not ask any questions about them
while he was actually in Utopia. He never found
out whether they had or had not become extinct.

As he heard on his first afternoon in that world
of this revision and editing, this weeding and cultivation of the kingdoms of nature by mankind, it
seemed to him to be the most natural and necessary
phase in human history. "After all," he said to
himself, "it was a good invention to say that man
was created a gardener."

And now man was weeding and cultivating his
own strain. . . .

The Utopians told of eugenic beginnings, of a
new and surer decision in the choice of parents, of
an increasing certainty in the science of heredity;
and as Mr. Barnstaple contrasted the firm clear

beauty of face and limb that every Utopian displayed with the carelessly assembled features and
bodily disproportions of his earthly associates, he
realized that already, with but three thousand years
or so of advantage, these Utopians were passing
beyond man towards a nobler humanity. They
were becoming different in kind.

§ 3

They were different in kind.

As the questions and explanations and exchanges
of that afternoon went on, it became more and more
evident to Mr. Barnstaple that the difference of
their bodies was as nothing to the differences of
their minds. Innately better to begin with, the
minds of these children of light had grown up uninjured by any such tremendous frictions, concealments, ambiguities and ignorances as cripple the
growing mind of an Earthling. They were clear
and frank and direct. They had never developed
that defensive suspicion of the teacher, that resistance to instruction, which is the natural response
to teaching that is half aggression. They were
beautifully unwary in their communications. The
ironies, concealments, insincerities, vanities and pretensions of earthly conversation seemed unknown
to them. Mr. Barnstaple found this mental nakedness of theirs as sweet and refreshing as the mountain air he was breathing. It amazed him that they
could be so patient and lucid with beings so underbred.

Underbred was the word he used in his mind.

Himself, he felt the most underbred of all; he was afraid of these Utopians; snobbish and abject before them, he was like a mannerless earthy lout in a drawing-room, and he was bitterly ashamed of his own abjection. All the other Earthlings except Mr. Burleigh and Lady Stella betrayed the defensive spite of consciously inferior creatures struggling against that consciousness.

Like Father Amerton, Mr. Burleigh's chauffeur was evidently greatly shocked and disturbed by the unclothed condition of the Utopians; his feelings expressed themselves by gestures, grimaces and an occasional sarcastic comment such as "I *don't* think!" or "What O!" These he addressed for the most part to Mr. Barnstaple, for whom, as the owner of a very little old car, he evidently mingled feelings of profound contempt and social fellowship. He would also direct Mr. Barnstaple's attention to anything that he considered remarkable in bearing or gesture, by means of a peculiar stare and grimace combined with raised eyebrows. He had a way of pointing with his mouth and nose that Mr. Barnstaple under more normal circumstances might have found entertaining.

Lady Stella, who had impressed Mr. Barnstaple at first as a very great lady of the modern type, he was now beginning to feel was on her defence and becoming rather too ladylike. Mr. Burleigh however retained a certain aristocratic sublimity. He had been a great man on earth for all his life and it was evident that he saw no reason why he should not be accepted as a great man in Utopia. On earth he had done little and had been intelligently

receptive with the happiest results. That alert,
questioning mind of his, free of all persuasions,
convictions or revolutionary desires, fell with the
utmost ease into the pose of a distinguished person
inspecting, in a sympathetic but entirely non-committal manner, the institutions of an alien state.
"Tell me," that engaging phrase, laced his conversation.

The evening was drawing on; the clear Utopian
sky was glowing with the gold of sunset and a towering mass of cloud above the lake was fading from
pink to a dark purple, when Mr. Rupert Catskill
imposed himself upon Mr. Barnstaple's attention.
He was fretting in his place. "I have something to
say," he said. "I have something to say."

Presently he jumped up and walked to the centre
of the semicircle from which Mr. Burleigh had
spoken earlier in the afternoon. "Mr. Serpentine,"
he said. "Mr. Burleigh. There are a few things
I should be glad to say—if you can give me this
opportunity of saying them."

§ 4

He took off his grey top hat, went back and placed
it on his seat and returned to the centre of the apse.
He put back his coat tails, rested his hands on his
hips, thrust his head forward, regarded his audience
for a moment with an expression half cunning, half
defiant, muttered something inaudible and began.

His opening was not prepossessing. There was
some slight impediment in his speech, the little
brother of a lisp, against which his voice beat gut-

turally. His first few sentences had an effect of
being jerked out by unsteady efforts. Then it became evident to Mr. Barnstaple that Mr. Catskill
was expressing a very definite point of view, he was
offering a reasoned and intelligible view of Utopia.
Mr. Barnstaple disagreed with that criticism, indeed
he disagreed with it violently, but he had to recognize that it expressed an understandable attitude
of mind.

Mr. Catskill began with a sweeping admission of
the beauty and order of Utopia. He praised the
"glowing health" he saw "on every cheek," the
wealth, tranquillity and comfort of Utopian life.
They had "tamed the forces of nature and subjugated them altogether to one sole end, to the
material comfort of the race."

"But Arden and Greenlake?" murmured Mr.
Barnstaple.

Mr. Catskill did not hear or heed the interruption. "The first effect, Mr. Speaker—Mr. Serpentine, I *should* say—the first effect upon an earthly
mind is overwhelming. Is it any wonder"—he
glanced at Mr. Burleigh and Mr. Barnstaple—"is
it any wonder that admiration has carried some of
us off our feet? Is it any wonder that for a time
your almost magic beauty has charmed us into forgetting much that is in our own natures—into forgetting deep and mysterious impulses, cravings,
necessities, so that we have been ready to say, 'Here
at last is Lotus Land. Here let us abide, let us
adapt ourselves to this planned and ordered splendour and live our lives out here and die.' I, too,
Mr.—Mr. Serpentine, succumbed to that magic for

a time. But only for a time. Already, Sir, I find
myself full of questionings." . . .

His bright, headlong mind had seized upon the
fact that every phase in the weeding and cleansing
of Utopia from pests and parasites and diseases had
been accompanied by the possibility of collateral
limitations and losses; or perhaps it would be juster
to say that that fact had seized upon his mind. He
ignored the deliberation and precautions that had
accompanied every step in the process of making
a world securely healthy and wholesome for human
activity. He assumed there had been losses with
every gain, he went on to exaggerate these losses
and ran on glibly to the inevitable metaphor of
throwing away the baby with its bath—inevitable,
that is, for a British parliamentarian. The Utopians, he declared, were living lives of extraordinary
ease, safety and "may I say so—indulgence" ("They
work," said Mr. Barnstaple), but with a thousand
annoyances and disagreeables gone had not something else greater and more precious gone also?
Life on earth was, he admitted, insecure, full of
pains and anxieties, full indeed of miseries and distresses and anguish, but also, and indeed by reason
of these very things, it had moments of intensity,
hopes, joyful surprises, escapes, attainments, such
as the ordered life of Utopia could not possibly afford. "You have been getting away from conflicts
and distresses. Have you not also been getting
away from the living and quivering realities of life?"

He launched out upon a eulogy of earthly life.
He extolled the vitality of life upon earth as though
there were no signs of vitality in the high splendour

about him. He spoke of the "thunder of our crowded cities," of the "urge of our teeming millions," of the "broad tides of commerce and industrial effort and warfare," that "swayed and came and went in the hives and harbours of our race."

He had the knack of the plausible phrase and that imaginative touch which makes for eloquence. Mr. Barnstaple forgot that slight impediment and the thickness of the voice that said these things. Mr. Catskill boldly admitted all the earthly evils and dangers that Mr. Burleigh had retailed. Everything that Mr. Burleigh had said was true. All that he had said fell indeed far short of the truth. Famine we knew, and pestilence. We suffered from a thousand diseases that Utopia had eliminated. We were afflicted by a thousand afflictions that were known to Utopia now only by ancient tradition. "The rats gnaw and the summer flies persecute and madden. At times life reeks and stinks. I admit it, Sir, I admit it. We go down far below your extremest experiences into discomforts and miseries, anxieties and anguish of soul and body, into bitterness, terror and despair. Yea. But do we not also go higher? I challenge you with that. What can you know in this immense safety of the intensity, the frantic, terror-driven intensity, of many of our efforts? What can you know of reprieves and interludes and escapes? Think of our many happinesses beyond your ken! What do you know here of the sweet early days of convalescence? Of going for a holiday out of disagreeable surroundings? Of taking some great risk to body or fortune and bringing it off? Of winning a bet against enormous odds?

Of coming out of prison? And, Sir, it has been said that there are those in our world who have found a fascination even in pain itself. Because our life is dreadfuller, Sir, it has, and it must have, moments that are infinitely brighter than yours. It is titanic, Sir, where this is merely tidy. And we are inured to it and hardened by it. We are tempered to a finer edge. That is the point to which I am coming. Ask us to give up our earthly disorder, our miseries and distresses, our high death-rates and our hideous diseases, and at the first question every man and woman in the world would say, 'Yes! Willingly, Yes!' At the first question, Sir!"

Mr. Catskill held his audience for a moment on his extended finger.

"And then we should begin to take thought. We should ask, as you say your naturalists asked about your flies and suchlike offensive small game, we should ask, 'What goes with it? What is the price?' And when we learnt that the price was to surrender that intensity of life, that tormented energy, that pickled and experienced toughness, that rat-like, wolf-like toughness our perpetual struggle engenders, we should hesitate. We should hesitate. In the end, Sir, I believe, I hope and believe, indeed I pray and believe, we should say, 'No!' We should say, 'No!' "

Mr. Catskill was now in a state of great cerebral exaltation. He was making short thrusting gestures with his clenched fist. His voice rose and fell and boomed; he swayed and turned about, glanced for the approval of his fellow Earthlings, flung stray smiles at Mr. Burleigh.

This idea that our poor wrangling, nerveless, chance-driven world was really a fierce and close-knit system of powerful reactions in contrast with the evening serenities of a made and finished Utopia, had taken complete possession of his mind. "Never before, Sir, have I realized, as I realize now, the high, the terrible and adventurous destinies of our earthly race. I look upon this Golden Lotus Land of yours, this divine perfected land from which all conflict has been banished——"

Mr. Barnstaple caught a faint smile on the face of the woman who had reminded him of the Delphic Sibyl.

"——and I admit and admire its order and beauty as some dusty and resolute pilgrim might pause, on his exalted and mysterious quest, and admit and admire the order and beauty of the pleasant gardens of some prosperous Sybarite. And like that pilgrim I may beg leave, Sir, to question the wisdom of your way of living. For I take it, Sir, that it is now a proven thing that life and all the energy and beauty of life are begotten by struggle and competition and conflict; we were moulded and wrought in hardship, and so, Sir, were you. And yet you dream here that you have eliminated conflict for ever. Your economic state, I gather, is some form of socialism; you have abolished competition in all the businesses of peace. Your political state is one universal unity; you have altogether cut out the bracing and ennobling threat and the purging and terrifying experience of war. Everything is ordered and provided for. Everything is secure. Everything is secure, Sir, except for one thing. . . .

"I grieve to trouble your tranquillity, Sir, but I must breathe the name of that one forgotten thing —*degeneration!* What is there here to prevent degeneration? Are you preventing degeneration?

"What penalties are there any longer for indolence? What rewards for exceptional energy and effort? What is there to keep men industrious, what watchful, when there is no personal danger and no personal loss but only some remote danger or injury to the community? For a time by a sort of inertia you may keep going. You may seem to be making a success of things. I admit it, you *do* seem to be making a success of things. Autumnal glory! Sunset splendour! *While about you in universes parallel to yours, parallel races still toil, still suffer, still compete and eliminate and gather strength and energy!*"

Mr. Catskill flourished his hand at the Utopians in rhetorical triumph.

"I would not have you think, Sir, that these criticisms of your world are offered in a hostile spirit. They are offered in the most amiable and helpful spirit. I am the skeleton, but the most friendly and apologetic skeleton, at your feast. I ask my searching and disagreeable question because I must. Is it indeed the wise way that you have chosen? You have sweetness and light—and leisure. Granted. But if there is all this multitude of Universes, of which you have told us, Mr. Serpentine, so clearly and illuminatingly, and if one may suddenly open into another as ours has done into yours, I would ask you most earnestly how safe is your sweetness, your light and your leisure? We talk here, separated by we know not how flimsy a partition from innumerable worlds. And at that thought, Sir, it seems to me that as I stand here in the great golden calm of this place I can almost hear the trampling of hungry myriads as fierce and persistent as rats or wolves, the snarling voices of races inured to every pain and cruelty, the threat of terrible heroisms and pitiless aggressions. . . ."

He brought his discourse to an abrupt end. He smiled faintly; it seemed to Mr. Barnstaple that he triumphed over Utopia. He stood with hands on his hips and, as if he bent his body by that method, bowed stiffly. "Sir," he said with that ghost of a lisp of his, his eye on Mr. Burleigh, "I have said my say."

He turned about and regarded Mr. Barnstaple for a moment with his face screwed up almost to the appearance of a wink. He nodded his head, as if he tapped a nail with a hammer, jerked himself into activity, and returned to his proper place.

§ 5

Urthred did not so much answer Mr. Catskill as sit, elbow on knee and chin on hand, thinking audibly about him.

"The gnawing vigour of the rat," he mused, "the craving pursuit of the wolf, the mechanical persistence of wasp and fly and disease germ, have gone out of our world. That is true. We have obliterated that much of life's devouring forces. And lost nothing worth having. Pain, filth, indignity for ourselves—or any creatures; they have gone or they go. But it is not true that competition has gone from our world. Why does he say it has? Everyone here works to his or her utmost—for service and distinction. None may cheat himself out of toil or duty as men did in the age of confusion, when the mean and acquisitive lived and bred in luxury upon the heedlessness of more generous types. Why does he say we degenerate? He has been told better already. The indolent and inferior do not procreate here. And why should he threaten us with fancies of irruptions from other, fiercer, more barbaric worlds? It is we who can open the doors into such other universes or close them as we choose. Because we know. We can go to them—when we know enough we shall—but they cannot come to us. There is no way but knowledge out of the cages of life. . . . What is the matter with the mind of this man?

"These Earthlings are only in the beginnings of science. They are still for all practical ends in that phase of fear and taboos that came also in the development of Utopia before confidence and understanding. Out of which phase our own world struggled during the Last Age of Confusion. The minds of these Earthlings are full of fears and prohibitions, and though it has dawned upon them that they may possibly control their universe, the thought is too terrible yet for them to face. They avert their minds from it. They still want to go on thinking, as their fathers did before them, that the universe is being managed for them better than they can control it for themselves. Because if that

is so, they are free to obey their own violent little
individual motives. Leave things to God, they cry,
or leave them to Competition."

"Evolution was our blessed word," said Mr. Barnstaple, deeply interested.

"It is all the same thing—God, or Evolution, or
what you will—so long as you mean a Power beyond your own which excuses you from your duty.
Utopia says, 'Do not leave things at all. Take hold.'
But these Earthlings still lack the habit of looking
at reality—undraped. This man with the white
linen fetter round his neck is afraid even to look
upon men and women as they are. He is disgust-
ingly excited by the common human body. This
man with the glass lens before his left eye struggles
to believe that there is a wise old Mother Nature
behind the appearances of things, keeping a Balance. It was fantastic to hear about his Balance
of Nature. Cannot he with two eyes and a lens
see better than that? This last man who spoke so
impressively, thinks that this old Beldame Nature
is a limitless source of will and energy if only we
submit to her freaks and cruelties and imitate her
most savage moods, if only we sufficiently thrust
and kill and rob and ravish one another. . . .
He too preaches the old fatalism and believes it is
the teaching of science. . . .

"These Earthlings do not yet dare to see what our
Mother Nature is. At the back of their minds is
still the desire to abandon themselves to her. They
do not see that except for our eyes and wills, she is
purposeless and blind. She is not awful, she is horrible. She takes no heed to our standards, nor to

any standards of excellence. She made us by accident; all her children are bastards—undesired; she will cherish or expose them, pet or starve or torment without rhyme or reason. She does not heed, she does not care. She will lift us up to power and intelligence, or debase us to the mean feebleness of the rabbit or the slimy white filthiness of a thousand of her parasitic inventions. There must be good in her because she made all that is good in us—but also there is endless evil. Do not you Earthlings see the dirt of her, the cruelty, the insane indignity of much of her work?"

"Phew! Worse than 'Nature red in tooth and claw,'" murmured Mr. Freddy Mush.

"These things are plain," mused Urthred. "If they dared to see.

"Half the species of life in our planet also, half and more than half of all the things alive, were ugly or obnoxious, inane, miserable, wretched, with elaborate diseases, helplessly ill-adjusted to Nature's continually fluctuating conditions, when first we took this old Hag, our Mother, in hand. We have, after centuries of struggle, suppressed her nastier fancies, and washed her and combed her and taught her to respect and heed the last child of her wantonings—Man. With Man came Logos, the Word and the Will into our universe, to watch it and fear it, to learn it and cease to fear it, to know it and comprehend it and master it. So that we of Utopia are no longer the beaten and starved children of Nature, but her free and adolescent sons. We have taken over the Old Lady's Estate. Every day we learn a little better how to master this little planet.

Every day our thoughts go out more surely to our inheritance, the stars. And the deeps beyond and beneath the stars."

"You have reached the stars?" cried Mr. Barnstaple.

"Not yet. Not even the other planets. But very plainly the time draws near when those great distances will cease to restrain us. . . ."

He paused. "Many of us will have to go out into the deeps of space. . . . And never return . . . Giving their lives. . . .

"And into these new spaces—countless brave men. . . ."

Urthred turned towards Mr. Catskill. "We find your frankly expressed thoughts particularly interesting today. You help us to understand the past of our own world. You help us to deal with an urgent problem that we will presently explain to you. There are thoughts and ideas like yours in our ancient literature of two or three thousand years ago, the same preaching of selfish violence as though it was a virtue. Even then intelligent men knew better, and you yourself might know better if you were not wilfully set in wrong opinions. But it is plain to see from your manner and bearing that you are very wilful indeed in your opinions.

"You are not, you must realize, a very beautiful person, and probably you are not very beautiful in your pleasures and proceedings. But you have superabundant energy, and so it is natural for you to turn to the excitements of risk and escape, to think that the best thing in life is the sensation of conflict and winning. Also in the economic confusion of such a world as yours there is an intolerable amount of toil that must be done, toil so disagreeable that it makes everyone of spirit anxious to thrust away as much of it as possible and to claim exemption from it on account of nobility, gallantry or good fortune. People in your world no doubt persuade themselves very easily that they are justifiably exempted, and you are under that persuasion. You live in a world of classes. Your badly trained mind has been under no necessity to invent its own excuses; the class into which you were born had all its excuses ready for you. So it is you take the best of everything without scruple and you adventure with life, chiefly at the expense of other people, with a mind trained by all its circumstances to resist the idea that there is any possible way of human living that can be steadfast and disciplined and at the same time vigorous and happy. You have argued against that persuasion all your life as though it were your personal enemy. It is your personal enemy; it condemns your way of life altogether, it damns you utterly for your adventures.

"Confronted now with an ordered and achieved beauty of living you still resist; you resist to escape dismay; you argue that this world of ours is unromantic, wanting in intensity, decadent, feeble. Now—in the matter of physical strength, grip hands with that young man who sits beside you."

Mr. Catskill glanced at the extended hand and shook his head knowingly. "You go on talking," he said.

"Yet when I tell you that neither our wills nor

our bodies are as feeble as yours, your mind resists
obstinately. You will not believe it. If for a
moment your mind admits it, afterwards it recoils
to the system of persuasions that protect your self-
esteem. Only one of you accepts our world at all,
and he does so rather because he is weary of yours
than willing for ours. So I suppose it has to be.
Yours are Age of Confusion minds, trained to
conflict, trained to insecurity and secret self-seeking. In that fashion Nature and your state have
taught you to live and so you must needs live until
you die. Such lessons are to be unlearnt only in
ten thousand generations, by the slow education of
three thousand years.

"And we are puzzled by the question, what are
we to do with you? We will try our utmost to deal
fairly and friendly with you if you will respect our
laws and ways.

"But it will be very difficult, we know, for you.
You do not realize yet how difficult your habits and
preconceptions will make it for you. Your party
so far has behaved very reasonably and properly,
in act if not in thought. But we have had another
experience of Earthling ways today of a much
more tragic kind. Your talk of fiercer, barbaric
worlds breaking in upon us has had its grotesque
parallel in reality today. It is true; there is something fierce and ratlike and dangerous about Earthly
men. You are not the only Earthlings who came
into Utopia through this gate that swung open for
a moment today. There are others——"

"Of course!" said Mr. Barnstaple. "I should
have guessed it! That third lot!"

"There is yet another of these queer locomotive machines of yours in Utopia."

"The grey car!" said Mr. Barnstaple to Mr. Burleigh. "It wasn't a hundred yards ahead of you."

"Raced us from Hounslow," said Mr. Burleigh's driver. "Real hot stuff."

Mr. Burleigh turned to Mr. Freddy Mush. "I think you said you recognized someone?"

"Lord Barralonga, Sir, almost to a certainty, and I *think* Miss Greeta Grey."

"There were two other men," said Mr. Barnstaple.

"They will complicate things," said Mr. Burleigh.

"They do complicate things," said Urthred. "They have killed a man."

"A Utopian?"

"These other people—there are five of them—whose names you seem to know, came into Utopia just in front of your two vehicles. Instead of stopping as you did when they found themselves on a new, strange road, they seem to have quickened their pace very considerably. They passed some men and women and they made extraordinary gestures to them and abominable noises produced by an instrument specially designed for that purpose. Further on they encountered a silver cheetah and charged at it and ran right over it, breaking its back. They do not seem to have paused to see what became of it. A young man named Gold came out into the road to ask them to stop. But their machine is made in the most fantastic way, very complex and very foolish. It is quite unable to stop short suddenly. It is not driven by a single engine that is completely controlled. It has a complicated internal conflict. It has a sort of engine that drives it forward by a complex cogged gear on the axle of the hind wheels and it has various clumsy stopping contrivances by means of friction at certain points. You can apparently drive the engine at the utmost speed and at the same time jam the wheels to prevent them going round. When this young man stepped forward in front of them, they were quite unable to stop. They may have tried to do so. They say they did. Their machine swerved dangerously and struck him with its side."

"And killed him?"

"And killed him instantly. His body was horribly injured. . . . But they did not stop even for that. They slowed down and had a hasty consultation, and then seeing that people were coming they set their machine in motion again and made off. They seem to have been seized with a panic fear of restraint and punishment. Their motives are very difficult to understand. At any rate they went on. They rode on and on into our country for some hours. An aeroplane was presently set to follow them and another to clear the road in front of them. It was very difficult to clear the road because neither our people nor our animals understand such vehicles as theirs—nor such behaviour. In the afternoon they got among mountains and evidently found our roads much too smooth and difficult for their machine. It made extraordinary noises as though it was gritting its teeth, and emitted a blue vapour with an offensive smell. At

one corner where it should have stopped short, it
skated about and slid suddenly sideways and rolled
over a cliff and fell for perhaps twice the height
of a man into a torrent."

"And they were killed?" asked Mr. Burleigh,
with, as it seemed to Mr. Barnstaple, a touch of
eagerness in his voice.

"Not one of them."

"Oh!" said Mr. Burleigh, "then what happened?"

"One of them has a broken arm and another is
badly cut about the face. The other two men and
the woman are uninjured except for fright and
shock. When our people came up to them the four
men held their hands above their heads. Apparently they feared they would be killed at once and
did this as an appeal for mercy."

"And what are you doing with them?"

"We are bringing them here. It is better, we
think, to keep all you Earthlings together. At present we cannot imagine what must be done to you.
We want to learn from you and we want to be
friendly with you if it is possible. It has been suggested that you should be returned to your world.
In the end that may be the best thing to do. But
at present we do not know enough to do this certainly. Arden and Greenlake, when they made the
attempt to rotate a part of our matter through
the F dimension, believed that they would rotate
it in empty space in that dimension. The fact that
you were there and were caught into our universe,
is the most unexpected thing that has happened in
Utopia for a thousand years."

CHAPTER THE SEVENTH

THE BRINGING IN OF LORD BARRALONGA'S PARTY

§ 1

The conference broke up upon this announcement, but Lord Barralonga and his party were not brought to the Conference Gardens until long after dark. No effort was made to restrain or control the movements of the Earthlings. Mr. Burleigh walked down to the lake with Lady Stella and the psychologist whose name was Lion, asking and answering questions. Mr. Burleigh's chauffeur wandered rather disconsolately, keeping within hail of his employer. Mr. Rupert Catskill took Mr. Mush off by the arm as if to give him instructions.

Mr. Barnstaple wanted to walk about alone to recall and digest the astounding realizations of the afternoon and to accustom himself to the wonder of this beautiful world, so beautiful and now in the twilight so mysterious also, with its trees and flowers becoming dim and shapeless notes of pallor and blackness and with the clear forms and gracious proportions of its buildings melting into a twilight indistinctness.

The earthliness of his companions intervened between him and this world into which he felt he might otherwise have been accepted and absorbed. He was in it, but in it only as a strange and discordant intruder. Yet he loved it already and desired it and was passionately anxious to become a part of it. He had a vague but very powerful feeling that if only he could get away from his companions, if only in some way he could cast off his earthly clothing and everything upon him that marked him as earthly and linked him to earth, he would by the very act of casting that off become himself native to Utopia, and then that this tormenting sense, this bleak, distressing strangeness would vanish out of his mind. He would suddenly find himself a Utopian in nature and reality, and it was Earth that would become the incredible dream, a dream that would fade at last completely out of his mind.

For a time, however, Father Amerton's need of a hearer prevented any such detachment from earthly thoughts and things. He stuck close to Mr. Barnstaple and maintained a stream of questions and comments that threw over this Utopian scene the quality of some Earl's Court exhibition that the two of them were visiting and criticizing together. It was evidently so provisional, so disputable and unreal to him, that at any moment Mr. Barnstaple felt he would express no astonishment if a rift in the scenery suddenly let in the clatter of the Earl's Court railway station or gave a glimpse of the conventional Gothic spire of St. Barnabas in the West.

At first Father Amerton's mind was busy chiefly with the fact that on the morrow he was to be "dealt with" on account of the scene in the conference. "How *can* they deal with me?" he said for the fourth time.

"I beg your pardon," said Mr. Barnstaple. Every time Mr. Amerton began speaking Mr. Barnstaple said, "I beg your pardon," in order to convey to him that he was interrupting a train of thought. But every time Mr. Barnstaple said, "I beg your pardon," Mr. Amerton would merely remark, "You ought to consult someone about your hearing," and then go on with what he had to say.

"How can I be *dealt with?*" he asked of Mr. Barnstaple and the circumambient dusk. "How can I be dealt with?"

"Oh! psycho-analysis or something of that sort," said Mr. Barnstaple.

"It takes two to play at that game," said Father Amerton, but it seemed to Mr. Barnstaple with a slight flavour of relief in his tone. "Whatever they ask me, whatever they suggest to me, I will not fail—I will bear my witness."

"I have no doubt they will find it hard to suppress you," said Mr. Barnstaple bitterly. . . .

For a time they walked among the tall sweet-smelling, white-flowered shrubs in silence. Now and then Mr. Barnstaple would quicken or slacken his pace with the idea of increasing his distance from Father Amerton, but quite mechanically Father Amerton responded to these efforts. "Promiscuity," he began again presently. "What other word could you use?"

"I really beg your pardon," said Mr. Barnstaple.

"What other word could I have used *but* 'promiscuity'? What else could one expect, with people running about in this amazing want of costume, but the morals of the monkeys' cage? They admit that our institution of marriage is practically unknown to them!"

"It's a different world," said Mr. Barnstaple irritably. "A different world."

"The Laws of Morality hold good for every conceivable world."

"But in a world in which people propagated by fission and there was no sex?"

"Morality would be simpler but it would be the same morality." . . .

Presently Mr. Barnstaple was begging his pardon again.

"I was saying that this is a lost world."

"It doesn't *look* lost," said Mr. Barnstaple.

"It has rejected and forgotten Salvation."

Mr. Barnstaple put his hands in his pocket and began to whistle the barcarolle from "The Tales of Hoffman," very softly to himself. Would Father Amerton never leave him? Could nothing be done with Father Amerton? At the old shows at Earl's Court there used to be wire baskets for waste paper and cigarette ends and bores generally. If one could only tip Father Amerton suddenly into some such receptacle!

"Salvation has been offered them, and they have rejected it and wellnigh forgotten it. And that is why we have been sent to them. We have been sent to them to recall them to the One Thing that Matters, to the One Forgotten Thing. Once more we have to raise the healing symbol as Moses raised it in the Wilderness. Ours is no light mission. We

have been sent into this Hell of sensuous material-
ism——"

"Oh, *Lord!*" said Mr. Barnstaple, and relapsed
into the barcarolle. . . .

"I *beg* your pardon," he exclaimed again presently.

"Where is the Pole Star? What has happened to
the Wain?"

Mr. Barnstaple looked up.

He had not thought of the stars before, and he
looked up prepared in this fresh Universe to see
the strangest constellations. But just as the life
and size of the planet they were on ran closely
parallel to the earth's, so he beheld above him a
starry vault of familiar forms. And just as the
Utopian world failed to be altogether parallel to
its sister universe, so did these constellations seem
to be a little out in their drawing. Orion, he
thought, straddled wider and with a great unfamiliar nebula at one corner, and it was true—
the Wain was flattened out and the pointers
pointed to a great void in the heavens.

"Their Pole Star gone! The Pointers, the Wain
askew! It is symbolical," said Father Amerton.

It was only too obviously going to be symbolical.
Mr. Barnstaple realized that a fresh storm of
eloquence was imminent from Father Amerton. At
any cost he felt this nuisance must be abated.

§ 2

On earth Mr. Barnstaple had been a passive victim to bores of all sorts, delicately and painfully

considerate of the mental limitations that made
their insensitive pressure possible. But the free
air of Utopia had already mounted to his head and
released initiatives that his excessively deferential
recognition of others had hitherto restrained. He
had had enough of Father Amerton; it was necessary to turn off Father Amerton, and he now proceeded to do so with a simple directness that surprised himself.

"Father Amerton," he said, "I have a confession
to make to you."

"Ah!" cried Father Amerton. "Please—anything?"

"You have been walking about with me and
shouting at my ears until I am strongly impelled
to murder you."

"If what I have said has struck home——"

"It hasn't struck home. It has been a tiresome,
silly, deafening jabbering in my ears. It wearies
me indescribably. It prevents my attending to
the marvellous things about us. I see exactly what
you mean when you say that there is no Pole Star
here and that that is symbolical. Before you begin
I appreciate the symbol, and a very obvious, weak
and ultimately inaccurate symbol it is. But you
are one of those obstinate spirits who believes in
spite of all evidence that the eternal hills are still
eternal and the fixed stars fixed for ever. I want
you to understand that I am entirely out of sympathy with all this stuff of yours. You seem to
embody all that is wrong and ugly and impossible in
Catholic teaching. I agree with these Utopians that
there is something wrong with your mind about

sex, in all probability a nasty twist given to it in early life, and that what you keep saying and hinting about sexual life here is horrible and outrageous. And I am equally hostile to you and exasperated and repelled by you when you speak of religion proper. You make religion disgusting just as you make sex disgusting. You are a dirty priest. What *you* call Christianity is a black and ugly superstition, a mere excuse for malignity and persecution. It is an outrage upon Christ. If you are a Christian, then most passionately I declare myself *not* a Christian. But there are other meanings for Christianity than those you put upon it, and in another sense this Utopia here is Christian beyond all dreaming. Utterly beyond your understanding. We have come into this glorious world, which, compared to our world, is like a bowl of crystal compared to an old tin can, and you have the insufferable impudence to say that we have been sent hither as missionaries to teach them—God knows what!"

"God *does* know what," said Father Amerton, a little taken aback, but coming up very pluckily.

"Oh!" cried Mr. Barnstaple, and was for a moment speechless.

"Listen to me, my Friend," said Father Amerton, catching at his sleeve.

"Not for my life!" cried Mr. Barnstaple, recoiling. "See! Down that vista, away there on the shore of the lake, those black figures are Mr. Burleigh, Mr. Mush and Lady Stella. They brought you here. They belong to your party and you belong to them. If they had not wanted your company you would not have been in their car. Go to

them. I will not have you with me any longer. I
refuse you and reject you. That is your way. This,
by this little building, is mine. Don't follow me, or
I will lay hands on you and bring in these Utopians
to interfere between us. . . . Forgive my plain-
ness, Mr. Amerton. But get away from me! Get
away from me!"

Mr. Barnstaple turned, and seeing that Father
Amerton stood hesitating at the parting of the
ways, took to his heels and ran from him.

He fled along an alley behind tall hedges, turned
sharply to the right and then to the left, passed over
a high bridge that crossed in front of a cascade that
flung a dash of spray in his face, blundered by two
couples of lovers who whispered softly in the darkling, ran deviously across flower-studded turf, and
at last threw himself down breathless upon the steps
that led up to a terrace that looked towards lake
and mountains, and was adorned, it seemed in the
dim light, with squat stone figures of seated vigilant
animals and men.

"Ye merciful stars!" cried Mr. Barnstaple. "At
last I am alone."

He sat on these steps for a long time with his eyes
upon the scene about him, drinking in the satisfying
realization that for a brief interval at any rate, with
no earthly presence to intervene, he and Utopia
were face to face.

§ 3

He could not call this world the world of his
dreams because he had never dared to dream of any

world so closely shaped to the desires and imaginations of his heart. But surely this world it was, or a world the very fellow of it, that had lain deep beneath the thoughts and dreams of thousands of sane and troubled men and women in the world of disorder from which he had come. It was no world of empty peace, no such golden decadence of indulgence as Mr. Catskill tried to imagine it; it was a world, Mr. Barnstaple perceived, intensely militant, conquering and to conquer, prevailing over the obduracy of force and matter, over the lifeless separations of empty space and all the antagonistic mysteries of being.

In Utopia in the past, obscured by the superficial exploits of statesmen like Burleigh and Catskill and the competition of traders and exploiters every whit as vile and vulgar as their earthly compeers, the work of quiet and patient thinkers and teachers had gone on and the foundations which sustained this serene intensity of activity had been laid. How few of these pioneers had ever felt more than a transitory gleam of the righteous loveliness of the world their lives made possible!

And yet even in the hate and turmoil and distresses of the Days of Confusion there must have been earnest enough of the exquisite and glorious possibilities of life. Over the foulest slums the sunset called to the imaginations of men, and from mountain ridges, across great valleys, from cliffs and hillsides and by the uncertain and terrible splendours of the sea, men must have had glimpses of the conceivable and attainable magnificence of being. Every flower petal, every sunlit leaf, the vitality of young things, the happy moments of the human mind transcending itself in art, all these things must have been material for hope, incentive to effort. And now at last—this world!

Mr. Barnstaple lifted up his hands like one who worships to the friendly multitude of the stars above him.

"I have seen," he whispered. "I have seen."

Little lights and soft glows of illumination were coming out here and there over this great park of flowerlike buildings and garden spaces that sloped down towards the lake. A circling aeroplane, itself a star, hummed softly overhead.

A slender girl came past him down the steps and paused at the sight of him.

"Are you one of the Earthlings?" came the question, and a beam of soft light shone momentarily upon Mr. Barnstaple from the bracelet on her arm.

"I came today," said Mr. Barnstaple, peering up at her.

"You are the man who came alone in a little machine of tin, with rubber air-bags round the wheels, very rusty underneath, and painted yellow. I have been looking at it."

"It is not a bad little car," said Mr. Barnstaple.

"At first we thought the priest came in it with you."

"He is no friend of mine."

"There were priests like that in Utopia many years ago. They caused much mischief among the people."

"He was with the other lot," said Mr. Barnstaple.

"For their week-end party I should think him—
rather a mistake."

She sat down a step or so above him.

"It is wonderful that you should come here out of
your world to us. Do you find this world of ours
very wonderful? I suppose many things that seem
quite commonplace to me because I have been born
among them seem wonderful to you."

"You are not very old?"

"I am eleven. I am learning the history of the
Ages of Confusion, and they say your world is still in
an Age of Confusion. It is just as though you came
to us out of the past—out of history. I was in the
Conference and I was watching your face. You love
this present world of ours—at least you love it much
more than your other people do."

"I want to live all the rest of my life in it."

"I wonder if that is possible?"

"Why should it not be possible? It will be easier
than sending me back. I should not be very much in
the way. I should only be here for twenty or thirty
years at the most, and I would learn everything I
could and do everything I was told."

"But isn't there work that you have to do in your
own world?"

Mr. Barnstaple made no answer to that. He did
not seem to hear it. It was the girl who presently
broke the silence.

"They say that when we Utopians are young,
before our minds and characters are fully formed and
matured, we are very like the men and women of
the Age of Confusion. We are more egotistical then,
they tell us; life about us is still so unknown, that

we are adventurous and romantic. I suppose I am
egotistical yet—and adventurous. And it does still
seem to me that in spite of many terrible and dreadful things there was much that must have been
wildly exciting and desirable in that past—which is
still so like your present. What can it have been
like to have been a general entering a conquered
city? Or a prince being crowned? Or to be rich
and able to astonish people by acts of power and
benevolence? Or to be a martyr led out to die for
some splendid misunderstood cause?"

"These things sound better in stories and histories
than in reality," said Mr. Barnstaple after due consideration. "Did you hear Mr. Rupert Catskill, the
last of the Earthlings to make a speech?"

"He thought romantically—but he did not look
romantic."

"He has lived most romantically. He has fought
bravely in wars. He has been a prisoner and escaped
wonderfully from prison. His violent imaginations
have caused the deaths of thousands of people. And
presently we shall see another romantic adventurer
in this Lord Barralonga they are bringing hither.
He is enormously rich and he tries to astonish people with his wealth—just as you have dreamt of
astonishing people."

"Are they not astonished?"

"Romance is not reality," said Mr. Barnstaple.
"He is one of a number of floundering, corrupting
rich men who are a weariness to themselves and an
intolerable nuisance to the rest of our world. They
want to do vulgar, showy things. This man Barralonga was an assistant to a photographer and

something of an actor when a certain invention
called moving pictures came into our world. He
became a great prospector in the business of showing these pictures, partly by accident, partly by the
unscrupulous cheating of various inventors. Then
he launched out into speculations in shipping and
in a trade we carry on in our world in frozen meat
brought from great distances. He made food costly
for many people and impossible for some, and so he
grew rich. For in our world men grow wealthy by
intercepting rather than by serving. And having
become ignobly rich, certain of our politicians, for
whom he did some timely services, ennobled him by
giving him the title of Lord. Do you understand
the things I am saying? Was your Age of Confusion
so like ours? *You did not know it was so ugly.* Forgive me if I disillusion you about the Age of Confusion and its romantic possibilities. But I have
just stepped out of the dust and disorder and
noise of its indiscipline, out of limitation, cruelties
and distresses, out of a weariness in which hope
dies. . . . Perhaps if my world attracts you you
may yet have an opportunity of adventuring out of
all this into its disorders. . . . That will be an
adventure indeed. . . . Who knows what may
happen between our worlds? . . . But you will
not like it, I am afraid. You cannot imagine how
dirty our world is. . . . Dirt and disease, these
are in the trailing skirts of all romance." . . .

A silence fell between them; he followed his own
thoughts and the girl sat and wondered over him.

At length he spoke again.

"Shall I tell you what I was thinking of when you spoke to me?"

"Yes?"

"Your world is the consummation of a million ancient dreams. It is wonderful! It is wonder, high as heaven. But it is a great grief to me that two dear friends of mine cannot be here with me to see what I am seeing. It is queer how strong the thought of them is in my mind. One has passed now beyond all the universes, alas!—but the other is still in my world. You are a student, my dear; everyone of your world, I suppose, is a student here, but in our world students are a class apart. We three were happy together because we were students and not yet caught into the mills of senseless toil, and we were none the less happy perhaps because we were miserably poor and often hungry together. We used to talk and dispute together and in our students' debating society, discussing the disorders of our world and how some day they might be bettered. Was there, in your Age of Confusion, that sort of eager, hopeful, poverty-struck student life?"

"Go on," said the girl with her eyes intent on his dim profile. "In old novels I have read of just that hungry, dreaming student world."

"We three agreed that the supreme need of our time was education. We agreed that was the highest service we could join. We all set about it in our various ways, I the least useful of the three. My friends and I drifted a little apart. They edited a great monthly periodical that helped to keep the world of science together, and my friend, serving a careful and grudging firm of publishers, edited school books for them, conducted an educational paper, and also inspected schools for our university. He was too heedless of pay and profit ever to become even passably well off though these publishers profited greatly by his work; his whole life was a continual service of toil for teaching; he did not take as much as a month's holiday in any year in his life. While he lived I thought little of the work he was doing, but since he died I have heard from teachers whose schools he inspected, and from book writers whom he advised, of the incessant high quality of his toil and the patience and sympathy of his work. On such lives as his this Utopia in which your sweet life is opening is founded; on such lives our world of earth will yet build its Utopia. But the life of this friend of mine ended abruptly in a way that tore my heart. He worked too hard and too long through a crisis in which it was inconvenient for him to take a holiday. His nervous system broke down with shocking suddenness, his mind gave way, he passed into a phase of acute melancholia and—died. For it is perfectly true, old Nature has neither righteousness nor pity. This happened a few weeks ago. That other old friend and I, with his wife, who had been his tireless helper, were chief among the mourners at his funeral. Tonight the memory of that comes back to me with extraordinary vividness. I do not know how you dispose of your dead here, but on earth the dead are mostly buried in the earth."

"We are burnt," said the girl.

"Those who are liberal-minded in our world burn also. Our friend was burnt, and we stood and took our part in a service according to the rites of our ancient religion in which we no longer believed, and presently we saw his coffin, covered with wreaths of flowers, slide from before us out of our sight through the gates that led to the furnaces of the crematorium, and as it went, taking with it so much of my youth, I saw that my other dear old friend was sobbing, and I too was wrung to the pitch of tears to think that so valiant and devoted and industrious a life should end, as it seemed, so miserably and thanklessly. The priest had been reading a long contentious discourse by a theological writer named Paul, full of bad arguments by analogy and weak assertions. I wished that instead of the ideas of this ingenious ancient we could have had some discourse upon the real nobility of our friend, on the pride and intensity of his work and on his scorn for mercenary things. All his life he had worked with unlimited devotion for such a world as this, and yet I doubt if he had ever had any realization of the clearer, nobler life for man that his life of toil and the toil of such lives as his were making sure and certain in the days to come. He lived by faith. He lived too much by faith. There was not enough sunlight in his life. If I could have him here now—and that other dear friend who grieved for him so bitterly; if I could have them both here; if I could give up my place here to them so that they could see, as I see, the real greatness of their lives reflected in these great consequences of such lives as theirs—then, then I could rejoice in Utopia indeed. . . . But I feel now as if I had taken my old friend's savings and was spending them on myself." . . .

Mr. Barnstaple suddenly remembered the youth of his hearer. "Forgive me, my dear child, for running on in this fashion. But your voice was kind."

The girl's answer was to bend down and brush his extended hand with her soft lips.

Then suddenly she sprang to her feet. "Look at that light," she said, "among the stars!"

Mr. Barnstaple stood up beside her.

"That is the aeroplane bringing Lord Barralonga and his party; Lord Barralonga who killed a man today! Is he a very big, strong man—ungovernable and wonderful?"

Mr. Barnstaple, struck by a sudden doubt, looked sharply at the sweet upturned face beside him.

"I have never seen him. But I believe he is a youngish, baldish, undersized man, who suffers very gravely from a disordered liver and kidneys. This has prevented the dissipation of his energies upon youthful sports and pleasures and enabled him to concentrate upon the acquisition of property. And so he was able to buy the noble title that touches your imagination. Come with me and look at him."

The girl stood still and met his eyes. She was eleven years old and she was as tall as he was.

"But was there no romance in the past?"

"Only in the hearts of the young. And it died."

"But is there no romance?"

"Endless romance—and it has all to come. It comes for you."

§ 4

The bringing in of Lord Barralonga and his party
was something of an anti-climax to Mr. Barnstaple's
wonderful day. He was tired and, quite unreason-
ably, he resented the invasion of Utopia by these
people.

The two parties of Earthlings were brought together in a brightly lit hall near the lawn upon which
the Barralonga aeroplane had come down. The newcomers came in in a group together, blinking, travel-
worn and weary-looking. But it was evident they
were greatly relieved to encounter other Earthlings
in what was to them a still intensely puzzling experience. For they had had nothing to compare
with the calm and lucid discussion of the Conference
Place. Their lapse into this strange world was still
an incomprehensible riddle for them.

Lord Barralonga was the owner of the gnome-like
face that had looked out at Mr. Barnstaple when the
large grey car had passed him on the Maidenhead
Road. His skull was very low and broad above his
brows so that he reminded Mr. Barnstaple of the
flat stopper of a glass bottle. He looked hot and
tired, he was considerably dishevelled as if from a
struggle, and one arm was in a sling; his little brown
eyes were as alert and wary as those of a wicked
urchin in the hands of a policeman. Sticking close
to him like a familiar spirit was a small, almost
jockey-like chauffeur, whom he addressed as "Ridley." Ridley's face also was marked by the stern
determination of a man in a difficult position not in
any manner to give himself away. His left cheek

and ear had been cut in the automobile smash and were liberally adorned with sticking-plaster. Miss Greeta Grey, the lady of the party, was a frankly blonde beauty in a white flannel tailor-made suit. She was extraordinarily unruffled by the circumstances in which she found herself; it was as if she had no sense whatever of their strangeness. She carried herself with the habitual hauteur of a beautiful girl almost professionally exposed to the risk of unworthy advances. Anywhere.

The other two people of the party were a grey-faced, grey-clad American, also very wary-eyed, who was, Mr. Barnstaple learnt from Mr. Mush, Hunker, the Cinema King, and a thoroughly ruffled-looking Frenchman, a dark, smartly dressed man, with an imperfect command of English, who seemed rather to have fallen into Lord Barralonga's party than to have belonged to it properly. Mr. Barnstaple's mind leapt to the conclusion, and nothing occurred afterwards to change his opinion, that some interest in the cinematograph had brought this gentleman within range of Lord Barralonga's hospitality and that he had been caught, as a foreigner may so easily be caught, into the embrace of a thoroughly uncongenial week-end expedition.

As Lord Barralonga and Mr. Hunker came forward to greet Mr. Burleigh and Mr. Catskill, this Frenchman addressed himself to Mr. Barnstaple with the inquiry whether he spoke French.

"I cannot understand," he said. "We were to have gone to Viltshire—Wiltshire, and then one 'orrible thing has happen after another. What is it we have come to and what sort of people are all

these people who speak most excellent French? Is
it a joke of Lord Barralonga, or a dream, or what
has happen to us?"

Mr. Barnstaple attempted some explanation.

"Another dimension," said the Frenchman, "another worl'. That is all very well. But I have my
business to attend to in London. I have no need to
be brought back in this way to France, some sort of
France, some other France in some other worl'. It
is too much of a joke altogether."

Mr. Barnstaple attempted some further exposition. It was clear from his interlocutor's puzzled
face that the phrases he used were too difficult. He
turned helplessly to Lady Stella and found her ready
to undertake the task. "This lady," he said, "will
be able to make things plain to you. Lady Stella,
this is Monsieur——"

"Emile Dupont," the Frenchman bowed. "I am
what you call a journalist and publicist. I am interested in the cinematograph from the point of view
of education and propaganda. It is why I am here
with his Lordship Barralonga."

French conversation was Lady Stella's chief ac-
complishment. She sailed into it now very readily.
She took over the elucidation of M. Dupont, and
only interrupted it to tell Miss Greeta Grey how
pleasant it was to have another woman with her in
this strange world.

Relieved of M. Dupont, Mr. Barnstaple stood
back and surveyed the little group of Earthlings in
the centre of the hall and the circle of tall, watchful
Utopians about them and rather aloof from them.
Mr. Burleigh was being distantly cordial to Lord

Barralonga, and Mr. Hunker was saying what a great pleasure it was to him to meet "Britain's foremost statesman." Mr. Catskill stood in the most friendly manner beside Barralonga; they knew each other well; and Father Amerton exchanged comments with Mr. Mush. Ridley and Penk, after some moments of austere regard, had gone apart to discuss the technicalities of the day's experience in undertones. Nobody paid any attention to Mr. Barnstaple.

It was like a meeting at a railway station. It was like a reception. It was utterly incredible and altogether commonplace. He was weary. He was saturated and exhausted by wonder.

"Oh, I am going to my bed!" he yawned suddenly. "I am going to my little bed."

He made his way through the friendly-eyed Utopians out into the calm starlight. He nodded to the strange nebula at the corner of Orion as a weary parent might nod to importunate offspring. He would consider it again in the morning. He staggered drowsily through the gardens to his own particular retreat.

He disrobed and went to sleep as immediately and profoundly as a tired child.

CHAPTER THE EIGHTH

EARLY MORNING IN UTOPIA

§ 1

Mr. Barnstaple awakened slowly out of profound slumber.

He had a vague feeling that a very delightful and wonderful dream was slipping from him. He tried to keep on with the dream and not to open his eyes. It was about a great world of beautiful people who had freed themselves from a thousand earthly troubles. But it dissolved and faded from his mind. It was not often nowadays that dreams came to Mr. Barnstaple. He lay very still with his eyes closed, reluctantly coming awake to the affairs of every day.

The cares and worries of the last fortnight resumed their sway. Would he ever be able to get away for a holiday by himself? Then he remembered that he had already got his valise stowed away in the Yellow Peril. But surely that was not last night; that was the night before last, and he had started—he remembered now starting and the little thrill of getting through the gate before Mrs. Barnstaple suspected anything. He opened his eyes and fixed them on a white ceiling, trying to recall that journey. He remembered turning into the Camberwell New Road and the bright exhilaration of the morning, Vauxhall Bridge and that nasty tangle of traffic at Hyde Park Corner. He always maintained that the west of London was far more difficult for motoring than the east. Then—had he gone to Uxbridge? No. He recalled the road to Slough and then came a blank in his mind.

What a very good ceiling this was! Not a crack nor a stain!

But how had he spent the rest of the day? He must have got somewhere because here he was in a thoroughly comfortable bed—an excellent bed. With a thrush singing. He had always maintained that a good thrush could knock spots off a nightingale, but this thrush was a perfect Caruso. And another answering it! In July! Pangbourne and Caversham were wonderful places for nightingales. In June. But this was July—and thrushes. . . . Across these drowsy thought-phantoms came the figure of Mr. Rupert Catskill, hands on hips, face and head thrust forward speaking, saying astonishing things. To a naked seated figure with a grave intent face. And other figures. One with a face like the Delphic Sibyl. Mr. Barnstaple began to remember that in some way he had got himself mixed up with a week-end party at Taplow Court. Now had this speech been given at Taplow Court? At Taplow Court they wear clothes. But perhaps the aristocracy in retirement and privacy——?

Utopia? . . . But was it possible?

Mr. Barnstaple sat up in his bed in a state of
extreme amazement. "Impossible!" he said. He
was lying in a little loggia half open to the air. Between the slender pillars of fluted glass he saw a
range of snow-topped mountains, and in the fore-
ground a great cluster of tall spikes bearing deep red
flowers. The bird was still singing—a glorified
thrush, in a glorified world. Now he remembered
everything. Now it was all clear. The sudden
twisting of the car, the sound like the snapping of
a fiddle string and—Utopia! Now he had it all,
from the sight of sweet dead Greenlake to the bringing in of Lord Barralonga under the strange unfamiliar stars. It was no dream. He looked at his
hand on the exquisitely fine coverlet. He felt his
rough chin. It was a world real enough for shaving—and for a very definite readiness for breakfast. Very—for he had missed his supper. And as
if in answer to his thought a smiling girl appeared
ascending the steps to his sleeping-place and bearing
a little tray. After all, there was much to be said
for Mr. Burleigh. To his swift statesmanship it
was that Mr. Barnstaple owed this morning cup
of tea.

"Good morning," said Mr. Barnstaple.

"Why not?" said the young Utopian, and put
down his tea and smiled at him in a motherly
fashion and departed.

"Why not a good morning, I suppose," said Mr.
Barnstaple and meditated for a moment, chin on
knees, and then gave his attention to the bread-and-
butter and tea.

§ 2

The little dressing-room in which he found his clothes lying just as he had dumped them overnight, was at once extraordinarily simple and extraordinarily full of interest for Mr. Barnstaple. He paddled about it humming as he examined it.

The bath was much shallower than an ordinary earthly bath; apparently the Utopians did not believe in lying down and stewing. And the forms of everything were different, simpler and more graceful. On earth he reflected art was largely wit. The artist had a certain limited selection of obdurate materials and certain needs, and his work was a clever reconciliation of the obduracy and the necessity and of the idiosyncrasy of the substance to the aesthetic preconceptions of the human mind. How delightful, for example, was the earthly carpenter dealing cleverly with the grain and character of this wood or that. But here the artist had a limitless control of material, and that element of witty adaptation had gone out of his work. His data were the human mind and body. Everything in this little room was unobtrusively but perfectly convenient—and difficult to misuse. If you splashed too much a thoughtful outer rim tidied things up for you.

In a tray by the bath was a very big fine sponge. So either Utopians still dived for sponges or they grew them or trained them (who could tell?) to come up of their own accord.

As he set out his toilet things a tumbler was pushed off a glass shelf on to the floor and did not

break. Mr. Barnstaple in an experimental mood
dropped it again and still it did not break.

He could not find taps at first though there was
a big washing basin as well as a bath. Then he
perceived a number of studs on the walls with black
marks that might be Utopian writing. He experi-
mented. He found very hot water and then very
cold water filling his bath, a fountain of probably
soapy warm water, and other fluids—one with an
odour of pine and one with a subdued odour of
chlorine. The Utopian characters on these studs
set him musing for a time; they were the first writing he had seen; they appeared to be word characters, but whether they represented sounds or were
greatly simplified hieroglyphics he could not imagine.
Then his mind went off at a tangent in another
direction because the only metal apparent in this
dressing-room was gold. There was, he noted, an
extraordinary lot of gold in the room. It was set
and inlaid in gold. The soft yellow lines gleamed
and glittered. Gold evidently was cheap in Utopia.
Perhaps they knew how to make it.

He roused himself to the business of his toilet.
There was no looking-glass in the room, but when
he tried what he thought was the handle of a cup-
board door, he found himself opening a triple full-
length mirror. Afterwards he was to discover that
there were no displayed mirrors in Utopia; Utopians, he was to learn, thought it indecent to be
reminded of themselves in that way. The Utopian
method was to scrutinize oneself, see that one was
all right and then forget oneself for the rest of the
day. He stood now surveying his pyjamad and

unshaven self with extreme disfavour. Why do respectable citizens favour such ugly pink-striped pyjamas? When he unpacked his nail brush and tooth brush, shaving brush and washing glove, they seemed to him to have the coarseness of a popular burlesque. His tooth brush was a particularly ignoble instrument. He wished now he had bought a new one at the chemist's shop near Victoria Station.

And what nasty queer things his clothes were!

He had a fantastic idea of adopting Utopian ideas of costume, but a reflective moment before his mirror restrained him. Then he remembered that he had packed a silk tennis shirt and flannels. Suppose he wore those, without a collar stud or tie—and went bare-footed?

He surveyed his feet. As feet went on earth they were not unsightly feet. But on earth they had been just wasted.

§ 3

A particularly clean and radiant Mr. Barnstaple, white-clad, bare-necked and bare-footed, presently emerged into the Utopian sunrise. He smiled, stretched his arms and took a deep breath of the sweet air. Then suddenly his face became hard and resolute.

From another little sleeping house not two hundred yards away Father Amerton was emerging. Intuitively Mr. Barnstaple knew he meant either to forgive or be forgiven for the overnight quarrel. It would be a matter of chance whether he would

select the rôle of offender or victim; what was certain was that he would smear a dreary mess of
emotional personal relationship over the jewel-like
clearness and brightness of the scene. A little to
the right of Mr. Barnstaple and in front of him
were wide steps leading down towards the lake.
Three strides and he was going down these steps two
at a time. It may have been his hectic fancy, but
it seemed to him that he heard the voice of Father
Amerton, "Mr. *Barn*—Staple," in pursuit.

Mr. Barnstaple doubled and doubled again and
crossed a bridge across an avalanche gully, a bridge
with huge masonry in back and roof and with delicate pillars of prismatic glass towards the lake.
The sunlight entangled in these pillars broke into
splashes of red and blue and golden light. Then at
a turfy corner gay with blue gentians, he narrowly
escaped a collision with Mr. Rupert Catskill. Mr.
Catskill was in the same costume that he had worn
on the previous day except that he was without
his grey top hat. He walked with his hands clasped
behind him.

" Hullo ! " he said. " What's the hurry? We
seem to be the first people up."

" I saw Father Amerton——"

" That accounts for it. You were afraid of being
caught up in a service, Matins or Prime or whatever
he calls it. Wise man to run. He shall pray for
the lot of us. Me too."

He did not wait for any endorsement from Mr.
Barnstaple, but went on talking.

" You have slept well? What did you think of
the old fellow's answer to my speech. Eh? Eva-

sive clichés. When in doubt, abuse the plaintiff's
attorney. We don't agree with him because we
have bad hearts."

" What old fellow do you mean? "

" The worthy gentleman who spoke after me."

" Urthred! But he's not forty."

" He's seventy-three. He told us afterwards.
They live long here, a lingering business. Our lives
are a fitful hectic fever from their point of view.
But as Tennyson said, 'Better fifty years of Europe
than a cycle of Cathay!' H'm? He evaded my
points. This is Lotus Land, Sunset Land; we
shan't be thanked for disturbing its slumbers."

" I doubt their slumbers."

" Perhaps the Socialist bug has bit you too. Yes
—I see it has! Believe me this is the most complete demonstration of decadence it would be possible to imagine. Complete. And we *shall* disturb
their slumbers, never fear. Nature, you will see, is
on our side—in a way no one has thought of yet."

" But I don't see the decadence," said Mr. Barnstaple.

" None so blind as those who won't see. It's
everywhere. Their large flushed pseudo-health.
Like fatted cattle. And their treatment of Barralonga. They don't know how to treat him. They
don't even arrest him. They've never arrested anyone for a thousand years. He careers through their
land, killing and slaying and frightening and disturbing and they're flabbergasted, Sir, simply flabbergasted. It's like a dog running amuck in a
world full of sheep. If he hadn't had a side-slip I
believe he would be hooting and snorting and

careering along now—killing people. They've lost the instinct of social defence."

"I wonder."

"A very good attitude of mind. If indulged in, in moderation. But when your wondering is over, you will begin to see that I am right. H'm? Ah! There on that terrace! Isn't that my Lord Barralonga and his French acquaintance? It is. Inhaling the morning air. I think with your permission I will go on and have a word with them. Which way did you say Father Amerton was? I don't want to disturb his devotions. This way? Then if I go to the right——"

He grimaced amiably over his shoulder.

§ 4

Mr. Barnstaple came upon two Utopians gardening.

They had two light silvery wheelbarrows, and they were cutting out old wood and overblown clusters from a line of thickets that sprawled over a rough-heaped ridge of rock and foamed with crimson and deep red roses. These gardeners had great leather gauntlets and aprons of tanned skin, and they carried hooks and knives.

Mr. Barnstaple had never before seen such roses as they were tending here; their fragrance filled the air. He did not know that double roses could be got in mountains; bright red single sorts he had seen high up in Switzerland, but not such huge loose-flowered monsters as these. They dwarfed their leaves. Their wood was in long, thorny, snaky-red

streaked stems that writhed wide and climbed to the
rocky lumps over which they grew. Their great
petals fell like red snow and like drifting moths and
like blood upon the soft soil that sheltered amidst
the brown rocks.

"You are the first Utopians I have actually seen
at work," he said.

"This isn't our work," smiled the nearer of the
two, a fair-haired, freckled, blue-eyed youth. "But
as we are for these roses we have to keep them in
order."

"Are they your roses?"

"Many people think these double mountain roses
too much trouble and a nuisance with their thorns
and sprawling branches, and many people think
only the single sorts of roses ought to be grown in
these high places and that this lovely sort ought
to be left to die out up here. Are you for our roses?"

"Such roses as these?" said Mr. Barnstaple. "Altogether."

"Good! Then just bring me up my barrow closer
for all this litter. We're responsible for the good
behaviour of all this thicket reaching right down
there almost to the water."

"And you have to see to it yourselves?"

"Who else?"

"But couldn't you get someone—pay someone to
see to it for you?"

"Oh, hoary relic from the ancient past!" the
young man replied. "Oh, fossil ignoramus from a
barbaric universe! Don't you realize that there is
no working class in Utopia? It died out fifteen
hundred years or so ago. Wages-slavery, pimping

and so forth are done with. We read about them in books. Who loves the rose must serve the rose—himself."

"But you work."

"Not for wages. Not because anyone else loves or desires something else and is too lazy to serve it or get it himself. We work, part of the brain, part of the will, of Utopia."

"May I ask at what?"

"I explore the interior of our planet. I study high-pressure chemistry. And my friend——"

He interrogated his friend, whose dark face and brown eyes appeared suddenly over a foam of blossom. "I do Food."

"A cook?"

"Of sorts. Just now I am seeing to your Earthling dietary. It's most interesting and curious—but I should think rather destructive. I plan your meals. . . . I see you look anxious, but I saw to your breakfast last night." He glanced at a minute wrist-watch under the gauntlet of his gardening glove. "It will be ready in about an hour. How was the early tea?"

"Excellent," said Mr. Barnstaple.

"Good," said the dark young man. "I did my best. I hope the breakfast will be as satisfactory. I had to fly two hundred kilometres for a pig last night and kill it and cut it up myself, and find out how to cure it. Eating bacon has gone out of fashion in Utopia. I hope you will find my rashers satisfactory."

"It seems very rapid curing—for a rasher," said Mr. Barnstaple. "We could have done without it."

"Your spokesman made such a point of it."

The fair young man struggled out of the thicket and wheeled his barrow away. Mr. Barnstaple wished the dark young man "Good morning."

"Why shouldn't it be?" asked the dark young man.

§ 5

He discovered Ridley and Penk approaching him. Ridley's face and ear were still adorned with sticking-plaster and his bearing was eager and anxious. Penk followed a little way behind him, holding one hand to the side of his face. Both were in their professional dress, white-topped caps, square-cut leather coats and black gaiters; they had made no concessions to Utopian laxity.

Ridley began to speak as soon as he judged Mr. Barnstaple was within earshot.

"You don't 'appen to know, Mister, where these 'ere decadents shoved our car?"

"I thought your car was all smashed up."

"Not a Rolls-Royce—not like that. Windscreen, mud-guards and the on-footboard perhaps. We went over sideways. I want to 'ave a look at it. And I didn't turn the petrol off. The carburettor was leaking a bit. My fault. I 'adn't been careful enough with the strainer. If she runs out of petrol, where's one to get more of it in this blasted Elysium? I ain't seen a sign anywhere. I know if I don't get that car into running form before Lord Barralonga wants it there's going to be trouble."

Mr. Barnstaple had no idea where the cars were.

" 'Aven't you a car of your own?" asked Ridley reproachfully.

" I have. But I've never given it a thought since I got out of it."

" Owner-driver," said Ridley bitterly.

" Anyhow, I can't help you find your cars. Have you asked any of the Utopians?"

" Not us. We don't like the style of 'em," said Ridley.

" They'll tell you."

" And watch us—whatever we do to our cars. They don't get a chance of looking into a Rolls-Royce every day in the year. Next thing we shall have them driving off in 'em. I don't like the place, and I don't like these people. They're queer. They ain't decent. His lordship says they're a lot of degenerates, and it seems to me his lordship is about right. I ain't a Puritan, but all this running about without clothes is a bit too thick for me. I wish I knew where they'd stowed those cars."

Mr. Barnstaple was considering Penk. "You haven't hurt your face?" he asked.

" Nothing to speak of," said Penk. " I suppose we ought to be getting on."

Ridley looked at Penk and then at Mr. Barnstaple. " He's had a bit of a contoosion," he remarked, a faint smile breaking through his sourness.

" We better be getting on if we're going to find those cars," said Penk.

A grin of intense enjoyment appeared upon Ridley's face. " 'E's bumped against something."

"Oh—*shut it!*" said Penk.

But the thing was too good to keep back. "One of these girls 'it 'im."

"What do you mean?" said Mr. Barnstaple. "You haven't been taking liberties——?"

"I 'ave *not*," said Penk. "But as Mr. Ridley's been so obliging as to start the topic I suppose I got to tell wot 'appened. It jest illustrates the uncertainties of being among a lot of arf-savage, arf-crazy people, like we got among."

Ridley smiled and winked at Mr. Barnstaple. "Regular 'ard clout she gave 'im. Knocked him over. 'E put 'is 'and on 'er shoulder and *clop!* over 'e went. Never saw anything like it."

"Rather unfortunate," said Mr. Barnstaple.

"It all 'appened in a second like."

"It's a pity it happened."

"Don't you go making any mistake about it, Mister, and don't you go running off with any false ideas about it," said Penk. "I don't want the story to get about—it might do me a lot of 'arm with Mr. Burleigh. Pity Mr. Ridley couldn't 'old 'is tongue. What provoked her I do not know. She came into my room as I was getting up, and she wasn't what you might call wearing anything, and she looked a bit saucy, to my way of thinking, and—well, something come into my head to say to her, something—well, just the least little bit sporty, so to speak. One can't always control one's thoughts—can one? A man's a man. If a man's expected to be civil in his private thoughts to girls without a stitch, so to speak—*well!* I dunno. I really do not know. It's against nature. I never

said it, whatever it was I thought of. Mr. Ridley
'ere will bear me out. I never said a word to her.
I 'adn't opened my lips when she hit me. Knocked
me over, she did—like a ninepin. Didn't even
seem angry about it. A 'ook-'it—sideways. It was
surprise as much as anything floored me."

"But Ridley says you touched her."

"Laid me 'and on 'er shoulder perhaps, in a sort
of fatherly way. As she was turning to go—not
being sure whether I wasn't going to speak to her,
I admit. And there you are! If I'm to get into
trouble because I was wantonly 'it——"

Penk conveyed despair of the world by an eloquent gesture.

Mr. Barnstaple considered. "I shan't make
trouble," he said. "But all the same I think we
must all be very careful with these Utopians. Their
ways are not our ways."

"Thank God!" said Ridley. "The sooner I get
out of this world back to Old England, the better
I shall like it."

He turned to go.

"You should 'ear 'is lordship," said Ridley over
his shoulder. "'E says it's just a world of bally
degenerates—rotten degenerates—in fact, if you'll
excuse me — § § * ! * ! * † * † ! degenerates.
Eh? That about gets 'em."

"The young woman's arm doesn't seem to have
been very degenerate," said Mr. Barnstaple, standing the shock bravely.

"Don't it?" said Ridley bitterly. "That's all
you know. Why! if there's one sign more sure
than another about degeneration it's when women

take to knocking men about. It's against instink.
In any respectable decent world such a thing
couldn't possibly 'ave 'appened. No 'ow! "

" No—'ow," echoed Penk.

" In *our* world, such a girl would jolly soon 'ave
'er lesson. Jolly soon. See? "

But Mr. Barnstaple's roving eye had suddenly
discovered Father Amerton approaching very
rapidly across a wide space of lawn and making
arresting gestures. Mr. Barnstaple perceived he
must act at once.

" Now here's someone who will certainly be able
to help you find your cars, if he cares to do so.
He's a most helpful man—Father Amerton. And
the sort of views he has about women are the sort
of views you have. You are bound to get on together. If you will stop him and put the whole
case to him—plainly and clearly. . . ."

He set off at a brisk pace towards the lake shore.

He could not be far now from the little summer-
house that ran out over the water against which
the gaily coloured boats were moored.

If he were to get into one of these and pull out
into the lake he would have Father Amerton at a
very serious disadvantage. Even if that good man
followed suit. One cannot have a really eloquent
emotional scene when one is pulling hard in pursuit of another boat.

§ 6

As Mr. Barnstaple untied the bright white canoe
with the big blue eye painted at its prow that he

had chosen, Lady Stella appeared on the landing-stage. She came out of the pavilion that stood over the water, and something in her quick movement as she emerged suggested to Mr. Barnstaple's mind that she had been hiding there. She glanced about her and spoke very eagerly. " Are you going to row out upon the lake, Mr. Bastable? May I come? "

She was attired, he noted, in a compromise between the Earthly and the Utopian style. She was wearing what might have been either a very simple custard-coloured tea robe or a very sophisticated bath wrap; it left her slender, pretty arms bare and free except for a bracelet of amber and gold, and on her bare feet—and they were unusually shapely feet—were sandals. Her head was bare, and her dark hair very simply done with a little black and gold fillet round it that suited her intelligent face. Mr. Barnstaple was an ignoramus about feminine costume, but he appreciated the fact that she had been clever in catching the Utopian note.

He helped her into the canoe. "We will paddle right out—a good way," she said with another glance over her shoulder, and sat down.

For a time Mr. Barnstaple paddled straight out so that he had nothing before him but sunlit water and sky, the low hills that closed in the lake towards the great plain, the huge pillars of the distant dam, and Lady Stella. She affected to be overcome by the beauty of the Conference garden slope with its houses and terraces behind him, but he could see that she was not really looking at the scene as

a whole, but searching it restlessly for some particular object or person.

She made conversational efforts, on the loveliness
of the morning and on the fact that birds were singing—"in July."

"But here it is not necessarily July," said Mr.
Barnstaple.

"How stupid of me! Of course not."

"We seem to be in a fine May."

"It is probably very early," she said. "I forgot
to wind my watch."

"Oddly enough we seem to be at about the same
hours in our two worlds," said Mr. Barnstaple. "My
wrist-watch says seven."

"No," said Lady Stella, answering her own
thoughts and with her eyes on the distant gardens.
"That is a Utopian girl. Have you met any others
—of our party—this morning?"

Mr. Barnstaple brought the canoe round so that
he too could look at the shore. From here they
could see how perfectly the huge terraces and avalanche walls and gullies mingled and interwove with
the projecting ribs and cliffs of the mountain masses
behind. The shrub tangles passed up into hanging
pinewoods; the torrents and cascades from the snow-
field above were caught and distributed amidst the
emerald slopes and gardens of the Conference Park.
The terraces that retained the soil and held the
whole design spread out on either hand to a great
distance and were continued up into the mountain
substance; they were built of a material that ranged
through a wide variety of colours from a deep red to
a purple-veined white, and they were diversified

by great arches over torrents and rock gullies, by huge round openings that spouted water and by cascades of steps. The buildings of the place were distributed over these terraces and over the grassy slopes they contained, singly or in groups and clusters, buildings of purple and blue and white as light and delicate as the Alpine flowers about them. For some moments Mr. Barnstaple was held silent by this scene, and then he attended to Lady Stella's question. "I met Mr. Rupert Catskill and the two chauffeurs," he said, "and I saw Father Amerton and Lord Barralonga and M. Dupont in the distance. I've seen nothing of Mr. Mush or Mr. Burleigh."

"Mr. Cecil won't be about for hours yet. He will lie in bed until ten or eleven. He always takes a good rest in the morning when there is any great mental exertion before him."

The lady hesitated and then asked: "I suppose you haven't seen Miss Greeta Grey?"

"No," said Mr. Barnstaple. "I wasn't looking for our people. I was just strolling about—and avoiding somebody."

"The censor of manners and costumes?"

"Yes. . . . That, in fact, is why I took to this canoe."

The lady reflected and decided on a confidence. "I was running away from someone too."

"Not the preacher?"

"Miss Grey!"

Lady Stella apparently went off at a tangent. "This is going to be a very difficult world to stay in. These people have very delicate taste. We may easily offend them."

"They are intelligent enough to understand."

"Do people who understand necessarily forgive? I've always doubted that proverb."

Mr. Barnstaple did not wish the conversation to drift away into generalities, so he paddled and said nothing.

"You see Miss Grey used to play Phryne in a Revue."

"I seem to remember something about it. There was a fuss in the newspapers."

"That perhaps gave her a bias."

Three long sweeps with the paddle.

"But this morning she came to me and told me that she was going to wear complete Utopian costume."

"Meaning?"

"A little rouge and face powder. It doesn't suit her the least little bit, Mr. Bastaple. It's a faux pas. It's indecent. But she's running about the gardens——. She might meet anyone. It's lucky Mr. Cecil isn't up. If she meets Father Amerton ——! But it's best not to think of that. You see, Mr. Bastaple, these Utopians and their sun-brown bodies—and everything, are in the picture. They don't embarrass me. But Miss Grey——. An earthly civilized woman taken out of her clothes *looks* taken out of her clothes. Peeled. A sort of *bleached* white. That nice woman who seems to hover round us, Lychnis, when she advised me what to wear, never for one moment suggested anything of the sort. . . . But, of course, I don't know Miss Grey well enough to talk to her and besides, one never knows how a woman of that sort is going to take a thing. . . ."

Mr. Barnstaple stared shoreward. Nothing was to be seen of an excessively visible Miss Greeta Grey. Then he had a conviction. "Lychnis will take care of her," he said.

"I hope she will. Perhaps, if we stay out here for a time——"

"She will be looked after," said Mr. Barnstaple. "But I think Miss Grey and Lord Barralonga's party generally are going to make trouble for us. I wish they hadn't come through with us."

"Mr. Cecil thinks that," said Lady Stella.

"Naturally we shall all be thrown very much together and judged in a lump."

"Naturally," Lady Stella echoed.

She said no more for a little while. But it was evident that she had more to say. Mr. Barnstaple paddled slowly.

"Mr. Bastable," she began presently.

Mr. Barnstaple's paddle became still.

"Mr. Bastable—are you *afraid?*"

Mr. Barnstaple judged himself. "I have been too full of wonder to be afraid."

Lady Stella decided to confess. "I *am* afraid," she said. "I wasn't at first. Everything seemed to go so easily and simply. But in the night I woke up—horribly afraid."

"No," considered Mr. Barnstaple. "No. It hasn't taken me like that—yet. . . . Perhaps it will."

Lady Stella leant forward and spoke confidentially, watching the effect of her words on Mr. Barnstaple. "These Utopians—I thought at first they were just simple, healthy human beings, artistic and innocent. But they are not, Mr. Bastable. There is something hard and complicated about them, something that goes beyond us and that we don't understand. And they don't care for us. They look at us with heartless eyes. Lychnis is kind, but hardly any of the others are the least bit kind. And I think they find us inconvenient."

Mr. Barnstaple thought it over. "Perhaps they do. I have been so preoccupied with admiration—so much of this is fine beyond dreaming—that I have not thought very much how we affected them. But—yes—they seem to be busy about other things and not very attentive to us. Except the ones who have evidently been assigned to watch and study us. And Lord Barralonga's headlong rush through the country must certainly have been inconvenient."

"He killed a man."

"I know."

They remained thoughtfully silent for some moments.

"And there are other things," Lady Stella resumed. "They think quite differently from our way of thinking. I believe they despise us already. I noted something. . . . Last evening you were not with us by the lake when Mr. Cecil asked them about their philosophy. He told them things about Hegel and Bergson and Lord Haldane and his own wonderful scepticism. He opened out—unusually. It was very interesting—to me. But I was watching Urthred and Lion and in the midst of it I saw—I am convinced—they were talking to each other in that silent way they have, about something quite different. They were just *shamming* attention. And when Freddy Mush tried to interest them in Neo-Georgian poetry and the effect of the war upon literature, and how he hoped that they had something *half* as beautiful as the Iliad in Utopia, though he confessed he couldn't believe they had, they didn't even pretend to listen. They did not answer him at all. . . . Our minds don't matter a bit to them."

"In these subjects. They are three thousand years further on. But we might be interesting as learners."

"Would it have been interesting to have taken a Hottentot about London explaining things to him— after one had got over the first fun of showing off his ignorance? Perhaps it would. But I don't think they want us here very much and I don't think they are going to like us very much, and I don't know what they are likely to do to us if we give too much trouble. And so I am afraid."

She broke out in a new place. "In the night I was reminded of my sister Mrs. Kelling's monkeys.

"It's a mania with her. They run about the gardens and come into the house and the poor things are always in trouble. They don't quite know what they may do and what they may not do; they all look frightfully worried and they get slapped and carried to the door and thrown out and all sorts of things like that. They spoil things and make her guests uneasy. You never seem to know what a monkey's going to do. And everybody hates to have them about except my sister. And she keeps

on scolding them. 'Come *down*, Jacko! Put that
down, Sadie'!"

Mr. Barnstaple laughed. "It isn't going to be
quite so bad as that with us, Lady Stella. We are
not monkeys."

She laughed too. "Perhaps it isn't. But all the
same—in the night—I felt it might be. We are
inferior creatures. One has to admit it. . . ."

She knitted her brows. Her pretty face expressed
great intellectual effort. "Do you realize how we
are cut off? . . . Perhaps you will think it silly of
me, Mr. Bastable, but last night before I went to
bed I sat down to write my sister a letter and tell
her all about things while they were fresh in my
mind. And suddenly I realized I might as well
write—to Julius Cæsar."

Mr. Barnstaple hadn't thought of that.

"That's a thing I can't get out of my head, Mr.
Bastable—no letters, no telegrams, no newspapers,
no Bradshaw in Utopia. All the things we care for
really—— All the people we live for. Cut off!
I don't know for how long. But completely cut
off. . . . How long are they likely to keep us here?"

Mr. Barnstaple's face became speculative.

"Are you *sure* they can ever send us back?" the
lady asked.

"There seems to be some doubt. But they are
astonishingly clever people."

"It seemed so easy coming here—just as if one
walked round a corner—but, of course, properly
speaking we are out of space and time. . . . More
out of it even than dead people. . . . The North
Pole or Central Africa is a whole universe nearer

home than we are. . . . It's hard to grasp that. In this sunlight it all seems so bright and familiar. . . . Yet last night there were moments when I wanted to scream. . . ."

She stopped short and scanned the shore. Then very deliberately she sniffed.

Mr. Barnstaple became aware of a peculiarly sharp and appetizing smell drifting across the water to him.

"Yes," he said.

"It's breakfast bacon!" cried Lady Stella with a squeak in her voice.

"Exactly as Mr. Burleigh told them," said Mr. Barnstaple, mechanically turning the canoe shoreward.

"Breakfast bacon! That's the most reassuring thing that has happened yet. . . . Perhaps after all it was silly to feel frightened. And there they are signalling to us!" She waved her arm.

"Greeta in a white robe—as you prophesied—and Mr. Mush in a sort of toga talking to her. . . . Where could he have got that toga?"

A faint sound of voices calling reached them.

"Com—*ing!*" cried Lady Stella.

"I hope I haven't been pessimistic," said Lady Stella. "But I felt *horrid* in the night."

BOOK THE SECOND

QUARANTINE CRAG

CHAPTER THE FIRST

THE EPIDEMIC

§ 1

The shadow of the great epidemic in Utopia fell upon our little band of Earthlings in the second day after their irruption. For more than twenty centuries the Utopians had had the completest freedom from infectious and contagious disease of all sorts. Not only had the graver epidemic fevers and all sorts of skin diseases gone out of the lives of animals and men, but all the minor infections of colds, coughs, influenzas and the like had also been mastered and ended. By isolation, by the control of carriers, and so forth, the fatal germs had been cornered and obliged to die out.

And there had followed a corresponding change in the Utopian physiology. Secretions and reactions that had given the body resisting power to infection had diminished; the energy that produced them had been withdrawn to other more serviceable applications. The Utopian physiology, relieved of these merely defensive necessities, had simplified itself and become more direct and efficient. This cleaning up of infections was such ancient history in Utopia that only those who specialized in the history of pathology understood anything of the miseries mankind had suffered under from this source, and even these specialists do not seem to have had any idea of how far the race had lost its former resistance to infection. The first person to think of this lost resisting power seems to have been Mr. Rupert Catskill. Mr. Barnstaple recalled that when they had met early on the first morning of their stay in the Conference Gardens, he had been hinting that Nature was in some unexplained way on the side of the Earthlings.

If making them obnoxious was being on their side then certainly Nature was on their side. By the evening of the second day after their arrival nearly everybody who had been in contact with the Earthlings, with the exception of Lychnis, Serpentine and three or four others who had retained something of their ancestral antitoxins, was in a fever with cough, sore throat, aching bones, headache and such physical depression and misery as Utopia had not known for twenty centuries. The first inhabitant of Utopia to die was that leopard which had sniffed at Mr. Rupert Catskill on his first arrival. It was found unaccountably dead on the second morning after that encounter. In the afternoon of the same day one of the girls who had helped Lady Stella to unpack her bags sickened suddenly and died. . . .

Utopia was even less prepared for the coming of these disease germs than for the coming of the Earthlings who brought them. The monstrous multitude of general and fever hospitals, doctors, drug shops, and so forth that had existed in the

last Age of Confusion had long since passed out of
memory; there was a surgical service for accidents
and a watch kept upon the health of the young,
and there were places of rest at which those who
were extremely old were assisted, but there remained scarcely anything of the hygienic organization that had formerly struggled against disease.
Abruptly the Utopian intelligence had to take up
again a tangle of problems long since solved and
set aside, to improvise forgotten apparatus and
organizations for disinfection and treatment, and
to return to all the disciplines of the war against
diseases that had marked an epoch in its history
twenty centuries before. In one respect indeed
that war had left Utopia with certain permanent
advantages. Nearly all the insect disease carriers
had been exterminated, and rats and mice and the
untidier sorts of small bird had passed out of the
problem of sanitation. That set very definite
limits to the spread of the new infections and to the
nature of the infections that could be spread. It
enabled the Earthlings only to communicate such
ailments as could be breathed across an interval, or
conveyed by a contaminating touch. Though not
one of them was ailing at all, it became clear that
some one among them had brought latent measles
into the Utopian universe, and that three or four
of them had liberated a long suppressed influenza.
Themselves too tough to suffer, they remained at
the focus of these two epidemics, while their victims
coughed and sneezed and kissed and whispered them
about the Utopian planet. It was not until the
afternoon of the second day after the irruption that

Utopia realized what had happened, and set itself
to deal with this relapse into barbaric solicitudes.

§ 2

Mr. Barnstaple was probably the last of the
Earthlings to hear of the epidemic. He was away
from the rest of the party upon an expedition of
his own.

It was early clear to him that the Utopians did
not intend to devote any considerable amount of
time or energy to the edification of their Earthling
visitors. After the *éclaircissement* of the afternoon
of the irruption there were no further attempts to
lecture to the visitors upon the constitution and
methods of Utopia and only some very brief questioning upon the earthly state of affairs. The
Earthlings were left very much together to talk
things out among themselves. Several Utopians
were evidently entrusted with their comfort and
well-being, but they did not seem to think that
their functions extended to edification. Mr. Barnstaple found much to irritate him in the ideas and
comments of several of his associates, and so he
obeyed his natural inclination to explore Utopia for
himself. There was something that stirred his
imagination in the vast plain below the lake that
he had glimpsed before his aeroplane descended into
the valley of the Conference, and on his second
morning he had taken a little boat and rowed out
across the lake to examine the dam that retained
its waters and to get a view of the great plain from
the parapet of the dam.

The lake was much wider than he had thought it
and the dam much larger. The water was crystalline clear and very cold, and there were but few fish
in it. He had come out immediately after his breakfast, but it was near midday before he had got to
the parapet of the great dam and could look down
the lower valley to the great plain.

The dam was built of huge blocks of red and gold-
veined rock, but steps at intervals gave access to the
roadway along its crest. The great seated figures
which brooded over the distant plain had been put
there, it would seem, in a mood of artistic light-
heartedness. They sat as if they watched or
thought, vast rude shapes, half mountainous, half
human. Mr. Barnstaple guessed them to be perhaps two hundred feet high; by pacing the distance
between two of them and afterwards counting the
number of them, he came to the conclusion that the
dam was between seven and ten miles long. On the
far side it dropped sheerly for perhaps five hundred
feet, and it was sustained by a series of enormous
buttresses that passed almost insensibly into native
rock. In the bays between these buttresses hummed
great batteries of water turbines, and then, its
first task done, the water dropped foaming and
dishevelled and gathered in another broad lake retained by a second great dam two miles or so away
and perhaps a thousand feet lower. Far away was
a third lake and a third dam and then the plain.
Only three or four minute-looking Utopians were
visible amidst all this Titanic engineering.

Mr. Barnstaple stood, the smallest of objects, in
the shadow of a brooding Colossus, and peered over

these nearer things at the hazy levels of the plain
beyond.

What sort of life was going on there? The relationship of plain to mountain reminded him very
strongly of the Alps and the great plain of Northern
Italy, down into which he had walked as the climax
of many a summer holiday in his youth. In Italy
he knew that those distant levels would be covered
with clustering towns and villages and carefully
irrigated and closely cultivated fields. A dense
population would be toiling with an ant-like industry in the production of food; for ever increasing
its numbers until those inevitable consequences of
overcrowding, disease and pestilence established a
sort of balance between the area of the land and the
number of families scraping at it for nourishment.
As a toiling man can grow more food than he can
actually eat, and as virtuous women can bear more
children than the land can possibly employ, a surplus of landless population would be gathered in
wen-like towns and cities, engaged there in legal and
financial operations against the agriculturalist or in
the manufacture of just plausible articles for sale.

Ninety-nine out of every hundred of this population would be concentrated from childhood to old
age upon the difficult task which is known as "getting a living." Amidst it, sustained by a pretence of
magical propitiations, would rise shrines and temples, supporting a parasitic host of priests and monks
and nuns. Eating and breeding, the simple routines
of the common life since human societies began,
complications of food-getting, elaborations of ac-
quisitiveness and a tribute paid to fear; such would

be the spectacle that any warm and fertile stretch
of earth would still display.   There would be gleams
of laughter and humour there, brief interludes of
holiday, flashes of youth before its extinction in
adult toil; but a driven labour, the spite and hates
of overcrowding, the eternal uncertainty of destitu-
tion, would dominate the scene.   Decrepitude would
come by sixty; women would be old and worn out
by forty.   But this Utopian plain below, sunlit and
fertile though it was, was under another law.   Here
that common life of mankind, its ancient traditions,
its hoary jests and tales repeated generation after
generation, its seasonal festivals, its pious fears and
spasmodic indulgences, its limited yet incessant and
pitifully childish hoping, and its abounding misery
and tragic futility, had come to an end.   It had
passed for ever out of this older world.   That high
tide of common living had receded and vanished
while the soil was still productive and the sun still
shone.

It was with something like awe that Mr. Barnstaple realized how clean a sweep had been made of
the common life in a mere score of centuries, how
boldly and dreadfully the mind of man had taken
hold, soul and body and destiny, of the life and
destiny of the race.   He knew himself now for the
creature of transition he was, so deep in the habits
of the old, so sympathetic with the idea of the new
that has still but scarcely dawned on earth.   For
long he had known how intensely he loathed and
despised that reeking peasant life which is our past;
he realized now for the first time how profoundly
he feared the high austere Utopian life which lies

before us. This world he looked out upon seemed
very clean and dreadful to him. What were they
doing upon those distant plains? What daily life
did they lead there?

He knew enough of Utopia now to know that the
whole land would be like a garden, with every
natural tendency to beauty seized upon and developed and every innate ugliness corrected and
overcome. These people could work and struggle
for loveliness, he knew, for his two rose growers had
taught him as much. And to and fro the food folk
and the housing people and those who ordered the
general life went, keeping the economic machine
running so smoothly that one heard nothing of the
jangling and jarring and internal breakages that
constitute the dominant melody in our Earth's affairs. The ages of economic disputes and experiments had come to an end; the right way to do
things had been found. And the population of this
Utopia, which had shrunken at one time to only two
hundred million, was now increasing again to keep
pace with the constant increase in human resources.
Having freed itself from a thousand evils that would
otherwise have grown with its growth, the race could
grow indeed.

And down there under the blue haze of the great
plain almost all those who were not engaged in the
affairs of food and architecture, health, education
and the correlation of activities, were busied upon
creative work; they were continually exploring the
world without or the world within, through scientific research and artistic creation. They were con-

tinually adding to their collective power over life
or to the realized worth of life.

Mr. Barnstaple was accustomed to think of our
own world as a wild rush of inventions and knowledge, but all the progress of earth for a hundred
years could not compare, he knew, with the forward swing of these millions of associated intelligences in one single year. Knowledge swept forward here and darkness passed as the shadow of a
cloud passes on a windy day. Down there they
were assaying the minerals that lie in the heart of
their planet, and weaving a web to capture the sun
and the stars. Life marched here; it was terrifying to think with what strides. Terrifying—
because at the back of Mr. Barnstaple's mind, as at
the back of so many intelligent minds in our world
still, had been the persuasion that presently everything would be known and the scientific process
come to an end. And then we should be happy for
ever after.

He was not really acclimatized to progress. He
had always thought of Utopia as a tranquillity with
everything settled for good. Even today it seemed
tranquil under that level haze, but he knew that
this quiet was the steadiness of a mill-race, which
seems almost motionless in its quiet onrush until a
bubble or a fleck of foam or some stick or leaf
shoots along it and reveals its velocity.

And how did it feel to be living in Utopia? The
lives of the people must be like the lives of very
successful artists or scientific workers in this world,
a continual refreshing discovery of new things, a
constant adventure into the unknown and untried.

For recreation they went about their planet, and there was much love and laughter and friendship in Utopia and an abundant easy informal social life. Games that did not involve bodily exercise, those substitutes of the half-witted for research and mental effort, had gone entirely out of life, but many active games were played for the sake of fun and bodily vigour. . . . It must be a good life for those who had been educated to live it, indeed a most enviable life.

And pervading it all must be the happy sense that it mattered; it went on to endless consequences. And they loved no doubt—subtly and deliciously—but perhaps a little hardly. Perhaps in those distant plains there was not much pity nor tenderness. Bright and lovely beings they were—in no way pitiful. There would be no need for those qualities. . . .

Yet the woman Lychnis looked kind. . . .

Did they keep faith or need to keep faith as earthly lovers do? What was love like in Utopia? Lovers still whispered in the dusk. . . . What was the essence of love? A preference, a sweet pride, a delightful gift won, the most exquisite reassurance of body and mind. . . .

What could it be like to love and be loved by one of these Utopian women?—to have her glowing face close to one's own—to be quickened into life by her kiss? . . .

Mr. Barnstaple sat in his flannels, bare-footed, in the shadow of a stone Colossus. He felt like some minute stray insect perched upon the big dam. It seemed to him that it was impossible that this

triumphant Utopian race could ever fall back again
from its magnificent attack upon the dominion of
all things. High and tremendously this world had
clambered and was still clambering. Surely it was
safe now in its attainment. Yet all this stupendous
security and mastery of nature had come about in
the little space of three thousand years. . . .

The race could not have altered fundamentally
in that brief interval. Essentially it was still a
stone-age race, it was not twenty thousand years
away from the days when it knew nothing of metals
and could not read nor write. Deep in its nature,
arrested and undeveloped, there still lay the seeds
of anger and fear and dissension. There must still
be many uneasy and insubordinate spirits in this
Utopia. Eugenics had scarcely begun here. He
remembered the keen sweet face of the young girl
who had spoken to him in the starlight on the night
of his arrival, and the note of romantic eagerness
in her voice when she had asked if Lord Barralonga
was not a very vigorous and cruel man.

Did the romantic spirit still trouble imaginations
here? Possibly only adolescent imaginations.

Might not some great shock or some phase of confusion still be possible to this immense order?
Might not its system of education become wearied
by its task of discipline and fall a prey to the
experimental spirit? Might not the unforeseen be
still lying in wait for this race? Suppose there
should prove to be an infection in Father Amerton's
religious fervour or Rupert Catskill's incurable
craving for fantastic enterprises!

No! It was inconceivable. The achievement of this world was too calmly great and assured.

Mr. Barnstaple stood up and made his way down the steps of the great dam to where, far below, his little skiff floated like a minute flower-petal upon the clear water.

§ 3

He became aware of a considerable commotion in the Conference places.

There were more than thirty aeroplanes circling in the air and descending and ascending from the park, and a great number of big white vehicles were coming and going by the pass road. Also people seemed to be moving briskly among the houses, but it was too far off to distinguish what they were doing. He stared for a time and then got into his little boat.

He could not watch what was going on as he returned across the lake because his back was towards the slopes, but once an aeroplane came down very close to him, and he saw its occupant looking at him as he rowed. And once when he rested from rowing and sat round to look he saw what he thought was a litter carried by two men.

As he drew near the shore a boat put off to meet him. He was astonished to see that its occupants were wearing what looked like helmets of glass with white pointed visors. He was enormously aston- ished and puzzled.

As they approached their message resonated into his mind. "Quarantine. You have to go into quar-

antine. You Earthlings have started an epidemic
and it is necessary to put you into quarantine."

Then these glass helmets must be a sort of gas-
mask!

When they came alongside him he saw that this
was so. They were made of highly flexible and
perfectly translucent material. . . .

§ 4

Mr. Barnstaple was taken past some sleeping
loggias where Utopians were lying in beds, while
others who wore gas-masks waited upon them. He
found that all the Earthlings and all their possessions, except their cars, were assembled in the hall
of the first day's Conference. He was told that the
whole party were to be removed to a new place
where they could be isolated and treated.

The only Utopians with the party were two who
wore gas-masks and lounged in the open portico in
attitudes disagreeably suggestive of sentries or cus-
todians.

The Earthlings sat about in little groups among
the seats, except for Mr. Rupert Catskill, who was
walking up and down in the apse talking. He was
hatless, flushed and excited, with his hair in some
disorder.

"It's what I foresaw would happen all along," he
repeated. "Didn't I tell you Nature was on our
side? Didn't I say it?"

Mr. Burleigh was shocked and argumentative.
"For the life of me I can't see the logic of it," he
declared. "Here are we—absolutely the only per-

fectly immune people here—and we—*we* are to be isolated."

"They say they catch things from us," said Lady Stella.

"Very well," said Mr. Burleigh, making his point with his long white hand. "Very well, then let *them* be isolated! This is—Chinese; this is topsy-turvy. I'm disappointed in them."

"I suppose it's their world," said Mr. Hunker, "and we've got to do things their way."

Mr. Catskill concentrated upon Lord Barralonga and the two chauffeurs. "I welcome this treatment. I welcome it."

"What's your idea, Rupert?" said his lordship. "We lose our freedom of action."

"Not at all," said Mr. Catskill. "Not at all. We gain it. We are to be isolated. We are to be put by ourselves in some island or mountain. Well and good. Well and good. This is only the beginning of our adventures. We shall see what we shall see."

"But how?"

"Wait a little. Until we can speak more freely. . . . These are panic measures. This pestilence is only in its opening stage. Everything is just beginning. Trust me."

Mr. Barnstaple sat sulkily by his valise, avoiding the challenge of Mr. Catskill's eye.

CHAPTER THE SECOND

THE CASTLE ON THE CRAG

§ 1

The quarantine place to which the Earthlings were taken must have been at a very considerable distance from the place of the Conference, because they were nearly six hours upon their journey, and all the time they were flying high and very swiftly. They were all together in one flying ship; it was roomy and comfortable and could have held perhaps four times as many passengers. They were accompanied by about thirty Utopians in gas-masks, among whom were two women. The aviators wore dresses of a white fleecy substance that aroused the interest and envy of both Miss Grey and Lady Stella. The flying ship passed down the valley and over the great plain and across a narrow sea and another land with a rocky coast and dense forests, and across a great space of empty sea. There was scarcely any shipping to be seen upon this sea at all; it seemed to Mr. Barnstaple that no earthly ocean would be so untravelled; only once or twice did he see very big drifting vessels quite unlike any earthly ships, huge rafts or platforms they seemed to be rather than ships, and once or twice he saw what was evidently a cargo boat—one with rigged masts and sails. And the air was hardly more frequented. After he was out of sight of land he saw only three aeroplanes until the final landfall.

They crossed a rather thickly inhabited, very delightful-looking coastal belt and came over what was evidently a rainless desert country, given over to mining and to vast engineering operations. Far away were very high snowy mountains, but the aeroplane descended before it came to these. For a time the Earthlings were flying over enormous heaps of slaggy accumulations, great mountains of them, that seemed to be derived from a huge well-like excavation that went down into the earth to an unknown depth. A tremendous thunder of machinery came out of this pit and much smoke. Here there were crowds of workers and they seemed to be living in camps among the debris. Evidently the workers came to this place merely for spells of work; there were no signs of homes. The aeroplane of the Earthlings skirted this region and flew on over a rocky and almost treeless desert deeply cut by steep gorges of the canyon type. Few people were to be seen, but there were abundant signs of engineering activity. Every torrent, every cataract was working a turbine, and great cables followed the cliffs of the gorges and were carried across the desert spaces. In the wider places of the gorges there were pine woods and a fairly abundant vegetation.

The high crag which was their destination stood out, an almost completely isolated headland, in the fork between two convergent canyons. It towered up to a height of perhaps two thousand feet above the foaming clash of the torrents below, a great mass of pale greenish and purple rocks, jagged and buttressed and cleft deeply by joint planes and white crystalline veins. The gorge on one side of it was much steeper than that on the other, it was so overhung indeed as to be darkened like a tunnel, and here within a hundred feet or so of the brow a slender metallic bridge had been flung across the gulf. Some yards above it were projections that might have been the remains of an earlier bridge of stone. Behind, the crag fell steeply for some hundreds of feet to a long slope covered with a sparse vegetation which rose again to the main masses of the mountain, a wall of cliffs with a level top.

It was on this slope that the aeroplane came down alongside of three or four smaller machines. The crag was surmounted by the tall ruins of an ancient castle, within the circle of whose walls clustered a number of buildings which had recently harboured a group of chemical students. Their researches, which had been upon some question of atomic structure quite incomprehensible to Mr. Barnstaple, were finished now and the place had become vacant. Their laboratory was still stocked with apparatus and material; and water and power were supplied to it from higher up the gorge by means of pipes and cables. There was also an abundant store of provisions. A number of Utopians were busily adapting the place to its new purpose of isolation and disinfection when the Earthlings arrived.

Serpentine appeared in the company of a man in a gas-mask whose name was Cedar. This Cedar was a cytologist, and he was in charge of the arrangements for this improvised sanatorium.

Serpentine explained that he himself had flown to the crag in advance, because he understood the equipment of the place and the research that had been going on there, and because his knowledge of the Earthlings and his comparative immunity to their infections made him able to act as an intermediary between them and the medical men who would now take charge of their case. He made these explanations to Mr. Burleigh, Mr. Barnstaple, Lord Barralonga and Mr. Hunker. The other Earthlings stood about in small groups beside the aeroplane from which they had alighted, regarding the castellated summit of the crag, the scrubby bushes of the bleak upland about them and the towering cliffs of the adjacent canyons with no very favourable expressions.

Mr. Catskill had gone apart nearly to the edge of the great canyon, and was standing with his hands behind his back in an attitude almost Napoleonic, lost in thought, gazing down into those sunless depths. The roar of the unseen waters below, now loud, now nearly inaudible, quivered in the air.

Miss Greeta Grey had suddenly produced a Kodak camera; she had been reminded of its existence when packing for this last journey, and she was taking a snapshot of the entire party.

Cedar said that he would explain the method of treatment he proposed to follow, and Lord Barralonga called "Rupert!" to bring Mr. Catskill into the group of Cedar's hearers.

Cedar was as explicit and concise as Urthred had been. It was evident, he said, that the Earthlings were the hosts of a variety of infectious organisms

which were kept in check in their bodies by immun-
izing counter substances, but against which the Utopians had no defences ready and could hope to
secure immunity only after a painful and disastrous
epidemic. The only way to prevent this epidemic
devastating their whole planet, indeed, was firstly
to gather together and cure all the cases affected,
which was being done by converting the Conference
Park into a big hospital, and next to take the Earthlings in hand and isolate them absolutely from the
Utopians until they could be cleaned of their infections. It was, he confessed, an inhospitable thing
to do to the Earthlings, but it seemed the only possible thing to do, to bring them into this peculiarly
high and dry desert air and there to devise methods
for their complete physical cleansing. If that was
possible it would be done, and then the Earthlings
would again be free to go and come as they pleased
in Utopia.

"But suppose it is not possible?" said Mr. Catskill abruptly.

"I think it will be."

"But if you fail?"

Cedar smiled at Serpentine. "Physical research
is taking up the work in which Arden and Greenlake
were foremost, and it will not be long before we
are able to repeat their experiment. And then to
reverse it."

"With us as your raw material?"

"Not until we are fairly sure of a safe landing for
you."

"You mean," said Mr. Mush, who had joined the

circle about Cedar and Serpentine, "that you are going to send us back?"

"If we cannot keep you," said Cedar, smiling.

"Delightful prospect!" said Mr. Mush unpleasantly. "To be shot across space in a gun. Experimentally."

"And may I ask," came the voice of Father Amerton, "may I ask the nature of this *treatment* of yours, these experiments of which we are to be the— guinea pigs, so to speak? Is it to be anything in the nature of vaccination?"

"Injections," explained Mr. Barnstaple.

"I have hardly decided yet," said Cedar. "The problem raises questions this world has forgotten for ages."

"I may say at once that I am a confirmed antivaccinationist," said Father Amerton. "Absolutely. Vaccination is an outrage on nature. If I had any doubts before I came into this world of—of *vitiation*, I have no doubts now. Not a doubt! If God had meant us to have these serums and ferments in our bodies He would have provided more natural and dignified means of getting them there than a squirt."

Cedar did not discuss the point. He went on to further apologies. For a time he must ask the Earthlings to keep within certain limits, to confine themselves to the crag and the slopes below it as far as the mountain cliffs. And further, it was impossible to set young people to attend to them as had hitherto been done. They must cook for themselves and see to themselves generally. The appliances were all to be found above upon the crest of the crag and he and Serpentine would make any

explanations that were needful. They would find
there was ample provision for them.

"I have come to my last clean collar," said M.
Catskill.

"For a time. When we have our problem clearer
we will come again and tell you what we mean to
do."

"Good," said Mr. Catskill. "Good."

"I wish I hadn't sent my maid by train," said
Lady Stella.

"I have come to my last clean collar," said M.
Dupont with a little humorous grimace. "It is no
joke this week-end with Lord Barralonga."

Lord Barralonga turned suddenly to his particular
minion. "I believe that Ridley has the makings of
a very good cook."

"I don't mind trying my hand," said Ridley. "I've
done most things—and once I used to look after a
steam car."

"A man who can keep one of those—those things
in order can do anything," said Mr. Penk with unusual emotion. "I've no objection to being a temporary general utility along of Mr. Ridley. I began
my career in the pantry and I ain't ashamed to
own it."

"If this gentleman will show us the gadgets,"
said Mr. Ridley, indicating Serpentine.

"Exactly," said Mr. Penk.

"And if all of us give as little trouble as possible,"
said Miss Greeta bravely.

"I think we shall be able to manage," said Mr.
Burleigh to Cedar. "If at first you can spare us a
little advice and help."

§ 2

Cedar and Serpentine remained with the Earthlings upon Quarantine Crag until late in the afternoon. They helped to prepare a supper and set it
out in the courtyard of the castle. They departed
with a promise to return on the morrow, and the
Earthlings watched them and their accompanying
aeroplanes soar up into the sky.

Mr. Barnstaple was surprised to find himself distressed at their going. He had a feeling that mischief was brewing amongst his companions and that
the withdrawal of these Utopians removed a check
upon this mischief. He had helped Lady Stella in
the preparation of an omelette; he had to carry
back a dish and a frying-pan to the kitchen after it
was served, so that he was the last to seat himself
at the supper-table. He found the mischief he
dreaded well afoot.

Mr. Catskill had finished his supper already and
was standing with his foot upon a bench orating
to the rest of the company.

"I ask you, Ladies and Gentlemen," Mr. Catskill
was saying; "I ask you: Is not Destiny writ large
upon this day's adventure? Not for nothing was
this place a fortress in ancient times. Here it is
ready to be a fortress again. M'm—a fortress.
. . . In such an adventure as will make the stories
of Cortez and Pizarro pale their ineffectual fires!"

"My dear Rupert!" cried Mr. Burleigh. "What
have you got in that head of yours now?"

Mr. Catskill waved two fingers dramatically.
"The conquest of a world!"

"Good God!" cried Mr. Barnstaple. "Are you mad?"

"As Clive," said Mr. Catskill, "or Sultan Baber when he marched to Panipat."

"It's a tall proposition," said Mr. Hunker, who seemed to have had his mind already prepared for these suggestions, "but I'm inclined to give it a hearing. The alternative so far as I can figure it out is to be scoured and whitewashed inside and out and then fired back into our own world—with a chance of hitting something hard on the way. You tell them, Mr. Catskill."

"Tell them," said Lord Barralonga, who had also been prepared. "It's a gamble, I admit. But there's situations when one has to gamble—or be gambled with. I'm all for the active voice."

"It's a gamble—certainly," said Mr. Catskill. "But upon this narrow peninsula, upon this square mile or so of territory, the fate, Sir, of two universes awaits decision. This is no time for the faint heart and the paralyzing touch of discretion. Plan swiftly—act swiftly. . . ."

"This is simply *thrilling!*" cried Miss Greeta Grey clasping her hands about her knees and smiling radiantly at Mr. Mush.

"These people," Mr. Barnstaple interrupted, "are three thousand years ahead of us. We are like a handful of Hottentots in a showman's van at Earl's Court, planning the conquest of London."

Mr. Catskill, hands on hips, turned with extraordinary good humour upon Mr. Barnstaple. "Three thousand years away from us—*yes!* Three thousand years ahead of us—*no!* That is where

you and I join issue. You say these people are
super-men. M'm—super-men. . . . I say they are
degenerate men. Let me call your attention to my
reasons for this belief—in spite of their beauty,
their very considerable material and intellectual
achievements and so forth. Ideal people, I admit.
. . . What then? . . . My case is that they have
reached a summit—and passed it, that they are
going on by inertia and that they have lost the
power not only of resistance to disease—that weakness we shall see develop more and more—but also
of meeting strange and distressing emergencies.
They are gentle. Altogether too gentle. They are
ineffectual. They do not know what to do. Here
is Father Amerton. He disturbed that first meeting in the most insulting way. (You know you did,
Father Amerton. I'm not blaming you. You are
morally—sensitive. And there were things to outrage you.) He was threatened—as a little boy is
threatened by a feeble old woman. Something was
to be done to him. Has anything been done to
him?"

"A man and a woman came and talked to me,"
said Father Amerton.

"And what did you do?"

"Simply confuted them. Lifted up my voice and
confuted them."

"What did they say?"

"What *could* they say?"

"We all thought tremendous things were going to
be done to poor Father Amerton. Well, and now
take a graver case. Our friend Lord Barralonga
ran amuck with his car—and killed a man. M'm.

Even at home they'd have endorsed your licence
you know. And fined your man. But here? . . .
The thing has scarcely been mentioned since.
Why? Because they don't know what to say about
it or do about it. And now they have put us here
and begged us to be good. Until they are ready to
come and try experiments upon us and inject things
into us and I don't know what. And if we submit,
Sir, if we submit, we lose one of our greatest powers
over these people, our power of at once giving and
resisting malaise, and in addition, I know not what
powers of initiative that may very well be associated
with that physiological toughness of which we are
to be robbed. They may trifle with our ductless
glands. But Science tells us that these very glands
secrete our personalities. Mentally, morally we
shall be dissolved. If we submit, Sir—if we submit.
But suppose we do not submit; what then?"

"Well," said Lord Barralonga, "what then?"

"They will not know what to do. Do not be
deceived by any outward shows of beauty and
prosperity. These people are living, as the ancient
Peruvians were living in the time of Pizarro, in
an enervating dream. They have drunken the
debilitating draught of Socialism and, as in ancient
Peru, there is no health nor power of will left in
them any more. A handful of resolute men and
women who can dare—may not only dare but
triumph in the face of such a world. And thus it
is I lay my plans before you."

"You mean to jump this entire Utopian planet?"
said Mr. Hunker.

"Big order," said Lord Barralonga.

"I mean, Sir, to assert the rights of a more vigorous form of social life over a less vigorous form of social life. Here we are—in a fortress. It is a real fortress and quite defensible. While you others have been unpacking, Barralonga and Hunker and I have been seeing to that. There is a sheltered well so that if need arises we can get water from the canyon below. The rock is excavated into chambers and shelters; the wall on the land side is sound and high, glazed so that it cannot be scaled. This great archway can easily be barricaded when the need arises. Steps go down through the rock to that little bridge which can if necessary be cut away. We have not yet explored all the excavations. In Mr. Hunker we have a chemist—he was a chemist before the movie picture claimed him as its master—and he says there is ample material in the laboratory for a store of bombs. This party, I find, can muster five revolvers with ammunition. I scarcely dared hope for that. We have food for many days."

"Oh! This is ridiculous!" cried Mr. Barnstaple standing up and then sitting down again. "This is preposterous! To turn on these friendly people! But they can blow this little headland to smithereens whenever they want to."

"Ah!" said Mr. Catskill and held him with his outstretched finger. "We've thought of that. But we can take a leaf from the book of Cortez—who, in the very centre of Mexico, held Montezuma as his prisoner and hostage. We too will have our hostage. Before we lift a finger——. First our hostage. . . ."

"Aerial bombs!"

"Is there such a thing in Utopia? Or such an idea? And again—we must have our hostage."

"Somebody of importance," said Mr. Hunker.

"Cedar and Serpentine are both important people," said Mr. Burleigh in tones of disinterested observation.

"But surely, Sir, you do not countenance this schoolboy's dream of piracy!" cried Mr. Barnstaple, sincerely shocked.

"Schoolboys!" cried Father Amerton. "A cabinet minister, a peer and a great entrepreneur!"

"My dear Sir," said Mr. Burleigh, "we are, after all, only envisaging eventualities. For the life of me, I do not see why we should not thresh out these possibilities. Though I pray to Heaven we may never have to realize them. You were saying, Rupert——?"

"We have to establish ourselves here and assert our independence and make ourselves *felt* by these Utopians."

"'Ear, 'ear!" said Mr. Ridley cordially. "One or two I'd like to make feel personally."

"We have to turn this prison into a capitol, into the first foothold of mankind in this world. It is like a foot thrust into a reluctant door that must never more close upon our race."

"It is closed," said Mr. Barnstaple. "Except by the mercy of these Utopians we shall never see our world again. And even with their mercy, it is doubtful."

"That's been keeping me awake nights," said Mr. Hunker.

"It's an idea that must have occurred to all of us," said Mr. Burleigh.

"And it's an idea that's so thundering disagreeable that one hasn't cared to talk about it," said Lord Barralonga.

"I never 'ad it until this moment," said Penk. "You don't reely mean to say, Sir, *we can't get back?*"

"Things will be as they will be," said Mr. Burleigh. "That is why I am anxious to hear Mr. Catskill's ideas."

Mr. Catskill rested his hands on his hips and his manner became very solemn. "For once," he said, "I am in agreement with Mr. Barnaby. I believe that the chances are *against* our ever seeing the dear cities of our world again."

"I felt that," said Lady Stella, with white lips. "I *knew* that two days ago."

"And so behold my week-end expand to an eternity!" said M. Dupont, and for a time no one said another word.

"It's as if——" Penk said at last. "Why! One might be dead!"

"But I *murst* be back," Miss Greeta Grey broke out abruptly, as one who sets aside a foolish idea. "It's absurd. I have to go on at the Alhambra on September the 2nd. It's imperative. We came here quite easily; it's ridiculous to say I can't go back in the same way."

Lord Barralonga regarded her with affectionate malignity. "You wait," he said.

"But I murst!" she sang.

"There's such things as impossibilities—even for Miss Greeta Grey."

"Charter a special aeroplane!" she said. "Anything."

He regarded her with an elfin grin and shook his head.

"My dear man," she said, "you've only seen me in a holiday mood, so far. Work is serious."

"My dear girl, that Alhambra of yours is about as far from us now as the Court of King Nebuchadnezzar. . . . It can't be done."

"But it *murst*," she said in her queenly way. "And that's all about it."

§ 3

Mr. Barnstaple got up from the table and walked apart to where a gap in the castle wall gave upon the darkling wilderness without. He sat down there. His eyes went from the little group talking around the supper-table to the sunlit crest of the cliffs across the canyon and to the wild and lonely mountain slopes below the headland. In this world he might have to live out the remainder of his days.

And those days might not be very numerous if Mr. Catskill had his way. Sydenham, and his wife and the boys were indeed as far—"as the Court of King Nebuchadnezzar."

He had scarcely given his family a thought since he had posted his letter at Victoria. Now he felt a queer twinge of desire to send them some word or token—if only he could. Queer that they would

never hear from him or of him again! How would
they get on without him? Would there be any
difficulty about the account at the bank? Or about
the insurance money? He had always intended to
have a joint and several account with his wife at
the bank, and he had never quite liked to do it.
Joint and several. . . . A thing every man ought
to do. . . . His attention came back to Mr.
Catskill unfolding his plans.

"We have to make up our minds to what may be
a prolonged, a very prolonged stay here. Do not
let us deceive ourselves upon that score. It may
last for years—it may last for generations."

Something struck Penk in that. "I don't 'ardly
see," he said, "how that can be—*generations?*"

"I am coming to that," said Mr. Catskill.

"Un'appily," said Mr. Penk, and became profoundly restrained and thoughtful with his eyes on
Lady Stella.

"We have to remain, a little alien community, in
this world until we dominate it, as the Romans
dominated the Greeks, and until we master its
science and subdue it to our purpose. That may
mean a long struggle. It may mean a very long
struggle indeed. And meanwhile we must maintain ourselves as a community; we must consider
ourselves a colony, a garrison, until that day of
reunion comes. We must hold our hostages, Sir,
and not only our hostages. It may be necessary
for our purpose, and if it is necessary for our purpose, so be it—to get in others of these Utopians, to
catch them young, before this so-called education

of theirs unfits them for our purpose, to train them
in the great traditions of our Empire and our race."

Mr. Hunker seemed on the point of saying something but refrained.

M. Dupont got up sharply from the table, walked
four paces away, returned and stood still, watching
Mr. Catskill.

"Generations?" said Mr. Penk.

"Yes," said Mr. Catskill.   "Generations.   For
here we are strangers—strangers, like that other
little band of adventurers who established their
citadel five-and-twenty centuries ago upon the
Capitol beside the rushing Tiber. This is our Capitol. A greater Capitol—of a greater Rome—in a
vaster world. And like that band of Roman adventurers we too may have to reinforce our scanty
numbers at the expense of the Sabines about us,
and take to ourselves servants and helpers and—
mates! No sacrifice is too great for the high possibilities of this adventure."

M. Dupont seemed to nerve himself for the sacrifice.

"Duly married," injected Father Amerton.

"Duly married," said Mr. Catskill in parenthesis.
"And so, Sir, we will hold out here and maintain
ourselves and dominate this desert countryside and
spread our prestige and our influence and our spirit
into the inert body of this decadent Utopian world.
Until at last we are able to master the secret that
Arden and Greenlake were seeking and recover the
way back to our own people, opening to the crowded
millions of our Empire——"

§ 4

"Just a moment," said Mr. Hunker. "Just a moment! About this empire——!"

"Exactly," said M. Dupont, recalled abruptly from some romantic day-dream. "About your Empire!"

Mr. Catskill regarded them thoughtfully and defensively. "When I say Empire I mean it in the most general sense."

"Exactly," snapped M. Dupont.

"I was thinking generally of our—Atlantic civilization."

"Before, Sir, you go on to talk of Anglo-Saxon unity and the English-speaking race," said M. Dupont, with a rising note of bitterness in his voice, "permit me to remind you, Sir, of one very important fact that you seem to be overlooking. The language of Utopia, Sir, is French. I want to remind you of that. I want to recall it to your mind. I will lay no stress here on the sacrifices and martyrdoms that France has endured in the cause of Civilization——"

The voice of Mr. Burleigh interrupted. "A very natural misconception. But, if you will pardon the correction, the language of Utopia is *not* French."

Of course, Mr. Barnstaple reflected, M. Dupont had not heard the explanation of the language difficulty.

"Permit me, Sir, to believe the evidence of my own ears," the Frenchman replied with dignified politeness. "These Utopians, I can assure you, speak French and nothing but French—and very excellent French it is."

"They speak no language at all," said Mr. Burleigh.

"Not even English?" sneered M. Dupont.

"Not even English."

"Not League of Nations, perhaps? But—Bah! Why do I argue? They speak French. Not even a Bosch would deny it. It needs an Englishman ——"

A beautiful wrangle, thought Mr. Barnstaple. There was no Utopian present to undeceive M. Dupont and he stuck to his belief magnificently. With a mixture of pity and derision and anger, Mr. Barnstaple listened to this little band of lost human beings, in the twilight of a vast, strange and possibly inimical world, growing more and more fierce and keen in a dispute over the claims of their three nations to "dominate" Utopia, claims based entirely upon greeds and misconceptions. Their voices rose to shouts and sank to passionate intensity as their lifelong habits of national egotism reasserted themselves. Mr. Hunker would hear nothing of any "Empire"; M. Dupont would hear of nothing but the supreme claim of France. Mr. Catskill twisted and turned. To Mr. Barnstaple this conflict of patriotic prepossessions seemed like a dog-fight on a sinking ship. But at last Mr. Catskill, persistent and ingenious, made headway against his two antagonists.

He stood at the end of the table explaining that he had used the word Empire loosely, apologizing for using it, explaining that when he said Empire he had all Western Civilization in mind. "When I said it," he said, turning to Mr. Hunker, "I meant a common brotherhood of understanding." He faced towards M. Dupont. "I meant our tried and imperishable Entente."

"There are at least no Russians here," said M. Dupont. "And no Germans."

"True," said Lord Barralonga. "We start ahead of the Hun here, and we can keep ahead."

"And I take it," said Mr. Hunker, "that Japanese are barred."

"No reason why we shouldn't start clean with a complete colour bar," reflected Lord Barralonga. "This seems to me a White Man's World."

"At the same time," said M. Dupont, coldly and insistently, "you will forgive me if I ask you for some clearer definition of our present relationship and for some guarantee, some effective guarantee, that the immense sacrifices France has made and still makes in the cause of civilized life, will receive their proper recognition and their due reward in this adventure. . . .

"I ask only for justice," said M. Dupont.

§ 5

Indignation made Mr. Barnstaple bold. He got down from his perch upon the wall and came up to the table.

"Are you mad," he said, "or am I?

"This squabble over flags and countries and fanciful rights and deserts—it is hopeless folly. Do you not realize even now the position we are in?"

His breath failed him for a moment and then he resumed.

"Are you incapable of thinking of human affairs except in terms of flags and fighting and conquest and robbery? Cannot you realize the proportion of things and the quality of this world into which we have fallen? As I have said already, we are like some band of savages in a show at Earl's Court, plotting the subjugation of London. We are like suppressed cannibals in the heart of a great city dreaming of a revival of our ancient and forgotten filthiness. What are our chances in this fantastic struggle?"

Mr. Ridley spoke reprovingly. "You're forgetting everythink you just been told. Everythink. 'Arf their population is laid out with flu and measles. And there's no such thing as a 'ealthy fighting will left in all Utopia."

"Precisely," said Mr. Catskill.

"Well, suppose you have chances? If that makes your scheme the more hopeful, it also makes it the more horrible. Here we are lifted up out of the troubles of our time to a vision, to a reality of civilization such as our own world can only hope to climb to in scores of centuries! Here is a world at peace, splendid, happy, full of wisdom and hope! If our puny strength and base cunning can contrive it, we are to shatter it all! We are proposing to wreck a world! I tell you it is not an adventure. It is a crime. It is an abomination. I will have no part in it. I am against you in this attempt."

Father Amerton would have spoken but Mr. Burleigh arrested him by a gesture.

"What would *you* have us do?" asked Mr. Burleigh.

"Submit to their science. Learn what we can from them. In a little while we may be cured of our inherent poisons and we may be permitted to return from this outlying desert of mines and turbines and rock, to those gardens of habitation we have as yet scarcely seen. There we too may learn something of civilization. . . . In the end we may even go back to our own disordered world—with knowledge, with hope and help, missionaries of a new order."

"But why——?" began Father Amerton.

Again Mr. Burleigh took the word. "Everything you say," he remarked, "rests on unproven assumptions. You choose to see this Utopia through rose-tinted glasses. We others—for it is"—he counted—"eleven to one against you—see things without such favourable preconceptions."

"And may I ask, Sir," said Father Amerton, springing to his feet and hitting the table a blow that set all the glasses talking. "May I ask, who *you* are, to set yourself up as a judge and censor of the common opinion of mankind? For I tell you, Sir, that here in this lonely and wicked and strange world, we here, we twelve, do represent mankind. We are the advance guard, the pioneers—in the new world that God has given us, even as He gave Canaan to Israel His chosen, three thousand years ago. Who are *you*——"

"Exactly," said Penk. "Who are you?"

And Mr. Ridley reinforced him with a shout: "Oo the 'ell are *you?*"

Mr. Barnstaple had no platform skill to meet so direct an attack. He stood helpless. Astonishingly Lady Stella came to his rescue.

"That isn't fair, Father Amerton," she said. "Mr. Barnstaple, whoever he is, has a perfect right to express his own opinion."

"And having expressed it," said Mr. Catskill, who had been walking up and down on the other side of the table to that on which Mr. Barnstaple stood, "M'm, having expressed it, to allow us to proceed with the business in hand. I suppose it was inevitable that we should find the conscientious objector in our midst—even in Utopia. The rest of us, I take it, are very much of one mind about our situation."

"We are," said Mr. Mush, regarding Mr. Barnstaple with a malevolent expression.

"Very well. Then I suppose we must follow the precedents established for such cases. We will not ask Mr.—Mr. Bastaple to share the dangers—and the honours—of a combatant. We will ask him merely to do civilian work of a helpful nature——"

Mr. Barnstaple held up his hand. "No," he said. "I am not disposed to be helpful. I do not recognize the analogy of the situation to the needs of the Great War, and, anyhow, I am entirely opposed to this project—this brigandage of a civilization. You cannot call me a conscientious objector to fighting, because I do not object to fighting in a just cause. But this adventure of yours is not a just cause. . . . I implore you, Mr. Burleigh, you who are not merely a politician, but a man of culture and a philosopher, to reconsider what it is we are being urged towards—towards acts of violence and mischief from which there will be no drawing back!"

"Mr. Barnstaple," said Mr. Burleigh with grave dignity and something like a note of reproach in his voice, "I *have* considered. But I think I may venture to say that I am a man of some experience, some traditional experience, in human affairs. I may not altogether agree with my friend Mr. Catskill. Nay! I will go further and say that in many respects I do *not* agree with him. If I were the autocrat here I would say that we have to offer these Utopians resistance—for our self-respect—but not to offer them the violent and aggressive resistance that he contemplates. I think we could be far more subtle, far more elaborate, and far more successful than Mr. Catskill is likely to be. But that is my own opinion. Neither Mr. Hunker nor Lord Barralonga, nor Mr. Mush, nor M. Dupont shares it. Nor do Mr.—our friends, the ah!—technical engineers here share it. And what I do perceive to be imperative upon our little band of Earthlings, lost here in a strange universe, is *unity of action*. Whatever else betide, dissension must not betray us. We must hold together and act together as one body. Discuss if you will, when there is any time for discussion, but in the end *decide*. And having decided abide loyally by the decision. Upon the need of securing a hostage or two I have no manner of doubt whatever. Mr. Catskill is right."

Mr. Barnstaple was a bad debater. "But these Utopians are as human as we are," he said. "All that is most sane and civilized in ourselves is with them."

Mr. Ridley interrupted in a voice designedly rough. "Oh Lord!" he said. "We can't go on jawing 'ere for ever. It's sunset, and Mr.—this gentleman 'as 'ad 'is say, and more than 'is say. We ought to have our places and know what is expected of us before night. May I propose that we elect Mr. Catskill our Captain with full military powers?"

"I second that," said Mr. Burleigh with grave humility.

"Perhaps M. Dupont," said Mr. Catskill, "will act with me as associated Captain, representing our glorious ally, his own great country."

"In the absence of a more worthy representative," acquiesced M. Dupont, "and to see that French interests are duly respected."

"And if Mr. Hunker would act as my lieutenant? . . . Lord Barralonga will be our quartermaster and Father Amerton our chaplain and censor. Mr. Burleigh, it goes without saying, will be our civil head."

Mr. Hunker coughed. He frowned with the expression of one who makes a difficult explanation. "I won't be exactly lieutenant," he said. "I'll take no official position. I've a sort of distaste for— foreign entanglements. I'll be a looker-on—who helps. But I think you will find you can count on me, Gentlemen—when help is needed."

Mr. Catskill seated himself at the head of the table and indicated the chair next to his for M. Dupont. Miss Greeta Grey seated herself on his other hand between him and Mr. Hunker. Mr. Burleigh remained in his place, a chair or so from

Mr. Hunker. The rest came and stood round the Captain except Lady Stella and Mr. Barnstaple.

Almost ostentatiously Mr. Barnstaple turned his back on the new command. Lady Stella, he saw, remained seated far down the table, looking dubiously at the little crowd of people at the end. Then her eyes went to the desolate mountain crest beyond.

She shivered violently and stood up. "It's going to be very cold here after sunset," she said, with nobody heeding her. "I shall go and unpack a wrap."

She walked slowly to her quarters and did not reappear.

§ 6

Mr. Barnstaple did not want to seem to listen to this Council of War. He walked to the wall of the old castle and up a flight of stone steps and along the rampart to the peak of the headland. Here the shattering and beating sound of the waters in the two convergent canyons was very loud.

There was still a bright upper rim of sunlit rock on the mountain face behind, but all the rest of the world was now in a deepening blue shadow, and a fleecy white mist was gathering in the canyons below and hiding the noisy torrents. It drifted up almost to the level of the little bridge that spanned the narrower canyon to a railed stepway from the crest on the further side. For the first time since he had arrived in Utopia Mr. Barnstaple felt a chill in the air. And loneliness like a pain.

Up the broader of the two meeting canyons some
sort of engineering work was going on and periodic
flashes lit the drifting mist. Far away over the
mountains a solitary aeroplane, very high, caught
the sun's rays ever and again and sent down quivering flashes of dazzling golden light, and then, as
it wheeled about, vanished again in the deepening
blue.

He looked down into the great courtyard of the
ancient castle below him. The modern buildings
in the twilight looked like phantom pavilions amidst
the archaic masonry. Someone had brought a
light, and Captain Rupert Catskill, the new Cortez,
was writing orders, while his Commando stood
about him.

The light shone on the face and shoulders and
arms of Miss Greeta Grey; she was peering over
the Captain's arm to see what he was writing.
And as Mr. Barnstaple looked he saw her raise her
hand suddenly to conceal an involuntary yawn.

CHAPTER THE THIRD

MR. BARNSTAPLE AS A TRAITOR TO MANKIND

§ 1

Mr. Barnstaple spent a large part of the night sitting upon his bed and brooding over the incalculable elements of the situation in which he found himself.

What could he do? What ought he to do? Where did his loyalty lie? The dark traditions and infections of the Earth had turned this wonderful encounter into an ugly and dangerous antagonism far too swiftly for him to adjust his mind to the new situation. Before him now only two possibilities seemed open. Either the Utopians would prove themselves altogether the stronger and the wiser and he and all his fellow pirates would be crushed and killed like vermin, or the desperate ambitions of Mr. Catskill would be realized and they would become a spreading sore in the fair body of this noble civilization, a band of robbers and destroyers, dragging Utopia year by year and age by age back to terrestrial conditions. There seemed only one escape from the dilemma; to get away from this fastness to the Utopians, to reveal the whole scheme of the Earthlings to them, and to throw himself and his associates upon their mercy.

But this must be done soon, before the hostages were seized and bloodshed began.

But in the first place it might be very difficult now to get away from the Earthling band. Mr. Catskill would already have organized watchers and sentinels, and the peculiar position of the crag exposed every avenue of escape. And in the next place Mr. Barnstaple had a lifelong habit of mind which predisposed him against tale-bearing and dissentient action. His school training had moulded him into subservience to any group or gang in which he found himself; his form, his side, his house, his school, his club, his party and so forth. Yet his intelligence and his limitless curiosities had always been opposed to these narrow conspiracies against the world at large. His spirit had made him an uncomfortable rebel throughout his whole earthly existence. He loathed political parties and political leaders, he despised and rejected nationalism and imperialism and all the tawdry loyalties associated with them; the aggressive conqueror, the grabbing financier, the shoving business man, he hated as he hated wasps, rats, hyenas, sharks, fleas, nettles and the like: all his life he had been a citizen of Utopia exiled upon Earth. After his fashion he had sought to serve Utopia. Why should he not serve Utopia now? Because his band was a little and desperate band, that was no reason why he should serve the things he hated. If they were a desperate crew, the fact remained that they were also, as a whole, an evil crew. There is no reason why liberalism should degenerate into a morbid passion for minorities. . . .

Only two persons among the Earthlings, Lady
Stella and Mr. Burleigh, held any of his sympathy.
And he had his doubts about Mr. Burleigh. Mr.
Burleigh was one of those strange people who seem
to understand everything and feel nothing. He impressed Mr. Barnstaple as being intelligently irresponsible. Wasn't that really more evil than being
unintelligently adventurous like Hunker or Barralonga?

Mr. Barnstaple's mind returned from a long ex-
cursion in ethics to the realities about him. Tomorrow he would survey the position and make his
plans, and perhaps in the twilight he would slip
away.

It was entirely in his character to defer action in
this way for the better part of the day. His life had
been one of deferred action almost from the beginning.

§ 2

But events could not wait for Mr. Barnstaple.

He was called at dawn by Penk, who told him
that henceforth the garrison would be aroused every
morning by an electric hooter he and Ridley had
contrived. As Penk spoke a devastating howl from
this contrivance inaugurated the new era. He
handed Mr. Barnstaple a slip of paper torn from a
note-book on which Mr. Catskill had written:—

"Non-comb. Barnaby. To assist Ridley prepare
breakfast, lunch and dinner, times and menu on
mess-room wall, clear away and wash up smartly

and at other times to be at disposal of Lt. Hunker, in chemical laboratory for experimenting and bomb-making. Keep laboratory clean."

"That's your job," said Penk. "Ridley's waitin' for you."

"Well," said Mr. Barnstaple, and got up. It was no use precipitating a quarrel if he was to escape. So he went to the scarred and bandaged Ridley, and they produced a very good imitation of a British military kitchen in that great raw year, 1914.

Everyone was turned out to breakfast at half-past six by a second solo on the hooter. The men were paraded and inspected by Mr. Catskill, with M. Dupont standing beside him; Mr. Hunker stood parallel with these two and a few yards away; all the other men fell in except Mr. Burleigh, who was to be civil commander in Utopia, and was, in that capacity, in bed, and Mr. Barnstaple the non-combatant. Miss Greeta Grey and Lady Stella sat in a sunny corner of the courtyard sewing at a flag. It was to be a blue flag with a white star, a design sufficiently unlike any existing national flag to avoid wounding the patriotic susceptibilities of any of the party. It was to represent the Earthling League of Nations.

After the parade the little garrison dispersed to its various posts and duties, M. Dupont assumed the chief command, and Mr. Catskill, who had watched all night, went to lie down. He had the Napoleonic quality of going off to sleep for an hour or so at any time in the day.

Mr. Penk went up to the top of the castle, where the hooter was installed, to keep a look out.

There were some moments to be snatched between the time when Mr. Barnstaple had finished with Ridley and the time when Hunker would discover his help was available, and this time he devoted to an inspection of the castle wall on the side of the slopes. While he was standing on the old rampart, weighing his chances of slipping away that evening in the twilight, an aeroplane appeared above the crag and came down upon the nearer slope. Two Utopians descended, talked with their aviator for a time, and then turned their faces towards the fastness of the Earthlings.

A single note of the hooter brought out Mr. Catskill upon the rampart beside Mr. Barnstaple. He produced a field-glass and surveyed the approaching figures.

"Serpentine and Cedar," he said, lowering his field-glass. "And they come alone. Good."

He turned round and signalled with his hand to Penk, who responded with two short whoops of his instrument. This was the signal for a general assembly.

Down below in the courtyard appeared the rest of the Allied force and Mr. Hunker and fell in with a reasonable imitation of discipline.

Mr. Catskill passed Mr. Barnstaple without taking any notice of him, joined M. Dupont, Mr. Hunker and their subordinates below and proceeded to instruct them in his plans for the forthcoming crisis. Mr. Barnstaple could not hear what was said. He noted with sardonic disapproval that each man, as Mr. Catskill finished with him, clicked his heels to-

gether and saluted. Then at a word of command
they dispersed to their posts.

There was a partly ruined flight of steps leading
down from the general level of the courtyard
through this great archway in the wall that gave
access to and from the slopes below. Ridley and
Mush went down to the right of these steps and
placed themselves below a projecting mass of
masonry so as to be hidden from anyone approaching from below. Father Amerton and Mr. Hunker
concealed themselves similarly to the left. Father
Amerton, Mr. Barnstaple noted, had been given a
coil of rope, and then his roving eye discovered Mr.
Mush glancing at a pistol in his hand and then re-
placing it in his pocket. Lord Barralonga took up
a position for himself some steps above Mr. Mush
and produced a revolver which he held in his one
efficient hand. Mr. Catskill remained at the head
of the stairs. He also was holding a revolver. He
turned to the citadel, considered the case of Penk for
a moment, and then motioned him down to join the
others. M. Dupont, armed with a stout table leg,
placed himself at Mr. Catskill's right hand.

For a time Mr. Barnstaple watched these dispositions without any realization of their significance.
Then his eyes went from the crouching figures within
the castle to the two unsuspecting Utopians who
were coming up towards them, and he realized that
in a couple of minutes Serpentine and Cedar would
be struggling in the grip of their captors. . . .

He perceived he had to act. And his had been a
contemplative, critical life with no habit of decision.
He found himself trembling violently.

§ 3

He still desired some mediatory intervention even in these fatal last moments. He raised an arm and cried "Hi!" as much to the Earthlings below as to the Utopians without. No one noticed either his gesture or his feeble cry.

Then his will seemed to break through a tangle of obstacles to one simple idea. Serpentine and Cedar must not be seized. He was amazed and indignant at his own vacillation. Of course they must not be seized! This foolery must be thwarted forthwith. In four strides he was on the wall above the archway and now he was shouting loud and clear. "Danger!" he shouted. "Danger!" and again "Danger!"

He heard Catskill's cry of astonishment and then a pistol bullet whipped through the air close to him.

Serpentine stopped short and looked up, touched Cedar's arm and pointed.

"These Earthlings want to imprison you. Don't come here! Danger!" yelled Mr. Barnstaple waving his arms and "*pat, pat, pat,*" Mr. Catskill experienced the disappointments of revolver shooting.

Serpentine and Cedar were turning back—but slowly and hesitatingly.

For a moment Mr. Catskill knew not what to do. Then he flung himself down the steps, crying, "After them! Stop them! Come on!"

"Go back!" cried Mr. Barnstaple to the Utopians. "Go back! Quickly! Quickly!"

Came a clatter of feet from below and then the eight men who constituted the combatant strength

of the Earthling forces in Utopia emerged from
under the archway running towards the two astonished Utopians. Mr. Mush led, with Ridley at his
heels; he was pointing his revolver and shouting.
Next came M. Dupont zealous and active. Father
Amerton brought up the rear with the rope.

"Go back!" screamed Mr. Barnstaple, with his
voice breaking.

Then he stopped shouting and watched—with his
hands clenched.

The aviator was running down the slope from his
machine to the assistance of Serpentine and Cedar.
And above out of the blue two other aeroplanes had
appeared.

The two Utopians disdained to hurry and in a
few seconds their pursuers had come up with them.
Hunker, Ridley and Mush led the attack. M. Dupont, flourishing his stick, was abreast with them
but running out to the right as though he intended
to get between them and the aviator. Mr. Catskill
and Penk were a little behind the leading three; the
one-armed Barralonga was perhaps ten yards behind
and Father Amerton had halted to re-coil his rope
more conveniently.

There seemed to be a moment's parley and then
Serpentine had moved quickly as if to seize Hunker.
A pistol cracked and then another went off rapidly
three times. "Oh God!" cried Mr. Barnstaple. "Oh
God!" as he saw Serpentine throw up his arms and
fall backward, and then Cedar had grasped and lifted
up Mush and hurled him at Mr. Catskill and Penk,
bowling both of them over into one indistinguishable
heap. With a wild cry M. Dupont closed in on

Cedar but not quickly enough. His club shot into the air as Cedar parried his blow, and then the Utopian stooped, caught him by a leg, overthrew him, lifted him and whirled him round as one might whirl a rabbit, to inflict a stunning blow on Mr. Hunker.

Lord Barralonga ran back some paces and began shooting at the approaching aviator.

The confusion of legs and arms on the ground became three separate people again. Mr. Catskill, shouting directions, made for Cedar, followed by Penk and Mush and, a moment after, by Hunker and Dupont. They clung to Cedar as hounds will cling to a boar. Time after time he flung them off him. Father Amerton hovered unhelpfully with his rope.

For some moments Mr. Barnstaple's attention was concentrated upon this swaying and staggering attempt to overpower Cedar, and then he became aware of other Utopians running down the slope to join the fray. . . . The other two aeroplanes had landed.

Mr. Catskill realized the coming of these reinforcements almost as soon as Mr. Barnstaple. His shouts of "Back! Back to the castle!" reached Mr. Barnstaple's ears. The Earthlings scattered away from the tall dishevelled figure, hesitated, and began to walk and then run back towards the Castle.

And then Ridley turned and very deliberately shot Cedar, who clutched at his breast and fell into a sitting position.

The Earthlings retreated to the foot of the steps

that led up through the archway into the castle, and
stood there in a panting, bruised and ruffled group.
Fifty yards away Serpentine lay still, the aviator
whom Barralonga had shot writhed and moaned, and
Cedar sat up with blood upon his chest trying to feel
his back. Five other Utopians came hurrying to
their assistance.

"What is all this firing?" said Lady Stella, suddenly at Mr. Barnstaple's elbow.

"Have they caught their hostages?" asked Miss
Greeta Grey.

"For the life of me!" said Mr. Burleigh, who had
come out upon the wall a yard or so away, "this
ought never to have happened. How did this get—
muffed, Lady Stella?"

"I called out to them," said Mr. Barnstaple.

"*You*—called—out—to them!" said Mr. Burleigh
incredulous.

"Treason I did not calculate upon," came the
wrathful voice of Mr. Catskill ascending out of the
archway.

§ 4

For some moments Mr. Barnstaple made no attempt to escape the danger that closed in upon him.
He had always lived a life of very great security
and with him, as with so many highly civilized
types, the power of apprehending personal danger
was very largely atrophied. He was a spectator by
temperament and training alike. He stood now as
if he looked at himself, the central figure of a great

and hopeless tragedy. The idea of flight came belatedly, in a reluctant and apologetic manner into his mind.

"Shot as a traitor," he said aloud. "Shot as a traitor."

There was that bridge over the narrow gorge. He might still get over that, if he went for it at once. If he was quick—quicker than they were. He was too intelligent to dash off for it; that would certainly have set the others running. He walked along the wall in a leisurely fashion past Mr. Burleigh, himself too civilized to intervene. In a quickening stroll he gained the steps that led to the citadel. Then he stood still for a moment to survey the situation. Catskill was busy setting sentinels at the gate. Perhaps he had not thought yet of the little bridge and imagined that Mr. Barnstaple was at his disposal at any time that suited him. Up the slope the Utopians were carrying off the dead or wounded men.

Mr. Barnstaple ascended the steps as if buried in thought and stood on the citadel for some seconds, his hands in his trouser pockets, as if he surveyed the view. Then he turned to the winding staircase that went down to a sort of guard-room below. As soon as he was surely out of sight he began to think and move very quickly.

The guard-room was perplexing. It had five doors, any one of which except the one by which he had just entered the room might lead down to the staircase. Against one, however, stood a pile of neat packing-cases. That left three to choose

from. He ran from one to the other leaving each
door open. In each case stone steps ran down to
a landing and a turning place. He stood hesitating
at the third and noted that a cold draught came
blowing up it. Surely that meant that this went
down to the cliff face, or whence came the air?
Surely this was it!

Should he shut the doors he had opened? No!
Leave them all open.

He heard a clatter coming down the staircase
from the citadel. Softly and swiftly he ran down
the steps and halted for a second at the corner
landing. He was compelled to stop and listen to
the movements of his pursuers. "This is the door
to the bridge, Sir!" he heard Ridley cry, and then
he heard Catskill say, "The Tarpeian Rock," and
Barralonga, "Exactly! Why should we waste a
cartridge? Are you sure this goes to the bridge,
Ridley?"

The footsteps pattered across the guard-room
and passed—down one of the other staircases.

"A reprieve!" whispered Mr. Barnstaple and then
stopped aghast.

He was trapped! The staircase they were on was
the staircase to the bridge!

They would go down as far as the bridge and as
soon as they got to it they would see that he was
neither on it nor on the steps on the opposite side
of the gorge and that therefore he could not possibly have escaped. They would certainly bar that
way either by closing and fastening any door there
might be or, failing such a barrier, by setting a

sentinel, and then they would come back and hunt
for him at their leisure.

What was it Catskill had been saying? The Tarpeian Rock? . . .

Horrible!

They mustn't take him alive. . . .

He must fight like a rat in a corner and oblige
them to shoot him. . . .

He went on down the staircase. It became very
dark and then grew light again. It ended in an
ordinary big cellar, which may once have been a
gun-pit or magazine. It was fairly well lit by two
unglazed windows cut in the rock. It now contained a store of provisions. Along one side stood
an array of the flask-like bottles that were used for
wine in Utopia; along the other was a miscellany
of packing-cases and cubes wrapped in gold-leaf.
He lifted one of the glass flasks by its neck. It
would make an effective club. Suppose he made a
sort of barrier of the packing-cases across the
entrance and stood beside it and clubbed the pursuers as they came in! Glass and wine would smash
over their skulls. . . . It would take time to
make the barrier. . . . He chose and carried
three of the larger flasks to the doorway where they
would be handy for him. Then he had an inspira-
tion and looked at the window.

He listened at the door of the staircase for a time.
Not a sound came from above. He went to the
window and lay down in the deep embrasure and
wriggled forward until he could see out and up and
down. The cliff below fell sheer; he could have
spat on to the brawling torrent fifteen hundred

feet perhaps below. The crag here was made up of almost vertical strata which projected and receded; a big buttress hid almost all of the bridge except the far end which seemed to be about twenty or thirty yards lower than the opening from which Mr. Barnstaple was looking. Mr. Catskill appeared upon this bridge, very small and distant, scrutinizing the rocky stair-way beyond the bridge. Mr. Barnstaple withdrew his head hastily. Then very discreetly he peeped again. Mr. Catskill was no longer to be seen. He was coming back.

To business! There was not much time.

In his earlier days before the great war had made travel dear and uncomfortable Mr. Barnstaple had done some rock climbing in Switzerland and he had also had some experience in Cumberland and Wales. He surveyed now the rocks close at hand with an intelligent expertness. They were cut by almost horizontal joint planes into which there had been a considerable infiltration chiefly of white crystalline material. This stuff, which he guessed was calcite, had weathered more rapidly than the general material of the rock, leaving a series of irregular horizontal grooves. With luck it might be possible to work along the cliff face, turn the buttress and scramble to the bridge.

And then came an even more hopeful idea. He could easily get along the cliff face to the first recess, flatten himself there and remain until the Earthlings had searched his cellar. After they had searched he might creep back to the cellar. Even if they looked out of the window they would not

see him and even if he left finger marks and so
forth in the embrasure, they would be likely to
conclude that he had either jumped or fallen down
the crag into the gorge below. But at first it might
be slow work negotiating the cliff face. . . .
And this would cut him off from his weapons, the
flasks. . . .

But the idea of hiding in the recess had taken a
strong hold upon his imagination. Very cautiously
he got out of the window, found a handhold, got
his feet on to his ledge and began to work his way
along towards his niche.

But there were unexpected difficulties, a gap of
nearly five yards in the handhold—nothing. He
had to flatten himself and trust to his feet and for
a time he remained quite still in that position.

Further on was a rotten lump of the vein mineral and it broke away under him very disconcert-
ingly, but happily his fingers had a grip and the
other foot was firm. The detached crystals slithered
down the rock face for a moment and then made no
further sound. They had dropped into the void.
For a time he was paralyzed.

"I'm not in good form," whispered Mr. Barnstaple. "I'm not in good form."

He clung motionless and prayed.

With an effort he resumed his traverse.

He was at the very corner of the recess when some
faint noise drew his eyes to the window from which
he had emerged. Ridley's face was poked out
slowly and cautiously, his eye red and fierce among
his white bandages.

He did not at first see Mr. Barnstaple. "Gawd!" he said when he did so and withdrew his head hastily.

Came a sound of voices saying indistinguishable things.

Some inappropriate instinct kept Mr. Barnstaple quite still, though he could have got into cover in the recess quite easily before Mr. Catskill looked out revolver in hand.

For some moments they stared at each other in silence.

"Come back or I shoot," said Mr. Catskill unconvincingly.

"Shoot!" said Mr. Barnstaple after a moment's reflection.

Mr. Catskill craned his head out and stared down into the shadowy blue depths of the canyon. "It isn't necessary," he answered. "We have to save cartridges."

"You haven't the guts," said Mr. Barnstaple.

"It's not quite that," said Mr. Catskill.

"No," said Mr. Barnstaple, "it isn't. You are fundamentally a civilized man."

Mr. Catskill scowled at him without hostility.

"You have a very good imagination," Mr. Barnstaple reflected. "The trouble is that you have been so damnably educated. What is the trouble with you? You are be-Kiplinged. Empire and Anglo-Saxon and boy-scout and sleuth are the stuff in your mind. If I had gone to Eton I might have been the same as you are, I suppose."

"Harrow," corrected Mr. Catskil.

"A perfectly *beastly* public school. Suburban place where the boys wear chignons and straw haloes. I might have guessed Harrow. But it's queer I bear you no malice. Given decent ideas you might have been very different from what you are. If I had been your schoolmaster—— But it's too late now."

"It is," said Mr. Rupert Catskill, smiling genially, and cocked his eye down into the canyon.

Mr. Barnstaple began to feel for his ledge round the corner with one foot.

"Don't go for a minute," said Mr. Catskill. "I'm not going to shoot."

A voice from within, probably Lord Barralonga's, said something about heaving a rock at Mr. Barnstaple. Someone else, probably Ridley, approved ferociously.

"Not without due form of trial," said Mr. Catskill over his shoulder. His face was inscrutable, but a fantastic idea began to run about in Mr. Barnstaple's mind that Mr. Catskill did not want to have him killed. He had thought about things and he wanted him now to escape—to the Utopians and perhaps rig up some sort of settlement with them.

"We intend to try you, Sir," said Mr. Catskill. "We intend to try you. We cite you to appear."

Mr. Catskill moistened his lips and considered. "The court will sit almost at once." His little bright brown eyes estimated the chances of Mr. Barnstaple's position very rapidly. He craned towards the bridge. "We shall not waste time over our procedure," he said. "And I have little doubt of our verdict. We shall condemn you to death. So— there you are, Sir. I doubt if we shall be more than a quarter of an hour before your fate is legally settled."

He glanced up trying to see the crest of the crag. "We shall probably throw rocks," he said.

"*Moriturus te saluo*," said Mr. Barnstaple with an air of making a witty remark. "If you will forgive me I will go on now to find a more comfortable position."

Mr. Catskill remained looking hard at him.

"I've never borne you any ill-will," said Mr. Barnstaple. "Had I been your schoolmaster everything might have been different. Thanks for the quarter of an hour more you give me. And if by any chance——"

"Exactly," said Mr. Catskill.

They understood one another.

When Mr. Barnstaple stepped round the bend into the recess Mr. Catskill was still looking out and Lord Barralonga was faintly audible advocating the immediate heaving of rocks.

§ 6

The ways of the human mind are past finding out. From desperation Mr. Barnstaple's mood had passed to exhilaration. His first sick horror of climbing above this immense height had given place now to an almost boyish assurance. His sense of immediate death had gone. He was appreciating this adventure,

indeed he was enjoying it, with an entire disregard
now of how it was to end.

He made fairly good time until he got to the angle
of the buttress, though his arms began to ache rather
badly, and then he had a shock. He had now a full
view of the bridge and up the narrow gorge. The
ledge he was working along did not run to the bridge
at all. It ran a good thirty feet below it. And what
was worse, between himself and the bridge were two
gullies and chimneys of uncertain depth. At this
discovery he regretted for the first time that he had
not stayed in the cellar and made a fight for it there.

He had some minutes of indecision—with the ache
in his arms increasing.

He was roused from his inaction by what he
thought at first was the shadow of a swift-flying bird
on the rock. Presently it returned. He hoped he
was not to be assailed by birds. He had read a story
—but never mind that now.

Then came a loud crack overhead, and he glanced
up to see a lump of rock which had just struck a
little bulge above him fly to fragments. From which
incident he gathered firstly that the court had de-
livered an adverse verdict rather in advance of Mr.
Catskill's time, and secondly that he was visible from
above. He resumed his traverse towards the shelter
of the gully with feverish energy.

The gully was better than he expected, a chimney;
difficult, he thought, to ascend, but quite practicable
downward. It was completely overhung. And perhaps a hundred feet below there was a sort of step in
it that gave a quite broad recess, sheltered from

above and with room enough for a man to sprawl on
it if he wanted to do so. There would be rest for
Mr. Barnstaple's arms, and without any needless
delay he clambered down to it and abandoned himself to the delightful sensation of not holding on to
anything. He was out of sight and out of reach of
his Earthling pursuers.

In the back of the recess was a trickle of water.
He drank and began to think of food and to regret
that he had not brought some provision with him
from the store in the cellar. He might have opened
one of those gold-leaf-covered cubes or pocketed a
small flask of wine. Wine would be very heartening
just now. But it did not do to think of that. He
stayed for a long time, as it seemed to him, on this
precious shelf, scrutinizing the chimney below very
carefully. It seemed quite practicable for a long
way down. The sides became very smooth, but they
seemed close enough together to get down with his
back against one side and his feet against the other.

He looked at his wrist-watch. It was still not nine
o'clock in the morning—it was about ten minutes to
nine. He had been called by Ridley before half-
past five. At half-past six he had been handing out
breakfast in the courtyard. Serpentine and Cedar
must have appeared about eight o'clock. In about
ten minutes Serpentine had been murdered. Then
the flight and the pursuit. How quickly things had
happened! . . .

He had all day before him. He would resume his
descent at half-past nine. Until then he would rest.
. . . It was absurd to feel hungry yet. . . . .

He was climbing again before half-past nine. For perhaps a hundred feet it was easy. Then by imperceptible degrees the gully broadened. He only realized it when he found himself slipping. He slipped, struggling furiously, for perhaps twenty feet, and then fell outright another ten and struck a rock and was held by a second shelf much broader than the one above. He came down on it with a jarring concussion and rolled—happily he rolled inward. He was bruised, but not seriously hurt. "My luck," he said. "My luck holds good."

He rested for a time, and then, confident that things would be all right, set himself to inspect the next stage of his descent. It was with a sort of incredulity that he discovered the chimney below his shelf was absolutely unclimbable. It was just a straight, smooth rock on either side for twenty yards at least and six feet wide. He might as well fling himself over at once as try to get down that. Then he saw that it was equally impossible to retrace his steps. He could not believe it; it seemed too silly. He laughed as one might laugh if one found one's own mother refusing to recognize one after a day's absence.

Then abruptly he stopped laughing.

He repeated every point in his examination. He fingered the smooth rocks about him. "But this is absurd," he said breaking out into a cold perspiration. There was no way out of this corner into which he had so painfully and laboriously got himself. He could neither go on nor go back. He was caught. His luck had given out.

§ 7

At midday by his wrist-watch Mr. Barnstaple was sitting in his recess as a weary invalid suffering from some incurable disease might sit up in an arm-chair during a temporary respite from pain, with nothing to do and no hope before him. There was not one chance in ten thousand that anything could happen to release him from this trap into which he had clambered. There was a trickle of water at the back but no food, not even a grass blade to nibble. Unless he saw fit to pitch himself over into the gorge, he must starve to death. . . . It would perhaps be cold at nights but not cold enough to kill him.

To this end he had come then out of the worried journalism of London and the domesticities of Sydenham.

Queer journey it was that he and the Yellow Peril had made!—Camberwell, Victoria, Hounslow, Slough, Utopia, the mountain paradise, a hundred fascinating and tantalizing glimpses of a world of real happiness and order, that long, long aeroplane flight half round a world. . . . And now—death.

The idea of abbreviating his sufferings by jumping over had no appeal for him. He would stay here and suffer such suffering as there might be before the end. And three hundred yards away or so were his fellow Earthlings, also awaiting their fate. . . . It was amazing. It was prosaic. . . .

After all to this or something like this most humanity had to come.

Sooner or later people had to lie and suffer, they

had to think and then think feverishly and then weakly, and so fade to a final cessation of thought.

On the whole, he thought, it was preferable to die in this fashion, preferable to a sudden death, it was worth while to look death in the face for a time, to have leisure to write *finis* in one's mind, to think over life and such living as one had done and to think it over with a detachment, an independence, that only an entire inability to alter one jot of it now could give.

At present his mind was clear and calm; a bleak serenity like a clear winter sky possessed him. There was suffering ahead, he knew, but he did not believe it would be intolerable suffering. If it proved intolerable the canyon yawned below. In that respect this shelf or rock was a better death bed than most, a more convenient death bed. Your sick bed presented pain with a wide margin, set it up for your too complete examination. But to starve was not so very dreadful, he had read; hunger and pain there would be, most distressful about the third day, and after that one became feeble and did not feel so much. It would not be like the torture of many cancer cases or the agony of brain fever; it would not be one tithe as bad as that. Lonely it would be. But is one much less lonely on a death bed at home? They come and say, "There! there!" and do little serviceable things—but are there any other interchanges? . . . You go your solitary way, speech and movement and the desire to speak or move passing from you, and their voices fade. . . . Everywhere death is a very solitary act, a going apart. . . .

A younger man would probably have found this

loneliness in the gorge very terrible, but Mr. Barnstaple had outlived the intenser delusions of com-
panionship. He would have liked a last talk with
his boys and to have put his wife into a good frame
of mind, but even these desires were perhaps more
sentimental than real. When it came to talks with
his boys he was apt to feel shy. As they had come
to have personalities of their own and to grow
through adolescence, he had felt more and more that
talking intimately to them was an invasion of their
right to grow up along their own lines. And they
too he felt were shy with him, defensively shy. Perhaps later on sons came back to a man—that was a
later on that he would never know now. But he
wished he could have let them know what had happened to him. That troubled him. It would set
him right in their eyes, it would perhaps be better
for their characters, if they did not think—as they
were almost bound to think—that he had run away
from them or lapsed mentally or even fallen into
bad company and been made away with. As it was
they might be worried and ashamed, needlessly, or
put to expense to find out where he was, and that
would be a pity.

One had to die. Many men had died as he was
going to die, fallen into strange places, lost in dark
caverns, marooned on desert islands, astray in the
Australian bush, imprisoned and left to perish. It
was good to die without great anguish or insult. He
thought of the myriads of men who had been cruci-
fied by the Romans—was it eight thousand or was
it ten thousand of the army of Spartacus that they
killed in that fashion along the Appian Way?—of

negroes hung in chains to starve, and of an endless
variety of such deaths. Shocking to young imaginations such things were and more fearful in thought
than in reality. It is all a matter of a little more
pain or a little less pain—but God will not have any
great waste of pain. Cross, wheel, electric chair or
bed of suffering—the thing is, *you die and have done*.

It was pleasant to find that one could think
stoutly of these things. It was good to be caught
and to find that one was not frantic. And Mr. Barnstaple was surprised to find how little he cared, now
that he faced the issue closely, whether he was immortal or whether he was not. He was quite prepared to find himself immortal or at least not ending
with death, in whole or in part. It was ridiculous to
be dogmatic and say that a part, an impression, of
his conscience and even of his willing life might not
go on in some fashion. But he found it impossible
to imagine how that could be. It was unimaginable.
It was not to be anticipated. He had no fear of that
continuation. He had no thought nor fear of the
possibility of punishment or cruelty. The universe
had at times seemed to him to be very carelessly put
together, but he had never believed that it was the
work of a malignant imbecile. It impressed him as
immensely careless but not as dominatingly cruel.
He had been what he had been, weak and limited
and sometimes silly, but the punishment of these
defects lay in the defects themselves.

He ceased to think about his own death. He began
to think of life generally, its present lowliness, its
valiant aspiration. He found himself regretting bitterly that he was not to see more of this Utopian

world, which was in so many respects so near an
intimation of what our own world may become. It
had been very heartening to see human dreams and
human ideals vindicated by realization, but it was
distressing to have had the vision snatched away
while he was still only beginning to examine it. He
found himself asking questions that had no answers
for him, about economics, about love and struggle.
Anyhow, he was glad to have seen as much as he
had. It was good to have been purged by this vision
and altogether lifted out of the dreary hopelessness
of Mr. Peeve, to have got life into perspective again.

The passions and conflicts and discomforts of A.D.
1921 were the discomforts of the fever of an uninocu-
lated world. The Age of Confusion on the Earth
also would, in its own time, work itself out, thanks
to a certain obscure and indomitable righteousness
in the blood of the human type. Squatting in a hole
in the cliff of the great crag, with unclimbable
heights and depths above him and below, chilly,
hungry and uncomfortable, this thought was a profound comfort to the strangely constituted mind of
Mr. Barnstaple.

But how miserably had he and his companions
failed to rise to the great occasions of Utopia! No
one had raised an effectual hand to restrain the
puerile imaginations of Mr. Catskill and the mere
brutal aggressiveness of his companions. How invincibly had Father Amerton headed for the rôle of
the ranting, hating, persecuting, quarrel-making
priest. How pitifully weak and dishonest Mr. Burleigh—and himself scarcely better! disapproving
always and always in ineffective opposition. What

an unintelligent beauty-cow that woman Greeta
Grey was, receptive, acquisitive, impenetrable to any
idea but the idea of what was due to her as a yielding
female! Lady Stella was of finer clay, but fired to
no service. Women, he thought, had not been well
represented in this chance expedition, just one
waster and one ineffective. Was that a fair sample
of Earth's womankind?

All the use these Earthlings had had for Utopia
was to turn it back as speedily as possible to the
aggressions, subjugations, cruelties and disorders of
the Age of Confusion to which they belonged. Serpentine and Cedar, the man of scientific power and
the man of healing, they had sought to make
hostages to disorder, and failing that they had killed
or sought to kill them.

They had tried to bring back Utopia to the state
of Earth, and indeed but for the folly, malice and
weakness of men Earth was now Utopia. Old Earth
was Utopia now, a garden and a glory, the Earthly
Paradise, except that it was trampled to dust and
ruin by its Catskills, Hunkers, Barralongas, Ridleys,
Duponts and their kind. Against their hasty
trampling folly nothing was pitted, it seemed, in the
whole wide world at present but the whinings of
the Peeves, the acquiescent disapproval of the Bur-
leighs and such immeasurable ineffectiveness as his
own protest. And a few writers and teachers who
produced results at present untraceable.

Once more Mr. Barnstaple found himself thinking of his old friend, the school inspector and school-
book writer, who had worked so steadfastly and

broken down and died so pitifully. He had worked
for Utopia all his days. Were there hundreds or
thousands of such Utopians yet on earth? What
magic upheld them?

"I wish I could get some message through to
them," said Mr. Barnstaple, "to hearten them."

For it was true, though he himself had to starve
and die like a beast fallen into a pit, nevertheless
Utopia triumphed and would triumph. The grab-
bers and fighters, the persecutors and patriots, the
lynchers and boycotters and all the riff-raff of short-
sighted human violence, crowded on to final defeat.
Even in their lives they know no happiness, they
drive from excitement to excitement and from
gratification to exhaustion. Their enterprises and
successes, their wars and glories, flare and pass.
Only the true thing grows, the truth, the clear idea,
year by year and age by age, slowly and invincibly
as a diamond grows amidst the darkness and pres-
sures of the earth, or as the dawn grows amidst the
guttering lights of some belated orgy.

What would be the end of those poor little people
up above there? Their hold on life was even more
precarious than his own, for he might lie and starve
here slowly for weeks before his mind gave its last
flicker. But they had openly pitted themselves
against the might and wisdom of Utopia, and even
now the ordered power of that world must be closing in upon them. He still had a faint irrational
remorse for his betrayal of Catskill's ambush. He
smiled now at the passionate conviction he had
felt at the time that if once Catskill could capture

his hostages, Earth might prevail over Utopia. That conviction had rushed him into action. His weak cries had seemed to be all that was left to avert this monstrous disaster. But suppose he had not béen there at all, or suppose he had obeyed the lingering instinct of fellowship that urged him to fight with the others; what then?

When he recalled the sight of Cedar throwing Mush about as one might throw a lap-dog about, and the height and shape of Serpentine, he doubted whether even upon the stairs in the archway it would have been possible for the Earthlings to have overpowered these two. The revolvers would have come into use just as they had come into use upon the slope, and Catskill would have got no hostages but only two murdered men.

How unutterably silly the whole scheme of Catskill had been! But it was no sillier than the behaviour of Catskill, Burleigh and the rest of the world's statesmen had been on earth, during the last few years. At times during the world agony of the great war it had seemed that Utopia drew near to earth. The black clouds and smoke of these dark years had been shot with the light of strange hopes, with the promise of a world reborn. But the nationalists, financiers, priests and patriots had brought all those hopes to nothing. They had trusted to old poisons and infections and to the weak resistances of the civilized spirit. They had counted their weapons and set their ambushes and kept their women busy sewing flags of discord. . . .

For a time they had killed hope, but only for a

time. For Hope, the redeemer of mankind, there is
perpetual resurrection.

"Utopia will win," said Mr. Barnstaple and for a
time he sat listening to a sound he had heard before
without heeding it very greatly, a purring throb in
the rocks about him, like the running of some great
machine. It grew louder and then faded down to
the imperceptible again.

His thoughts came back to his erstwhile companions. He hoped they were not too miserable or
afraid up there. He was particularly desirous that
something should happen to keep up Lady Stella's
courage. He worried affectionately about Lady
Stella. For the rest it would be as well if they
remained actively combative to the end. Possibly
they were all toiling at some preposterous and
wildly hopeful defensive scheme of Catskill's. Except Mr. Burleigh who would be resting—convinced
that for him at least there would still be a gentle-
manly way out. And probably not much afraid if
there wasn't. Amerton and possibly Mush might
lapse into a religious revival—that would irritate
the others a little, or possibly even provide a mental
opiate for Lady Stella and Miss Greeta Grey. Then
for Penk there was wine in the cellar. . . .

They would follow the laws of their being, they
would do the things that nature and habit would
require of them. What else was possible?

Mr. Barnstaple plunged into a metaphysical
gulf. . . .

Presently he caught himself looking at his wrist-
watch. It was twenty minutes past twelve. He
was looking at his watch more and more frequently

234   MEN LIKE GODS

—or time was going more slowly. . . . Should
he wind his watch or let it run down? He was
already feeling very hungry. That could not be
real hunger yet; it must be his imagination getting
out of control.

CHAPTER THE FOURTH

THE END OF QUARANTINE CRAG

§ 1

Mr. Barnstaple awoke slowly and reluctantly from a dream about cookery. He was Soyer, the celebrated chef of the Reform Club, and he was inventing and tasting new dishes. But in the pleasant way of dreamland he was not only Soyer, but at the same time he was a very clever Utopian biologist and also God Almighty. So that he could not only make new dishes, but also make new vegetables and meats to go into them. He was particularly interested in a new sort of fowl, the Chateaubriand breed of fowls, which was to combine the rich quality of very good beefsteak with the size and delicacy of a fowl's breast. And he wanted to stuff it with a blend of pimento, onion and mushroom—except that the mushroom wasn't quite the thing. The mushrooms—he tasted them—indeed just the least little modification. And into the dream came an assistant cook, several assistant cooks, all naked as Utopians, bearing fowls from the pantry and saying that they had not kept, they had gone "high" and they were going higher. In order to illustrate this idea of their going higher these assistant cooks

235

lifted the fowls above their heads and then began to climb the walls of the kitchen, which were rocky and for a kitchen remarkably close together. Their figures became dark. They were thrown up in black outline against the luminous steam arising from a cauldron of boiling soup. It was boiling soup, and yet it was cold soup and cold steam.

Mr. Barnstaple was awake.

In the place of luminous steam there was mist, brightly moonlit mist, filling the gorge. It threw up the figures of the two Utopians in black silhouette. . . .

What Utopians?

His mind struggled between dreaming and waking. He started up rigidly attentive. They moved with easy gestures, quite unaware of his presence so close to them. They had already got a thin rope ladder fixed to some point overhead, but how they had managed to do this he did not know. One still stood on the shelf, the other swayed above him stretched across the gully clinging to the rope with his feet against the rock. The head of a third figure appeared above the edge of the shelf. It swayed from side to side. He was evidently coming up by a second rope ladder. Some sort of discussion was in progress. It was borne in upon Mr. Barnstaple that this last comer thought that he and his companions had clambered high enough, but that the uppermost man insisted they should go higher. In a few moments the matter was settled.

The uppermost Utopian became very active, lunged upward, swung out and vanished by jerks out of Mr. Barnstaple's field of view. His com-

panions followed him and one after the other was
lost to sight, leaving nothing visible but the con-
vulsively agitated rope ladder and a dangling rope
that they seemed to be dragging up the crag with
them.

Mr. Barnstaple's taut muscles relaxed.   He
yawned silently, stretched his painful limbs and
stood up very cautiously. He peered up the gully.
The Utopians seemed to have reached the shelf
above and to be busy there. The rope that had
dangled became taut. They were hauling up something from below. It was a large bundle, possibly
of tools or weapons or material wrapped in something that deadened its impacts against the rock.
It jumped into view, hung spinning for a moment
and was then snatched upward as the Utopians took
in a fresh reef of rope. A period of silence followed.

He heard a metallic clang and then, thud, thud,
a dull intermittent hammering.   Then he jumped
back as the end of a thin rope, apparently running
over a pulley, dropped past him. The sounds from
above now were like filing and then some bits of
rock fell past him into the void.

§ 2

He did not know what to do. He was afraid to
call to these Utopians and make his presence known
to them. After the murder of Serpentine he was
very doubtful how a Utopian would behave to an
Earthling found hiding in a dark corner.

He examined the rope ladder that had brought

these Utopians to his level. It was held by a long
spike the end of which was buried in the rock at
the side of the gully. Possibly this spike had been
fired at the rock from below while he was asleep.
The ladder was made up of straight lengths and
rings at intervals of perhaps two feet. It was of
such light material that he would have doubted its
capacity to bear a man if he had not seen the Utopians upon it. It occurred to him that he might
descend by this now and take his chances with any
Utopians who might be below. He could not very
well bring himself to the attention of these three
Utopians above except by some sudden and startling action which might provoke sudden and unpleasant responses, but if he appeared first clambering slowly from above any Utopians beneath would
have time to realize and consider the fact of his
proximity before they dealt with him. And also
he was excessively eager to get down from this
dreary ledge.

He gripped a ring, thrust a leg backwards over
the edge of the shelf, listened for some moments to
the little noises of the three workers above him, and
then began his descent.

It was an enormous descent. Presently he found
himself regretting that he had not begun counting
the rings of the ladder. He must already have
handed himself down hundreds. And still when
he craned his neck to look down, the dark gulf
yawned below. It had become very dark now. The
moonlight did not cut down very deeply into the
canyon and the faint reflection from the thin mists
above was all there was to break the blackness.

And even overhead the moonlight seemed to be passing.

Now he was near the rock, now it fell away and the rope ladder seemed to fall plumb into lightless bottomless space. He had to feel for each ring, and his bare feet and hands were already chafed and painful. And a new and disagreeable idea had come into his head—that some Utopian might presently come rushing up the ladder. But he would get notice of that because the rope would tighten and quiver, and he would be able to cry out, "I am an Earthling coming down. I am a harmless Earthling."

He began to cry out these words experimentally. The gorge re-echoed them, and there was no answering sound.

He became silent again, descending grimly and as steadily as possible, because now an intense desire to get off this infernal rope ladder and rest his hot hands and feet was overmastering every other motive.

Clang, clang and a flash of green light.

He became rigid peering into the depths of the canyon. Came the green flash again. It revealed the depths of the gorge, still as it seemed an immense distance below him. And up the gorge—something; he could not grasp what it was during that momentary revelation. At first he thought it was a huge serpent writhing its way down the gorge, and then he concluded it must be a big cable that was being brought along the gorge by a handful of Utopians. But how the three or four figures he had indistinctly seen could move this colossal rope he could not imagine. The head of this cable serpent seemed to be lifting itself obliquely up the cliff. Perhaps it was being dragged up by ropes he had not observed. He waited for a third flash, but none came. He listened. He could hear nothing but a throbbing sound he had already noted before, like the throbbing of an engine running very smoothly.

He resumed his descent.

When at last he reached a standing place it took him by surprise. The rope ladder fell past it for some yards and ended. He was swaying more and more and beginning to realize that the rope ladder came to an end, when he perceived the dim indication of a nearly horizontal gallery cut along the rock face. He put out a foot and felt an edge and swung away out from it. He was now so weary and exhausted that for a time he could not relinquish his grip on the rope ladder and get a footing on the shelf. At last he perceived how this could be done. He released his feet and gave himself a push away from the rock with them. He swung back into a convenient position for getting a foothold. He repeated this twice, and then had enough confidence to abandon his ladder and drop on to the shelf. The ladder dangled away from him into the darkness and then came wriggling back to tap him playfully and startlingly on the shoulder blade.

The gallery he found himself in seemed to follow a great vein of crystalline material along the cliff face. Borings as high as a man ran into the rock. He peered and felt his way along the gallery for a time. Manifestly if this was a mine there would be some way of ascending to it and descending from it into the gorge. The sound of the torrent was much louder now, and he judged he had perhaps come down two-thirds of the height of the crag. He was inclined to wait for daylight. The illuminated dial of his wrist-watch told him it was now four o'clock. It would not be long before dawn. He found a comfortable face of rock for his back and squatted down.

Dawn seemed to come very quickly, but in reality he dozed away the interval. When he glanced at his watch again it was half-past five.

He went to the edge of the gallery and peered up the gorge to where he had seen the cable. Things were pale and dim and very black and white, but perfectly clear. The walls of the canyon seemed to go up for ever and vanish at last in cloud. He had a glimpse of a Utopian below, who was presently hidden by the curve of the gorge. He guessed that the great cable must have been brought so close up to the Quarantine Crag as to be invisible to him.

He could find no down-going steps from the gallery, but some thirty or forty yards off were five or six cable ways running at a steep angle from the gallery to the opposite side of the gorge. They looked very black and distinct. He went along to them. Each was a carrier cable on which ran a small carrier trolley with a big hook below. Three of the carrier cables were empty, but on two the trolley was hauled up. Mr. Barnstaple examined the trolleys and found a catch retained them. He turned over one of these catches and the trolley ran away promptly, nearly dropping him into the gulf. He saved himself by clutching the carrier cable. He watched the trolley swoop down like a bird to a broad stretch of sandy beach on the other side of the torrent and come to rest there. It seemed all right. Trembling violently, he turned to the remaining trolley.

His nerves and will were so exhausted now that it was a long time before he could bring himself to trust to the hook of the remaining trolley and to release its catch. Then smoothly and swiftly he swept across the gorge to the beach below. There were big heaps of crystalline mineral on this beach and a cable—evidently for raising it—came down out of the mists above from some invisible crane, but not a Utopian was in sight. He relinquished his hold and dropped safely on his feet. The beach broadened down-stream and he walked along it close to the edge of the torrent.

The light grew stronger as he went. The world ceased to be a world of greys and blacks; colour came back to things. Everything was heavily bedewed. And he was hungry and almost intolerably weary. The sand changed in its nature and became soft and heavy for his feet. He felt he could walk no further. He must wait for help. He sat down on a rock and looked up towards Quarantine Crag towering overhead.

§ 3

Sheer and high the great headland rose like the prow of some gigantic ship behind the two deep blue canyons; a few wisps and layers of mist still hid from Mr. Barnstaple its crest and the little bridge

across the narrower gorge.   The sky above between
the streaks of mist was now an intense blue.   And
even as he gazed the mists swirled and dissolved,
the rays of the rising sun smote the old castle to
blinding gold, and the fastness of the Earthlings
stood out clear and bright.

The bridge and the castle were very remote and
all that part of the crag was like a little cap on the
figure of a tall upstanding soldier.   Round beneath
the level of the bridge at about the height at which
the three Utopians had worked or were still working
ran something dark, a rope-like band.   He jumped
to the conclusion that this must be the cable he had
seen lit up by those green flashes in the night.   Then
he noted a peculiar body upon the crest of the more
open of the two gorges.   It was an enormous vertical
coil, a coil flattened into a disc, which had appeared
on the edge of the cliff opposite to Coronation Crag.
Less plainly seen because of a projecting mass of
rock, was a similar coil in the narrower canyon
close to the steps that led up from the little bridge.
Two or three Utopians, looking very small because
they were so high and very squat because they were
so foreshortened, were moving along the cliff edge
and handling something that apparently had to do
with these coils.

Mr. Barnstaple stared at these arrangements with
much the same uncomprehending stare as that with
which some savage who had never heard a shot
fired in anger might watch the loading of a gun.

Came a familiar sound, faint and little.   It was
the hooter of Quarantine Castle sounding the re-
veille.   And almost simultaneously the little Na-

poleonic figure of Mr. Rupert Catskill emerged against the blue. The head and shoulders of Penk rose and halted and stood at attention behind him. The captain of the Earthlings produce dhis field-glasses and surveyed the coils through them.

"I wonder what he makes of them," said Mr. Barnstaple.

Mr. Catskill turned and gave some direction to Penk, who saluted and vanished.

A click from the nearer gorge jerked his attention back to the little bridge. It had gone. His eye dropped and caught it up within a few yards of the water. He saw the water splash and the metal framework crumple up and dance two steps and lie still, and then a moment later the crash and clatter of the fall reached his ears.

"Now who did that?" asked Mr. Barnstaple and Mr. Catskill answered his question by going hastily to that corner of the castle and staring down. Manifestly he was surprised. Manifestly therefore it was the Utopians who had cut the bridge.

Mr. Catskill was joined almost immediately by Mr. Hunker and Lord Barralonga. Their gestures suggested an animated discussion.

The sunlight was creeping by imperceptible degrees down the front of Quarantine Crag. It had now got down to the cable that encircled the crest; in the light this shone with a coppery sheen. The three Utopians who had awakened Mr. Barnstaple in the night became visible descending the rope ladder very rapidly. And once more Mr. Barnstaple was aware of that humming sound he had heard ever and again during the night, but now it was much

louder and it sounded everywhere about him, in the
air, in the water, in the rocks and in his bones.

Abruptly something black and spear-shaped appeared beside the little group of Earthlings above.
It seemed to jump up beside them, it paused and
jumped again half the height of a man and jumped
again. It was a flag being hauled up a flag staff,
that Mr. Barnstaple had not hitherto observed. It
reached the top of the staff and hung limp.

Then some eddy in the air caught it. It flapped
out for a moment, displayed a white star on a blue
ground and dropped again.

This was the flag of Earth—this was the flag of
the crusade to restore the blessings of competition,
conflict and warfare to Utopia. Beneath it appeared
the head of Mr. Burleigh, examining the Utopian
coils through his glasses.

§ 4

The throbbing and humming in Mr. Barnstaple's
ears grew rapidly louder and rose acutely to an extreme intensity. Suddenly great flashes of violet
light leapt across from coil to coil, passing through
Quarantine Castle as though it was not there.

For a moment longer it *was* there.

The flag flared out madly and was torn from its
staff. Mr. Burleigh lost his hat. A half length of
Mr. Catskill became visible struggling with his coat
tails which had blown up and enveloped his head.
At the same time Mr. Barnstaple saw the castle
rotating upon the lower part of the crag, exactly as
though some invisible giant had seized the upper

tenth of the headland and was twisting it round.
And then it vanished.

As it did so, a great column of dust poured up into
its place; the waters in the gorge sprung into the
air in tall fountains and were splashed to spray, and
a deafening thud smote Mr. Barnstaple's ears. Aerial
powers picked him up and tossed him a dozen yards
and he fell amidst a rain of dust and stones and
water. He was bruised and stunned.

"My God!" he cried, "My God," and struggled to
his knees, feeling violently sick.

He had a glimpse of the crest of Quarantine Crag,
truncated as neatly as though it had been cheese cut
with a sharp knife. And then fatigue and exhaustion
had their way with him and he sprawled forward and
lay insensible.

BOOK THE THIRD

A NEOPHYTE IN UTOPIA

CHAPTER THE FIRST

THE PEACEFUL HILLS BESIDE THE RIVER

§ 1

"God has made more universes than there are pages in all the libraries of earth; man may learn and grow for ever amidst the multitude of His worlds."

Mr. Barnstaple had a sense of floating from star to star and from plane to plane, through an incessant variety and wonder of existences. He passed over the edge of being; he drifted for ages down the faces of immeasurable cliffs; he travelled from everlasting to everlasting in a stream of innumerable little stars. At last came a phase of profound restfulness. There was a sky of level clouds, warmed by the light of a declining sun, and a skyline of gently undulating hills, golden grassy upon their crests and carrying dark purple woods and thickets and patches of pale yellow like ripening corn upon their billowing slopes. Here and there were domed buildings and terraces, flowering gardens and little villas and great tanks of gleaming water.

There were many trees like the eucalyptus—only that they had darker leaves—upon the slopes immediately below and round and about him; and all the land fell at last towards a very broad valley down which a shining river wound leisurely in great semicircular bends until it became invisible in the evening haze.

A slight movement turned his eyes to discover Lychnis seated beside him. She smiled at him and put her finger on her lips. He had a vague desire to address her, and smiled faintly and moved his head. She got up and slipped away from him past the head of his couch. He was too feeble and incurious to raise his head and look to see where she had gone. But he saw that she had been sitting at a white table on which was a silver bowl full of intensely blue flowers, and the colour of the flowers held him and diverted his first faint impulse of curiosity.

He wondered whether colours were really brighter in this Utopian world or whether something in the air quickened and clarified his apprehension.

Beyond the table were the white pillars of the loggia. A branch of one of these eucalyptus-like trees, with leaves bronze black, came very close outside.

And there was music. It was a little trickle of sound, that dripped and ran, a mere unobtrusive rivulet of little clear notes upon the margin of his consciousness, the song of some fairyland Debussy.

Peace. . . .

§ 2

He was awake again.

He tried hard to remember.

He had been knocked over and stunned in some manner too big and violent for his mind to hold as yet.

Then people had stood about him and talked
about him. He remembered their feet. He must
have been lying on his face with his face very close
to the ground. Then they had turned him over,
and the light of the rising sun had been blinding
in his eyes.

Two gentle goddesses had given him some restora-
tive in a gorge at the foot of high cliffs. He had
been carried in a woman's arms as a child is carried.
After that there were cloudy and dissolving memories of a long journey, a long flight through the air.
There was something next to this, a vision of huge
complicated machinery that did not join on to anything else. For a time his mind held this up in an
interrogative fashion and then dropped it wearily.
There had been voices in consultation, the prick
of an injection and some gas that he had had to in-
hale. And sleep—or sleeps, spells of sleep interspersed with dreams. . . .

Now with regard to that gorge; how had he got
there?

The gorge—in another light, a greenish light—
with Utopians who struggled with a great cable.

Suddenly hard and clear came the vision of the
headland of Coronation Crag towering up against
the bright blue morning sky, and then the crest of
it grinding round, with its fluttering flags and its
dishevelled figures, passing slowly and steadily, as
some great ship passes out of a dock, with its flags
and passengers into the invisible and unknown.
All the wonder of his great adventure returned to
Mr. Barnstaple's mind.

§ 3

He sat up in a state of interrogation and Lychnis reappeared at his elbow.

She seated herself on his bed close to him, shook up some pillows behind him and persuaded him to lie back upon them. She conveyed to him that he was cured of some illness and no longer infectious, but that he was still very weak. Of what illness? he asked himself. More of the immediate past became clear to him.

"There was an epidemic," he said. "A sort of mixed epidemic—of all our infections."

She smiled reassuringly. It was over. The science and organization of Utopia had taken the danger by the throat and banished it. Lychnis, however, had had nothing to do with the preventive and cleansing work that had ended the career of these invading microbes so speedily; her work had been the help and care of the sick. Something came through to the intelligence of Mr. Barnstaple that made him think that she was faintly sorry that this work of pity was no longer necessary. He looked up into her beautiful kindly eyes and met her affectionate solicitude. She was not sorry Utopia was cured again; that was incredible; but it seemed to him that she was sorry that she could no longer spend herself in help and that she was glad that he at least was still in need of assistance.

"What became of those people on the rock?" he asked. "What became of the other Earthlings?"

She did not know. They had been cast out of Utopia, she thought.

"Back to earth?"

She did not think they had gone back to earth. They had perhaps gone into yet another universe. But she did not know. She was one of those who had no mathematical aptitudes, and physico-chemical science and the complex theories of dimensions that interested so many people in Utopia were outside her circle of ideas. She believed that the crest of Coronation Crag had been swung out of the Utopian universe altogether. A great number of people were now intensely interested in this experimental work upon the unexplored dimensions into which physical processes might be swung, but these matters terrified her. Her mind recoiled from them as one recoils from the edge of a cliff. She did not want to think where the Earthlings had gone, what deeps they had reeled over, what immensities they had seen and swept down into. Such thoughts opened dark gulfs beneath her feet where she had thought everything fixed and secure. She was a conservative in Utopia. She loved life as it was and as it had been. She had given herself to the care of Mr. Barnstaple when she had found that he had escaped the fate of the other Earthlings, and she had not troubled very greatly about the particulars of that fate. She had avoided thinking about it.

"But where are they? Where have they gone?"

She did not know.

She conveyed to him haltingly and imperfectly her own halting and unsympathetic ideas of these new discoveries that had inflamed the Utopian imagination. The crucial moment had been the experiment of Arden and Greenlake that had brought the

Earthlings into Utopia. That had been the first rupture of the hitherto invincible barriers that had held their universe in three spatial dimensions. That had opened these abysses. That had been the moment of release for all the new work that now filled Utopia. That had been the first achievement of practical results from an intricate network of theory and deduction. It sent Mr. Barnstaple's mind back to the humbler discoveries of earth, to Franklin snapping the captive lightning from his kite and Galvani, with his dancing frog's legs, puzzling over the miracle that brought electricity into the service of men. But it had taken a century and a half for electricity to make any sensible changes in human life because the earthly workers were so few and the ways of the world so obstructive and slow and spiteful. In Utopia to make a novel discovery was to light an intellectual conflagration. Hundreds of thousands of experimentalists in free and open cooperation were now working along the fruitful lines that Arden and Greenlake had made manifest. Every day, every hour now, new and hitherto fantastic possibilities of interspatial relationship were being made plain to the Utopians.

Mr. Barnstaple rubbed his head and eyes with both hands and then lay back, blinking at the great valley below him, growing slowly golden as the sun sank. He felt himself to be the most secure and stable of beings at the very centre of a sphere of glowing serenity. And that effect of an immense tranquillity was a delusion; that still evening peace was woven of incredible billions of hurrying and clashing atoms.

All the peace and fixity that man has ever known
or will ever know is but the smoothness of the face
of a torrent that flies along with incredible speed
from cataract to cataract. Time was when men
could talk of everlasting hills. Today a schoolboy
knows that they dissolve under the frost and wind
and rain and pour seaward, day by day and hour by
hour. Time was when men could speak of Terra
Firma and feel the earth fixed, adamantine beneath
their feet. Now they know that it whirls through
space eddying about a spinning, blindly driven sun
amidst a sheeplike drift of stars. And this fair cur-
tain of appearance before the eyes of Mr. Barnstaple, this still and level flush of sunset and the
great cloth of starry space that hung behind the
blue; that too was now to be pierced and torn and
rent asunder. . . .

The extended fingers of his mind closed on the
things that concerned him most.

"But where are my people?" he asked. "Where
are their bodies? Is it just possible they are still
alive?"

She could not tell him.

He lay thinking. . . . It was natural that he
should be given into the charge of a rather back-
ward-minded woman. The active-minded here had
no more use for him in their lives than active-minded
people on earth have for pet animals. She did not
want to think about these spatial relations at all;
the subject was too difficult for her; she was one of
Utopia's educational failures. She sat beside him
with a divine sweetness and tranquillity upon her
face, and he felt his own judgment upon her like a

committed treachery. Yet he wanted to know very
badly the answer to his question.

He supposed the crest of Coronation Crag had
been twisted round and flung off into some outer
space. It was unlikely that this time the Earthlings would strike a convenient planet again. In
all probability they had been turned off into the
void, into the interstellar space of some unknown
universe. . . .

What would happen then? They would freeze.
The air would instantly diffuse right out of them.
Their own gravitation would flatten them out, crush
them together, collapse them! At least they would
have no time to suffer. A gasp, like someone flung
into ice-cold water. . . .

He contemplated these possibilities.

"Flung out!" he said aloud. "Like a cageful of
mice thrown over the side of a ship!"

"I don't understand," said Lychnis, turning to
him.

He appealed to her. "And now—tell me. What
is to become of me?"

§ 4

For a time Lychnis gave him no answer. She sat
with her soft eyes upon the blue haze into which
the great river valley had now dissolved. Then she
turned to him with a question:

"You want to stay in this world?"

"Surely any Earthling would want to stay in this
world. My body has been purified. Why should
I not stay?"

"It seems a good world to you?"

"Loveliness, order, health, energy and wonder; it has all the good things for which my world groans and travails."

"And yet our world is not content."

"I could be contented."

"You are tired and weak still."

"In this air I could grow strong and vigorous. I could almost grow young in this world. In years, as you count them here, I am still a young man."

Again she was silent for a time. The mighty lap of the landscape was filled now with indistinguishable blue, and beyond the black silhouettes of the trees upon the hillside only the skyline of the hills was visible against the yellow green and pale yellow of the evening sky. Never had Mr. Barnstaple seen so peaceful a nightfall. But her words denied that peace. "Here," she said, "there is no rest. Every day men and women awake and say: What new thing shall we do to-day? What shall we change?"

"They have changed a wild planet of disease and disorder into a sphere of beauty and safety. They have made the wilderness of human motives bear union and knowledge and power."

"And research never rests, and curiosity and the desire for more power and still more power consumes all our world."

"A healthy appetite. I am tired now, as weak and weary and soft as though I had just been born; but presently when I have grown stronger I too may share in that curiosity and take a part in these great discoveries that now set Utopia astir. Who knows?"

He smiled at her kind eyes.

"You will have much to learn," she said.

She seemed to measure her own failure as she said these words.

Some sense of the profound differences that three thousand years of progress might have made in the fundamental ideas and ways of thinking of the race dawned upon Mr. Barnstaple's mind. He remembered that in Utopia he heard only the things he could understand, and that all that found no place in his terrestrial circle of ideas was inaudible to his mind. The gulfs of misunderstanding might be wider and deeper than he was assuming. A totally illiterate Gold Coast negro trying to master thermo-electricity would have set himself a far more hopeful task.

"After all it is not the new discoveries that I want to share," he said; "quite possibly they are altogether beyond me; it is this perfect, beautiful daily life, this life of all the dreams of my own time come true, that I want. I just want to be alive here. That will be enough for me."

"You are weak and tired yet," said Lychnis. "When you are stronger you may face other ideas."

"But what other ideas——?"

"Your mind may turn back to your own world and your own life."

"Go back to Earth!"

Lychnis looked out at the twilight again for a while before she turned to him with, "You are an Earthling born and made. What else can you be?"

"What else can I be?" Mr. Barnstaple's mind rested upon that, and he lay feeling rather than thinking amidst its implications as the pinpoint lights of Utopia pricked the darkling blue below and ran into chains and groups and coalesced into nebulous patches.

He resisted the truth below her words. This glorious world of Utopia, perfect and assured, poised ready for tremendous adventures amidst untravelled universes, was a world of sweet giants and uncompanionable beauty, a world of enterprises in which a poor muddy-witted, weak-willed Earthling might neither help nor share. They had plundered their planet as one empties a purse; they thrust out their power amidst the stars. . . . They were kind. They were very kind. . . . But they were different. . . .

CHAPTER THE SECOND

A LOITERER IN A LIVING WORLD

§ 1

In a few days Mr. Barnstaple had recovered strength of body and mind. He no longer lay in bed in a loggia, filled with self-pity and the beauty of a world subdued; he went about freely and was soon walking long distances over the Utopian countryside, seeking acquaintances and learning more and more of this wonderland of accomplished human desires.

For that is how it most impressed him. Nearly all the greater evils of human life had been conquered; war, pestilence and malaise, famine and poverty had been swept out of human experience. The dreams of artists, of perfected and lovely bodies and of a world transfigured to harmony and beauty had been realized; the spirits of order and organization ruled triumphant. Every aspect of human life had been changed by these achievements.

The climate of this Valley of Rest was bland and sunny like the climate of South Europe, but nearly everything characteristic of the Italian or Spanish scene had gone. Here were no bent and aged crones carrying burthens, no chattering pursuit by beggars, no ragged workers lowering by the wayside. The puny terracing, the distressing accumulations of hand cultivation, the gnarled olives, hacked vines, the little patches of grain or fruit, and the grudged litigious irrigation of those primitive conditions, gave place to sweeping schemes of conservation, to a broad and subtle handling of slope and soil and sunshine. No meagre goats nor sheep, child-tended, cropped among the stones, no tethered cattle ate their apportioned circles of herbage and no more. There were no hovels by the wayside, no shrines with tortured, blood-oozing images, no slinking misbegotten curs nor beaten beasts sweating and panting between their overloaded paniers at the steeper places of rutted, rock-strewn and dung-strewn roads. Instead the great smooth indestructible ways swept in easy gradients through the land, leaping gorges and crossing valleys upon wide-arched viaducts, piercing cathedral-like aisles through the hillsides, throwing off bastions to command some special splendour of the land. Here were resting places and shelters, stairways clambering to pleasant arbours and summer-houses where friends might talk and lovers shelter and rejoice. Here were groves and avenues of such trees as he had never seen before. For on earth as yet there is scarcely such a thing as an altogether healthy fully grown tree, nearly all our trees are bored and consumed by parasites, rotten and tumorous with fungi, more gnarled and crippled and disease-twisted even than mankind.

The landscape had absorbed the patient design of five-and-twenty centuries. In one place Mr. Barnstaple found great works in progress; a bridge was being replaced, not because it was outworn, but because someone had produced a bolder, more delightful design.

For a time he did not observe the absence of telephonic or telegraphic communication; the posts and wires that mark a modern countryside had disappeared. The reasons for that difference he was to learn later. Nor did he at first miss the railway, the railway station and the wayside inn. He perceived that the frequent buildings must have specific functions, that people came and went from them with an appearance of interest and preoccupation, that from some of them seemed to come a hum and whir of activity; work of many sorts was certainly in progress; but his ideas of the mechanical organization of this new world were too vague and tentative as yet for him to attempt to fix any significance to this sort of place or that. He walked agape like a savage in a garden.

He never came to nor saw any towns. The reason for any such close accumulations of human beings had largely disappeared. In certain places, he learnt, there were gatherings of people for studies, mutual stimulation, or other convenient exchanges, in great series of communicating buildings; but he never visited any of these centres.

And about this world went the tall people of Utopia, fair and wonderful, smiling or making some friendly gesture as they passed him but giving him little chance for questions or intercourse. They travelled swiftly in machines upon the high road or walked, and ever and again the shadow of a silent soaring aeroplane would pass over him. He went a

little in awe of these people and felt himself a queer
creature when he met their eyes. For like the gods
of Greece and Rome theirs was a cleaned and perfected humanity, and it seemed to him that they
were gods. Even the great tame beasts that walked
freely about this world had a certain divinity that
checked the expression of Mr. Barnstaple's friendli-
ness.

§ 2

Presently he found a companion for his rambles,
a boy of thirteen, a cousin of Lychnis, named Crystal. He was a curly-headed youngster, brown-eyed
as she was; and he was reading history in a holiday
stage of his education.

So far as Mr. Barnstaple could gather the more
serious part of his intellectual training was in mathematical work interrelated to physical and chemical
science, but all that was beyond an Earthling's range
of ideas. Much of this work seemed to be done in
co-operation with other boys, and to be what we
should call research on earth. Nor could Mr. Barnstaple master the nature of some other sort of study
which seemed to turn upon refinements of expression. But the history brought them together. The
boy was just learning about the growth of the
Utopian social system out of the efforts and experiences of the Ages of Confusion. His imagination
was alive with the tragic struggles upon which the
present order of Utopia was founded, he had a
hundred questions for Mr. Barnstaple, and he was

full of explicit information which was destined presently to sink down and become part of the foundations of his adult mind. Mr. Barnstaple was as
good as a book to him, and he was as good as a
guide to Mr. Barnstaple. They went about together
talking upon a footing of the completest equality,
this rather exceptionally intelligent Earthling ·and
this Utopian stripling, who topped him by perhaps
an inch when they stood side by side.

The boy had the broad facts of Utopian history at
his fingers' ends. He could explain and find an interest in explaining how artificial and upheld the
peace and beauty of Utopia still were. Utopians
were in essence, he said, very much what their ancestors had been in the beginnings of the newer stone
age, fifteen thousand or twenty thousand years ago.
They were still very much what Earthlings had been
in the corresponding period. Since then there had
been only 600 or 700 generations and no time for
any very fundamental changes in the race. There
had not been even a general admixture of races.
On Utopia as on earth there had been dusky and
brown peoples, and they remained distinct. The
various races mingled socially but did not interbreed
very much; rather they purified and intensified their
racial gifts and beauties. There was often very passionate love between people of contrasted race, but
rarely did such love come to procreation. There
had been a certain deliberate elimination of ugly,
malignant, narrow, stupid and gloomy types during
the past dozen centuries or so; but except for the
fuller realization of his latent possibilities, the common man in Utopia was very little different from

the ordinary energetic and able people of a later
stone-age or early bronze-age community. They
were infinitely better nourished, trained and educated, and mentally and physically their condition
was clean and fit, but they were the same flesh
and nature as we are.

"But,'" said Mr. Barnstaple, and struggled with
that idea for a time. "Do you mean to tell me
that half the babies born on earth to-day might
grow to be such gods as these people I meet?"

"Given our air, given our atmosphere."

"Given your heritage."

"Given our freedom."

In the past of Utopia, in the Age of Confusion, Mr.
Barnstaple had to remember, everyone had grown
up with a crippled or a thwarted will, hampered by
vain restrictions or misled by plausible delusions.
Utopia still bore it in mind that human nature was
fundamentally animal and savage and had to be
adapted to social needs, but Utopia had learnt the
better methods of adaptation—after endless failures
of compulsion, cruelty and deception. "On Earth
we tame our animals with hot irons and our fellow
men by violence and fraud," said Mr. Barnstaple,
and described the schools and books, newspapers and
public discussions of the early twentieth century to
his incredulous companion. "You cannot imagine
how beaten and fearful even decent people are upon
Earth. You learn of the Age of Confusion in your
histories but you do not know what the realities of
a bad mental atmosphere, an atmosphere of feeble
laws, hates and superstitions, are. As night goes
round the Earth always there are hundreds of thou-

sands of people who should be sleeping, lying awake, fearing a bully, fearing a cruel competition, dreading lest they cannot make good, ill of some illness they cannot comprehend, distressed by some irrational quarrel, maddened by some thwarted instinct or some suppressed and perverted desire." . . .

Crystal admitted that it was hard to think now of the Age of Confusion in terms of misery. Much of the every-day misery of Earth was now inconceivable. Very slowly Utopia had evolved its present harmony of law and custom and education. Man was no longer crippled and compelled; it was recognized that he was fundamentally an animal and that his daily life must follow the round of appetites satisfied and instincts released. The daily texture of Utopian life was woven of various and interesting foods and drinks, of free and entertaining exercise and work, of sweet sleep and of the interest and happiness of fearless and spiteless love-making. Inhibition was at a minimum. But where the power of Utopian education began was after the animal had been satisfied and disposed of. The jewel on the reptile's head that had brought Utopia out of the confusions of human life was curiosity, the play impulse, prolonged and expanded in adult life into an insatiable appetite for knowledge and an habitual creative urgency. All Utopians had become as little children, learners and makers.

It was strange to hear this boy speaking so plainly and clearly of the educational process to which he was being subjected, and particularly to find he could talk so frankly of love.

An earthly bashfulness almost prevented Mr.

Barnstaple from asking, "But you——. You do not make Love?"

"I have had curiosities," said the boy, evidently saying what he had been taught to say. "But it is not necessary nor becoming to make love too early in life nor to let desire take hold of one. It weakens youth to become too early possessed by desire—which often will not leave one again. It spoils and cripples the imagination. I want to do good work as my father has done before me."

Mr. Barnstaple glanced at the beautiful young profile at his side and was suddenly troubled by memories of a certain study number four at school, and of some ugly phases of his adolescence, the stuffy, secret room, the hot and ugly fact. He felt a beastlier Earthling than ever. "Heigho!" he sighed. "But this world of yours is as clean as starlight and as sweet as cold water on a dusty day."

"Many people I love," said the boy, "but not with passion. Some day that will come. But one must not be too eager and anxious to meet passionate love or one might make-believe and give or snatch at a sham. . . . There is no hurry. No one will prevent me when my time comes. All good things come to one in this world in their own good time."

But work one does not wait for; one's work, since it concerns one's own self only, one goes to meet. Crystal thought very much about the work that he might do. It seemed to Mr. Barnstaple that work, in the sense of uncongenial toil, had almost disappeared from Utopia. Yet all Utopia was working. Everyone was doing work that fitted natural aptitudes and appealed to the imagination of the worker.

Everyone worked happily and eagerly—as those people we call geniuses do on our Earth.

For suddenly Mr. Barnstaple found himself telling Crystal of the happiness of the true artist, of the true scientific worker, of the original man even on earth as it is today. They, too, like the Utopians, do work that concerns themselves and is in their own nature for great ends. Of all Earthlings they are the most enviable.

"If such men are not happy on earth," said Mr. Barnstaple, "it is because they are touched with vulgarity and still heed the soiled successes and honours and satisfactions of vulgar men, still feel neglect and limitation that should concern them no more. But to him who has seen the sun shine in Utopia surely the utmost honour and glory of earth can signify no more and be no more desirable than the complimentary spittle of the chieftain and a string of barbaric beads."

§ 3

Crystal was still of an age to be proud of his *savoir faire*. He showed Mr. Barnstaple his books and told him of his tutors and exercises.

Utopia still made use of printed books; books were still the simplest, clearest way of bringing statement before a tranquil mind. Crystal's books were very beautifully bound in flexible leather that his mother had tooled for him very prettily, and they were made of hand-made paper. The lettering was some fluent phonetic script that Mr. Barnstaple could not understand. It reminded him of Arabic;

and frequent sketches, outline maps and diagrams
were interpolated.   Crystal was advised in his holiday reading by a tutor for whom he prepared a sort
of exercise report, and he supplemented his reading
by visits to museums; but there was no educational
museum convenient in the Valley of Peace for Mr.
Barnstaple to visit.

Crystal had passed out of the opening stage of
education which was carried on, he said, upon large
educational estates given up wholly to the lives of
children.   Education up to eleven or twelve seemed
to be much more carefully watched and guarded
and taken care of in Utopia than upon earth.
Shocks to the imagination, fear and evil suggestions
were warded off as carefully as were infection and
physical disaster; by eight or nine the foundations
of a Utopian character were surely laid, habits of
cleanliness, truth, candour and helpfulness, confidence in the world, fearlessness and a sense of
belonging to the great purpose of the race.

Only after nine or ten did the child go outside
the garden of its early growth and begin to see the
ordinary ways of the world.   Until that age the care
of the children was largely in the hands of nurses
and teachers, but after that time the parents became
more of a factor than they had been in a youngster's
life.   It was always a custom for the parents of a
child to be near and to see that child in its nursery
days, but just when earthly parents tended to separate from their children as they went away to school
or went into business, Utopian parentage grew to be
something closer.   There was an idea in Utopia
that between parent and child there was a necessary

temperamental sympathy; children looked forward
to the friendship and company of their parents, and
parents looked forward to the interest of their children's adolescence, and though a parent had practically no power over a son or daughter, he or she
took naturally the position of advocate, adviser and
sympathetic friend. The friendship was all the
franker and closer because of that lack of power,
and all the easier because age for age the Utopians
were so much younger and fresher-minded than
Earthlings. Crystal it seemed had a very great passion for his mother. He was very proud of his
father, who was a wonderful painter and designer;
but it was his mother who possessed the boy's heart.

On his second walk with Mr. Barnstaple he said
he was going to hear from his mother, and Mr.
Barnstaple was shown the equivalent of correspondence in Utopia. Crystal carried a little bundle of
wires and light rods; and presently coming to a
place where a pillar stood in the midst of a lawn he
spread this affair out like a long cat's cradle and
tapped a little stud in the pillar with a key that he
carried on a light gold chain about his neck. Then
he took up a receiver attached to his apparatus, and
spoke aloud and listened and presently heard a
voice.

It was a very pleasant woman's voice; it talked to
Crystal for a time without interruption, and then
Crystal talked back, and afterwards there were other
voices, some of which Crystal answered and some
which he heard without replying. Then he gathered
up his apparatus again.

This Mr. Barnstaple learnt was the Utopian

equivalent of letter and telephone. For in Utopia, except by previous arrangement, people do not talk together on the telephone. A message is sent to the station of the district in which the recipient is known to be, and there it waits until he chooses to tap his accumulated messages. And any that one wishes to repeat can be repeated. Then he talks back to the senders and dispatches any other messages he wishes. The transmission is wireless. The little pillars supply electric power for transmission or for any other purpose the Utopians require. For example, the gardeners resort to them to run their mowers and diggers and rakes and rollers.

Far away across the valley Crystal pointed out the district station at which this correspondence gathered and was dispersed. Only a few people were on duty there; almost all the connexions were automatic. The messages came and went from any part of the planet.

This set Mr. Barnstaple going upon a long string of questions.

He discovered for the first time that the message organization of Utopia had a complete knowledge of the whereabouts of every soul upon the planet. It had a record of every living person and it knew in what message district he was. Everyone was indexed and noted.

To Mr. Barnstaple, accustomed to the crudities and dishonesties of earthly governments, this was an almost terrifying discovery. "On earth that would be the means of unending blackmail and tyranny," he said. "Everyone would lie open to espionage. We had a fellow at Scotland Yard. If he had been in your communication department he would have made life in Utopia intolerable in a week. You cannot imagine the nuisance he was." . . .

Mr. Barnstaple had to explain to Crystal what blackmail meant. It was like that in Utopia to begin with, Crystal said. Just as on earth so in Utopia there was the same natural disposition to use knowledge and power to the disadvantage of one's fellows, and the same jealousy of having one's personal facts known. In the Stone Age in Utopia men kept their true names secret and could only be spoken of by nicknames. They feared magic abuses. "Some savages still do that on earth," said Mr. Barnstaple. It was only very slowly that Utopians came to trust doctors and dentists and only very slowly that doctors and dentists became trustworthy. It was a matter of scores of centuries before the chief abuses of the confidences and trusts necessary to a modern social organization could be effectively corrected.

Every young Utopian had to learn the Five Principles of Liberty, without which civilization is impossible. The first was the Principle of Privacy. This is that all individual personal facts are private between the citizen and the public organization to which he entrusts them, and can be used only for his convenience and with his sanction. Of course all such facts are available for statistical uses, but not as individual personal facts. And the second principle is the Principle of Free Movement. A citizen, subject to the due discharge of his public obligations, may go without permission or explana-

tion to any part of the Utopian planet. All the
means of transport are freely at his service. Every
Utopian may change his surroundings, his climate
and his social atmosphere as he will. The third
principle is the Principle of Unlimited Knowledge.
All that is known in Utopia, except individual personal facts about living people, is on record and as
easily available as a perfected series of indices,
libraries, museums, and inquiry offices can make it.
Whatever the Utopian desires to know he may know
with the utmost clearness, exactness and facility so
far as his powers of knowing and his industry go.
Nothing is kept from him and nothing is misrepre-
sented to him. And that brought Mr. Barnstaple
to the fourth Principle of Liberty, which was that
Lying is the Blackest Crime.

Crystal's definition of lying was a sweeping one;
the inexact statement of facts, even the suppression
of a material fact, was lying.

"Where there are lies there cannot be freedom."

Mr. Barnstaple was mightily taken by this idea.
It seemed at once quite fresh to him and one that
he had always unconsciously entertained. Half the
difference between Utopia and our world he asserted
lay in this, that our atmosphere was dense and
poisonous with lies and shams.

"When one comes to think of it," said Mr. Barnstaple, and began to expatiate to Crystal upon all
the falsehoods of human life. The fundamental
assumptions of earthly associations were still largely
lies, false assumptions of necessary and unavoidable
differences in flags and nationality, pretences of
function and power in monarchy; impostures of

organized learning, religious and moral dogmas and
shams. And one must live in it; one is a part of it.
You are restrained, taxed, distressed and killed by
these insane unrealities. "Lying the Primary
Crime! How simple that is! How true and necessary it is! That dogma is the fundamental distinction of the scientific world-state from all preceding
states." And going on from that Mr. Barnstaple
launched out into a long and loud tirade against the
suppression and falsifications of earthly newspapers.

It was a question very near his heart. The London newspapers had ceased to be impartial vehicles
of news; they omitted, they mutilated, they mis-
stated. They were no better than propaganda rags.
Rags! *Nature,* within its field, was shiningly accu-
rate and full, but that was a purely scientific paper;
it did not touch the every-day news. The Press, he
held, was the only possible salt of contemporary
life, and if the salt had lost its savour——!

The poor man found himself orating as though
he was back at his Sydenham breakfast-table after a
bad morning's paper.

"Once upon a time Utopia was in just such a
tangle," said Crystal consolingly. "But there is a
proverb, 'Truth comes back where once she has
visited.' You need not trouble so much as you do.
Some day even your press may grow clear."

"How do *you* manage about newspapers and criticism?" said Mr. Barnstaple.

Crystal explained that there was a complete distinction between news and discussion in Utopia.
There were houses—one was in sight—which were
used as reading-rooms. One went to these places

to learn the news. Thither went the reports of all
the things that were happening on the planet, things
found, things discovered, things done. The reports
were made as ' they were needed; there were no
advertisement contracts to demand the same bulk
of news every day. For some time Crystal said the
reports had been very full and amusing about the
Earthlings, but he had not been reading the paper
for many days because of the interest in history the
Earthling affair had aroused in him. There was
always news of fresh scientific discoveries that stirred
the imagination. One frequent item of public interest and excitement was the laying out of some wide
scheme of research. The new spatial work that
Arden and Greenlake had died for was producing
much news. And when people died in Utopia it
was the custom to tell the story of their lives.
Crystal promised to take Mr. Barnstaple to a news
place and entertain him by reading him some of the
Utopian descriptions of earthly life which had been
derived from the Earthlings, and Mr. Barnstaple
asked that when this was done he might also hear
about Arden and Greenlake, who had been not only
great discoverers, but great lovers, and of Serpentine
and Cedar, for whom he had conceived an intense
admiration. Utopian news lacked of course the
high spice of an earthly newspaper; the intriguing
murders and amusing misbehaviours, the entertaining and exciting consequences of sexual ignorance
and sexual blunderings, the libel cases and detected
swindles, the great processional movements of
Royalty across the general traffic, and the romantic
fluctuations of the stock exchange and sport. But

where the news of Utopia lacked liveliness, the liveliness of discussion made up for it. For the Fifth
Principle of Liberty in Utopia was Free Discussion
and Criticism.

Any Utopian was free to criticize and discuss anything in the whole universe provided he told no lies
about it directly or indirectly; he could be as respect-
ful or disrespectful as he pleased; he could propose
anything however subversive. He could break into
poetry or fiction as he chose. He could express himself in any literary form he liked or by sketch or
caricature as the mood took him. Only he must
refrain from lying; that was the one rigid rule of
controversy. He could get what he had to say
printed and distributed to the news rooms. There
it was read or neglected as the visitors chanced to
approve of it or not. Often if they liked what they
read they would carry off a copy with them. Crystal
had some new fantastic fiction about the exploration
of space among his books; imaginative stories
that boys were reading very eagerly; they were
pamphlets of thirty or forty pages printed on a
beautiful paper that he said was made directly from
flax and certain reeds. The librarians noted what
books and papers were read and taken away, and
these they replaced with fresh copies. The piles
that went unread were presently reduced to one or
two copies and the rest went back to the pulping
mills. But many of the poets and philosophers
and story-tellers whose imaginations found no wide
popularity were nevertheless treasured and their
memories kept alive by a few devoted admirers.

§ 4

"I am not at all clear in my mind about one thing," said Mr. Barnstaple. "I have seen no coins and nothing like money passing in this world. By all outward appearance this might be a Communism such as was figured in a book we used to value on Earth, a book called *News from Nowhere* by an Earthling named William Morris. It was a graceful impossible book. In that dream everyone worked for the joy of working and took what he needed. But I have never believed in Communism because I recognize, as here in Utopia you seem to recognize, the natural fierceness and greediness of the untutored man. There is joy in creation for others to use, but no natural joy in unrequited service. The sense of justice to himself is greater in man than the sense of service. Somehow here you must balance the work anyone does for Utopia against what he destroys or consumes. How do you do it?"

Crystal considered. "There were Communists in Utopia in the Last Age of Confusion. In some parts of our planet they tried to abolish money suddenly and violently and brought about great economic confusion and want and misery. To step straight to communism failed—very tragically. And yet Utopia today is practically a communism, and except by way of curiosity I have never had a coin in my hand in all my life."

In Utopia just as upon earth, he explained, money came as a great discovery; as a method of freedom. Hitherto, before the invention of money, all service

between man and man had been done through bond-
age or barter.   Life was a thing of slavery and narrow choice.   But money opened up the possibility
of giving a worker a free choice in his reward.   It
took Utopia three thousand years and more to
realize that possibility.   The idea of money
abounded in pitfalls and was easily corruptible;
Utopia floundered its way to economic lucidity
through long centuries of credit and debt, false and
debased money; extravagant usury and every possibility of speculative abuse.   In the matter of money
more than in any other human concern, human cunning has set itself most vilely and treacherously to
prey upon human necessity.   Utopia once carried,
as earth carries now, a load of parasitic souls, specu-
lators, forestallers, gamblers and bargain-pressing
Shylocks, exacting every conceivable advantage out
of the weaknesses of the monetary system; she had
needed centuries of economic sanitation.   It was
only when Utopia had got to the beginnings of
world-wide political unity and when there were sufficiently full statistics of world resources and world
production, that human society could at last give
the individual worker the assurance of a coin of
steadfast significance, a coin that would mean for
him today or tomorrow or at any time the certainty of a set quantity of elemental values.   And
with peace throughout the planet and increasing
social stability, interest, which is the measure of
danger and uncertainty, dwindled at last to nothing.   Banking became a public service perforce,
because it no longer offered profit to the individual
banker.   "Rentier classes," Crystal conveyed, "are

not a permanent element in any community. They mark a phase of transition between a period of insecurity and high interest and a period of complete security and no interest. They are a dawn phenomenon."

Mr. Barnstaple digested this statement after an interval of incredulity. He satisfied himself by a few questions that young Utopia really had some idea of what a rentier class was, what its moral and imaginative limitations were likely to be and the rôle it may have played in the intellectual development of the world by providing a class of independent minds.

"Life is intolerant of all independent classes," said Crystal, evidently repeating an axiom. "Either you must earn or you must rob. . . . We have got rid of robbing."

The youngster still speaking by his book went on to explain how the gradual disuse of money came about. It was an outcome of the general progressive organization of the economic system, the substitution of collective enterprises for competitive enterprises and of wholesale for retail dealing. There had been a time in Utopia when money changed hands at each little transaction and service. One paid money if one wanted a newspaper or a match or a bunch of flowers or a ride on a street conveyance. Everybody went about the world with pockets full of small coins paying on every slight occasion. Then as economic science became more stable and exact the methods of the club and the covering subscription extended. People were able to buy passes that carried them by all the available means of transport for a year or for ten years or for life. The State learnt from clubs and hotels to provide matches, newspapers, stationery and transport for a fixed annual charge. The same inclusive system spread from small and incidental things to great and essential matters, to housing and food and even clothing. The State postal system, which knew where every Utopian citizen was, was presently able in conjunction with the public banking system to guarantee his credit in any part of the world. People ceased to draw coin for their work; the various departments of service, and of economic, educational and scientific activity would credit the individual with his earnings in the public bank and debit him with his customary charges for all the normal services of life.

"Something of this sort is going on on earth even now," said Mr. Barnstaple. "We use money in the last resort, but a vast volume of our business is already a matter of book-keeping."

Centuries of unity and energy had given Utopia a very complete control of many fountains of natural energy upon the planet, and this was the heritage of every child born therein. He was credited at his birth with a sum sufficient to educate and maintain him up to four- or five-and-twenty, and then he was expected to choose some occupation to replenish his account.

"But if he doesn't?" said Mr. Barnstaple.

"Everyone does."

"But if he didn't?"

"He'd be miserable and uncomfortable. I've never heard of such a case. I suppose he'd be dis-

cussed. Psychologists might examine him. . . .
But one must do something."

"But suppose Utopia had no work for him to do?"

Crystal could not imagine that. "There is always
something to be done."

"But in Utopia once, in the old times, you had
unemployment?"

"That was part of the Confusion. There was a
sort of hypertrophy of debt; it had become paralysis.
Why, when they had unemployment at that same
time there was neither enough houses nor food nor
clothing. They had unemployment and shortage
at one and the same time. It is incredible."

"Does everyone earn about the same amount of
pay?"

"Energetic and creative people are often given big
grants if they seem to need the help of others or a
command of natural resources. . . . And artists
sometimes grow rich if their work is much desired."

"Such a gold chain as yours you had to buy?"

"From the maker in his shop. My mother bought
it."

"Then there are shops?"

"You shall see some. Places where people go to
see new and delightful things."

"And if an artist grows rich, what can he do with
his money?"

"Take time and material to make some surpass-
ingly beautiful thing to leave the world. Or collect
and help with the work of other artists. Or do
whatever else he pleases to teach and fine the common sense of beauty in Utopia. Or just do nothing. . . . Utopia can afford it—if he can."

§ 5

"Cedar and Lion," said Mr. Barnstaple, "explained
to the rest of us how it is that your government is
as it were broken up and dispersed among the people
who have special knowledge of the matters involved.
The balance between interests, we gathered, was
maintained by those who studied the general psychology and the educational organization of Utopia.
At first it was very strange to our earthly minds that
there should be nowhere a pretended omniscience
and a practical omnipotence, that is to say a sov-
ereign thing, a person or an assembly whose *fiat*
was final. Mr. Burleigh and Mr. Catskill thought
that such a thing was absolutely necessary, and so,
less surely, did I. 'Who will decide?' was their
riddle. They expected to be taken to see the President or the Supreme Council of Utopia. I suppose
it seems to you the most natural of things that there
should be nothing of the sort, and that a question
should go simply and naturally to the man who
knows best about it."

"Subject to free criticism," said Crystal.

"Subject to the same process that has made him
eminent and responsible. But don't people thrust
themselves forward even here—out of vanity? And
don't people get thrust forward in front of the best—
out of spite?"

"There is plenty of spite and vanity in every
Utopian soul," said Crystal. "But people speak
very plainly and criticism is very searching and free.
So that we learn to search our motives before we
praise or question."

"What you say and do shows up here plainly at its true value," said Mr. Barnstaple. "You cannot throw mud in the noise and darkness unchallenged or get a false claim acknowledged in the disorder."

"Some years ago there was a man, an artist, who made a great trouble about the work of my father. Often artistic criticism is very bitter here, but he was bitter beyond measure. He caricatured my father and abused him incessantly. He followed him from place to place. He tried to prevent the allocation of material to him. He was quite ineffective. Some people answered him, but for the most part he was disregarded. . . ."

The boy stopped short.

"Well?"

"He killed himself. He could not escape from his own foolishness. Everyone knew what he had said and done. . . ."

"But in the past there were kings and councils and conferences in Utopia," said Mr. Barnstaple, returning to the main point.

"My books teach me that our state could have grown up in no other way. We had to have these general dealers in human relationship, politicians and lawyers, as a necessary stage in political and social development. Just as we had to have soldiers and policemen to save people from mutual violence. It was only very slowly that politicians and lawyers came to admit the need for special knowledge in the things they had to do. Politicians would draw boundaries without any proper knowledge of ethnology or economic geography, and lawyers decide about will and purpose with the crudest knowledge of psychology. They produced the most preposterous and unworkable arrangements in the gravest fashion."

"Like Tristram Shandy's parish bull—which set about begetting the peace of the world at Versailles," said Mr. Barnstaple.

Crystal looked puzzled.

"A complicated allusion to a purely earthly matter," said Mr. Barnstaple. "This complete diffusion of the business of politics and law among the people with knowledge, is one of the most interesting things of all to me in this world. Such a diffusion is beginning upon earth. The people who understand world-health for instance are dead against political and legal methods, and so are many of our best economists. And most people never go into a law court, and wouldn't dream of doing so upon business of their own, from their cradles to their graves. What became of your politicians and lawyers? Was there a struggle?"

"As light grew and intelligence spread they became more and more evidently unnecessary. They met at last only to appoint men of knowledge as assessors and so forth, and after a time even these appointments became foregone conclusions. Their activities melted into the general body of criticism and discussion. In places there are still old buildings that used to be council chambers and law courts. The last politician to be elected to a legislative assembly died in Utopia about a thousand years ago. He was an eccentric and garrulous old gentleman; he was the only candidate and one man voted for him, and he insisted upon assembling in solitary state and having all his speeches and proceedings taken down in shorthand. Boys and girls who were learning stenography used to go to report him. Finally he was dealt with as a mental case."

"And the last judge?"

"I have not learnt about the last judge," said Crystal. "I must ask my tutor. I suppose there was one, but I suppose nobody asked him to judge anything. So he probably got something more respectable to do."

§ 6

"I begin to apprehend the daily life of this world," said Mr. Barnstaple. "It is a life of demi-gods, very free, strongly individualized, each following an individual bent, each contributing to great racial ends. It is not only cleanly naked and sweet and lovely but full of personal dignity. It is, I see, a practical communism, planned and led up to through long centuries of education and discipline and collectivist preparation. I had never thought before that socialism could exalt and ennoble the individual and individualism degrade him, but now I see plainly that here the thing is proved. In this fortunate world—it is indeed the crown of all its health and happiness—there is no Crowd. The old world, the world to which I belong, was and in my universe alas still is, the world of the Crowd, the world of that detestable crawling mass of un-featured, infected human beings.

"You have never seen a Crowd, Crystal; and in all your happy life you never will. You have never

seen a Crowd going to a football match or a race
meeting or a bull-fight or a public execution or the
like crowd joy; you have never watched a Crowd
wedge and stick in a narrow place or hoot or howl
in a crisis. You have never watched it stream slug-
gishly along the streets to gape at a King, or yell for
a war, or yell quite equally for a peace. And you
have never seen the Crowd, struck by some Panic
breeze, change from Crowd proper to Mob and
begin to smash and hunt. All the Crowd celebra-
tions have gone out of this world; all the 'Crowd's
gods, there is no Turf here, no Sport, no war demon-
strations, no Coronations and Public Funerals, no
great shows, but only your little theatres. . . .
Happy Crystal! who will never see a Crowd!"

"But I have seen Crowds," said Crystal.

"Where?"

"I have seen cinematograph films of Crowds,
photographed thirty centuries ago and more. They
are shown in our history museums. I have seen
Crowds streaming over downs after a great race
meeting, photographed from an aeroplane, and
Crowds rioting in some public square and being
dispersed by the police. Thousands and thousands
of swarming people. But it is true what you say.
There are no more Crowds in Utopia. Crowds and
the crowd-mind have gone for ever."

§ 7

When after some days Crystal had to return to
his mathematical studies, his departure left Mr.
Barnstaple very lonely. He found no other com-

panion. Lychnis seemed always near him and ready
to be with him, but her want of active intellectual
interests, so remarkable in this world of vast intellectual activities, estranged him from her. Other
Utopians came and went, friendly, amused, polite,
but intent upon their own business. They would
question him curiously, attend perhaps to a question
or so of his own, and depart with an air of being
called away.

Lychnis, he began to realize, was one of Utopia's
failures. She was a lingering romantic type and
she cherished a great sorrow in her heart. She had
had two children whom she had loved passionately.
They were adorably fearless, and out of foolish
pride she had urged them to swim out to sea and
they had been taken by a current and drowned.
Their father had been drowned in attempting their
rescue and Lychnis had very nearly shared their
fate. She had been rescued. But her emotional
life had stopped short at that point, had, as it were,
struck an attitude and remained in it. Tragedy
possessed her. She turned her back on laughter
and gladness and looked for distress. She had redis-
covered the lost passion of pity, first pity for herself
and then a desire to pity others. She took no interest any more in vigorous and complete people, but
her mind concentrated upon the consolation to be
found in consoling pain and distress in others. She
sought her healing in healing them. She did not
want to talk to Mr. Barnstaple of the brightness of
Utopia; she wanted him to talk to her of the miseries
of earth and of his own miseries. That she might
sympathize. But he would not tell her of his own

miseries because indeed, such was his temperament, he had none; he had only exasperations and regrets.

She dreamt, he perceived, of being able to come to earth and give her beauty and tenderness to the sick and poor. Her heart went out to the spectacle of human suffering and weakness. It went out to these things hungrily and desirously. . . .

Before he detected the drift of her mind he told her many things about human sickness and poverty. But he spoke of these matters not with pity but indignation, as things that ought not to be. And when he perceived how she feasted on these things he spoke of them hardly and cheerfully as things that would presently be swept away. "But they will still have suffered," she said. . . .

Since she was always close at hand, she filled for him perhaps more than her legitimate space in the Utopian spectacle. She lay across it like a shadow. He thought very frequently about her and about the pity and resentment against life and vigour that she embodied. In a world of fear, weakness, infection, darkness and confusion, pity, the act of charity, the alms and the refuge, the deed of stark devotion, might show indeed like sweet and gracious presences; but in this world of health and brave enterprises, pity betrayed itself a vicious desire. Crystal, Utopian youth, was as hard as his name. When he had slipped one day on some rocks and twisted and torn his ankle, he had limped but he had laughed. When Mr. Barnstaple was winded on a steep staircase Crystal was polite rather than sympathetic. So Lychnis had found no confederate in the dedication of her life to sorrow; even from Mr. Barnstaple

she could win no sympathy. He perceived that
indeed so far as temperament went he was a better
Utopian than she was. To him as to Utopia it
seemed rather an occasion for gladness than sorrow
that her man and her children had met death fear-
lessly. They were dead; a brave stark death; the
waters still glittered and the sun still shone. But
her loss had revealed some underlying racial taint in
her, something very ancient in the species, something
that Utopia was still breeding out only very slowly,
the dark sacrificial disposition that bows and re-
sponds to the shadow. It was strange and yet perhaps it was inevitable that Mr. Barnstaple should
meet again in Utopia that spirit which Earth knows
so well, the spirit that turns from the Kingdom of
Heaven to worship the thorns and the nails, which
delights to represent its God not as the Resurrection
and the Life but as a woeful and defeated cadaver.

She would talk to him of his sons as if she envied
him because of the loss of her own, but all she said
reminded him of the educational disadvantages and
narrow prospects of his boys and how much stouter
and finer and happier their lives would have been in
Utopia. He would have risked drowning them a
dozen times to have saved them from being clerks
and employees of other men. Even by earthly
standards he felt now that he had not done his best
by them; he had let many things drift in their lives
and in the lives of himself and his wife that he now
felt he ought to have controlled. Could he have
his time over again he felt that he would see to it
that his sons took a livelier interest in politics and
science and were not so completely engulfed in the

trivialities of suburban life, in tennis playing, amateur theatricals, inane flirtations and the like. They were good boys in substance he felt, but he had left them to their mother; and he had left their mother too much to herself instead of battling with her for the sake of his own ideas. They were living trivially in the shadow of one great catastrophe and with no security against another; they were living in a world of weak waste and shabby insufficiency. And his own life also had been—weak waste.

His life at Sydenham began to haunt him. "I criticized everything but I altered nothing," he said. "I was as bad as Peeve. Was I any more use in that world than I am in this? But on Earth we are all wasters. . . ."

He avoided Lychnis for a day or so and wandered about the valley alone. He went into a great reading-room and fingered books he could not read; he was suffered to stand in a workshop, and he watched an artist make a naked girl of gold more lovely than any earthly statuette and melt her again dissatisfied; here he came upon men building, and here was work upon the fields, here was a great shaft in the hillside and something deep in the hill that flashed and scintillated strangely; they would not let him go in to it; he saw a thousand things he could not understand. He began to feel as perhaps a very intelligent dog must sometimes feel in the world of men, only that he had no master and no instincts that could find a consolation in canine abjection. The Utopians went about their business in the day-time, they passed him smiling and they filled him with intolerable envy. They knew what to do. They belonged. They went by in twos and threes in the evening, communing together and sometimes singing together. Lovers would pass him, their sweetly smiling faces close together, and his loneliness became an agony of hopeless desires.

Because, though he fought hard to keep it below the threshold of his consciousness, Mr. Barnstaple desired greatly to love and be loved in Utopia. The realization that no one of these people could ever conceive of any such intimacy of body or spirit with him was a humiliation more fundamental even than his uselessness. The loveliness of the Utopian girls and women who glanced at him curiously or passed him with a serene indifference, crushed down his self-respect and made the Utopian world altogether intolerable to him. Mutely, unconsciously, these Utopian goddesses concentrated upon him the uttermost abasement of caste and race inferiority. He could not keep his thoughts from love where everyone it seemed had a lover, and in this Utopian world love for him was a thing grotesque and inconceivable. . . .

Then one night as he lay awake distressed beyond measure by the thought of such things, an idea came to him whereby it seemed to him he might restore his self-respect and win a sort of citizenship in Utopia.

So that they might even speak of him and remember him with interest and sympathy.

CHAPTER THE THIRD

THE SERVICE OF THE EARTHLING

§ 1

The man to whom Mr. Barnstaple, after due inquiries, went to talk was named Sungold. He was probably very old, because there were lines of age about his eyes and over his fine brow. He was a ruddy man, bearded with an auburn beard that had streaks of white, and his eyes were brown and nimble under his thick eyebrows. His hair had thinned but little and flowed back like a mane, but its copper-red colour had gone. He sat at a table with papers spread before him, making manuscript notes. He smiled at Mr. Barnstaple, for he had been expecting him, and indicated a seat for him with his stout and freckled hand. Then he waited smilingly for Mr. Barnstaple to begin.

"This world is one triumph of the desire for order and beauty in men's minds," said Mr. Barnstaple. "But it will not tolerate one useless soul in it. Everyone is happily active. Everyone but myself. . . . I belong nowhere. I have nothing to do. And no one—is related to me."

Sungold moved his head slightly to show that he understood.

"It is hard for an Earthling, with an earthly want of training, to fall into any place here. Into any

usual work or any usual relationship. One is—a
stranger. . . . But it is still harder to have no
place at all. In the new work, of which I am told
you know most of anyone and are indeed the centre
and regulator, it has occurred to me that I might be
of some use, that I might indeed be as good as a
Utopian. . . . If so, I want to be of use. You
may want someone just to risk death—to take the
danger of going into some strange place—someone
who desires to serve Utopia—and who need not have
skill or knowledge—or be a beautiful or able
person?"

Mr. Barnstaple stopped short.

Sungold conveyed the completest understanding
of all that was in Mr. Barnstaple's mind.

Mr. Barnstaple sat interrogative while for a time
Sungold thought.

Then words and phrases began to string themselves together in Mr. Barnstaple's mind.

Sungold wondered if Mr. Barnstaple understood
either the extent or the limitations of the great
discoveries that were now being made in Utopia.
Utopia, he said, was passing into a phase of intense
intellectual exaltation. New powers and possibilities intoxicated the imagination of the race, and it
was indeed inconceivable that an unteachable and
perplexed Earthling could be anything but distressed
and uncomfortable amidst the vast strange activities
that must now begin. Even many of their own
people, the more backward Utopians, were disturbed.
For centuries Utopian philosophers and experimentalists had been criticizing, revising and reconstruct-
ing their former instinctive and traditional ideas of

space and time, of form and substance, and now very
rapidly the new ways of thinking were becoming
clear and simple and bearing fruit in surprising
practical applications. The limitations of space
which had seemed for ever insurmountable were
breaking down; they were breaking down in a
strange and perplexing way but they were breaking
down. It was now theoretically possible, it was
rapidly becoming practically possible, to pass from
the planet Utopia to which the race had hitherto
been confined, to other points in its universe of
origin, that is to say to remote planets and distant
stars. . . . That was the gist of the present situation.

"I cannot imagine that," said Mr. Barnstaple.

"You cannot imagine it," Sungold agreed, quite
cordially. "But it is so. A hundred years ago it
was inconceivable—here."

"Do you get there by some sort of backstairs in
another dimension?" said Mr. Barnstaple.

Sungold considered this guess. It was a grotesque
image, he said, but from the point of view of an
Earthling it would serve. That conveyed something
of its quality. But it was so much more wonderful. . . .

"A new and astounding phase has begun for life
here. We learnt long ago the chief secrets of happiness upon this planet. Life is good in this world.
You find it good? . . . For thousands of years yet
it will be our fastness and our home. But the wind
of a new adventure blows through our life. All this
world is in a mood like striking camp in the winter
quarters when spring approaches."

He leant over his papers towards Mr. Barnstaple,
and held up a finger and spoke audible words as if to
make his meaning plainer. It seemed to Mr. Barnstaple that each word translated itself into English
as he spoke it. At any rate Mr. Barnstaple understood. "The collision of our planet Utopia with
your planet Earth was a very curious accident, but
an unimportant accident, in this story. I want you
to understand that. Your universe and ours are
two out of a great number of gravitation-time
universes, which are translated together through the
inexhaustible infinitude of God. They are similar
throughout, but they are identical in nothing. Your
planet and ours happen to be side by side, so to
speak, but they are not traveling at exactly the same
pace nor in a strictly parallel direction. They will
drift apart again and follow their several destinies.
When Arden and Greenlake made their experiment
the chances of their hitting anything in your universe were infinitely remote. They had disregarded
it, they were merely rotating some of our matter
out of and then back into our universe. You fell
into us—as amazingly for us as for you. The importance of our discoveries for us lies in our own
universe and not in yours. We do not want to
come into your universe nor have more of your
world come into ours. You are too like us, and
you are too dark and troubled and diseased—you
are too contagious—and we, we cannot help you
yet because we are not gods but men."

Mr. Barnstaple nodded.

"What could Utopians do with the men of Earth?
We have no strong instinct in us to teach or domi-

nate other adults. That has been bred out of us by long centuries of equality and free co-operation. And you would be too numerous for us to teach and much of your population would be grown up and set in bad habits. Your stupidities would get in our way, your quarrels and jealousies and traditions, your flags and religions and all your embodied spites and suppressions, would hamper us in everything we should want to do. We should be impatient with you, unjust, overbearing. You are too like us for us to be patient with your failures. It would be hard to remember constantly how ill-bred you were. In Utopia we found out long ago that no race of human beings was sufficiently great, subtle and powerful to think and act for any other race. Perhaps already you are finding out the same thing on Earth as your races come into closer contact. And much more would this be true between Utopia and Earth. From what I know of your people and their ignorance and obstinacies it is clear our people would despise you; and contempt is the cause of all injustice. We might end by exterminating you. . . . But why should we make that possible? . . . We must leave you alone. We cannot trust ourselves with you. . . . Believe me this is the only reasonable course for us."

Mr. Barnstaple assented silently.

"You and I—two individuals—can be friends and understand."

"What you say is true," said Mr. Barnstaple. "It is true. But it grieves me it is true. . . . Greatly. . . . Nevertheless, I gather, I at least may be of service in Utopia?"

"You can."

"How?"

"By returning to your own world."

Mr. Barnstaple thought for some moments. It was what he had feared. But he had offered himself. "I will do that."

"By attempting to return, I should say. There is risk. You may be killed."

"I must take that."

"We want to verify all the data we have of the relations of our universe to yours. We want to reverse the experiment of Arden and Greenlake and see if we can return a living being to your world. We are almost certain now that we can do so. And that human being must care for us enough and care for his own world enough to go back and give us a sign that he has got there."

Mr. Barnstaple spoke huskily. "I can do that," he said.

"We can put you into that machine of yours and into the clothes you wore. You can be made again exactly as you left your world."

"Exactly. I understand."

"And because your world is vile and contentious and yet has some strangely able brains in it, here and there, we do not want your people to know of us, living so close to you—for we shall be close to you yet for some hundreds of years at least—we do not want them to know for fear that they should come here presently, led by some poor silly genius of a scientific man, come in their greedy, foolish, breeding swarms, hammering at our doors, threatening our lives, and spoiling our high adventures, and so have to be beaten off and killed like an invasion of rats or parasites."

"Yes," said Mr. Barnstaple. "Before men can come to Utopia, they must learn the way here. Utopia, I see, is only a home for those who have learnt the way."

He paused and answered some of his own thoughts. "When I have returned," he said, "shall I begin to forget Utopia?"

Sungold smiled and said nothing.

"All my days the nostalgia of Utopia will distress me."

"And uphold you."

"I shall take up my earthly life at the point where I laid it down, but—on Earth—I shall be a Utopian. For I feel that having offered my service and had it accepted, that I am no longer an outcast in Utopia. I belong. . . ."

"Remember you may be killed. You may die in the trial."

"As it may happen."

"Well—Brother!"

The friendly paw took Mr. Barnstaple's and pressed it and the deep eyes smiled.

"After you have returned and given us your sign, several of the other Earthlings may also be sent back."

Mr. Barnstaple sat up. *"But!"* he gasped. His voice rose high in amazement. "I thought they were hurled into the blank space of some outer universe and altogether destroyed!"

"Several were killed. They killed themselves by rushing down the side of the old fortress in the outer

darkness as the Crag rotated.   The men in leather.
The man you call Long Barrow——"

"Barralonga?"

"Yes.   And the man who shrugged his shoulders
and said, 'What would you?'   The others came back
as the rotation was completed late in the day—
asphyxiated and frozen but not dead.   They have
been restored to life, and we are puzzled now how
to dispose of them. .|. . They are of no use what-
ever in this world.   They encumber us."

"It is only too manifest," said Mr. Barnstaple.

"The man you call Burleigh seems to be of some
importance in your earthly affairs.   We have
searched his mind.   His powers of belief are very
small.   He believes in very little but the life of a
cultivated wealthy gentleman who holds a position
of modest distinction in the councils of a largely
fictitious empire.   It is doubtful if he will believe
in the reality of any of this experience.   We will
make sure anyhow that he thinks it has been an
imaginative dream.   He will consider it too fantastic to talk about because it is plain he is already
very afraid of his imagination.   He will find himself
back in your world a few days after you reach it
and he will make his way to his own home unobtrusively.   He will come next after you.   You will see
him reappear in political affairs.   Perhaps a little
wiser."

"It might well be," said Mr. Barnstaple.

"And—what are the sounds of his name?—Rupert
Catskill; he too will return.   Your world would
miss him."

"Nothing will make *him* wiser," said Mr. Barnstaple with conviction.

"Lady Stella will come."

"I am glad she has escaped. She will say nothing about Utopia. She is very discreet."

"The priest is mad. His behaviour became offensive and obscene and he is under restraint."

"What did he do?"

"He made a number of aprons of black silk and set out with them to attack our young people in an undignified manner."

"You can send him back," said Mr. Barnstaple after reflection.

"But will your world allow that sort of thing?"

"*We* call that sort of thing Purity," said Mr. Barnstaple. "But of course if you like to keep him. . . ."

"He shall come back," said Sungold.

"The others you can keep," said Mr. Barnstaple. "In fact you will have to keep them. Nobody on Earth will trouble about them very much. In our world there are so many people that always a few are getting lost. As it is, returning even the few you propose to do may excite attention. Local people may begin to notice all these wanderers coming from nowhere in particular and asking their way home upon the Maidenhead Road. They might give way under questions. . . . You cannot send any more. Put the rest on an island. Or something of that sort. I wish I could advise you to keep the priest also. But many people would miss him. They would suffer from suppressed Purity and begin to behave queerly. The pulpit of St. Barnabas satisfies a recognized craving. And it will be quite

easy to persuade him that Utopia is a dream and
delusion. All priests believe that naturally of all
Utopias. He will think of it, if he thinks of it at all,
as—what would he call it?—as a moral nightmare."

§ 2

Their business was finished, but Mr. Barnstaple
was loth to go.

He looked Sungold in the eye and found something kindly there.

"You have told me all that I have to do," he said,
"and it is fully time that I went away from you, for
any moment in your life is more precious than a day
of mine. Yet because I am to go so soon and so
obediently out of this vast and splendid world of
yours back to my native disorders, I could find it in
my heart to ask you to unbend if you could, to come
down to me a little, and to tell me simply and
plainly of the greater days and greater achievements
that are now dawning upon this planet. You speak
of your being able presently to go out of this Utopia
to remote parts in your universe. That perplexes
my mind. Probably I am unfitted to grasp that
idea, but it is very important to me. It has been a
belief in our world that at last there must be an end
to life because our sun and planets are cooling, and
there seems no hope of escape from the little world
upon which we have arisen. We were born with
it and we must die with it. That robbed many of
us of hope and energy: for why should we work for
progress in a world that must freeze and die?"

Sungold laughed. "Your philosophers concluded too soon."

He sprawled over the table towards his hearer and looked him earnestly in the face.

"Your earthly science has been going on for how long?"

"Two hundred—three hundred years."

Sungold held up two fingers. "And men? How many men?"

"A few hundred who mattered in each generation."

"We have gone on for three thousand years now, and a hundred million good brains have been put like grapes into the wine-press of science. And we know today—how little we know. There is never an observation made but a hundred observations are missed in the making of it; there is never a measurement but some impish truth mocks us and gets away from us in the margin of error. I know something of where your scientific men are, all power to the poor savages! because I have studied the beginnings of our own science in the long past of Utopia. How can I express our distances? Since those days we have examined and tested and tried and retried a score of new ways of thinking about space, of which time is only a specialized form. We have forms of expression that we cannot get over to you so that things that used to seem difficult and paradoxical to us—that probably seem hopelessly difficult and paradoxical to you, lose all their difficulty in our minds. It is hard to convey to you. We think in terms of a space in which the space and time system, in terms of which you think, is only a specialized case. So far as our feelings and instincts and daily habits go we too live in another such system as you do—but not so far as our knowledge goes, not so far as our powers go. Our minds have exceeded our lives—as yours will. We are still flesh and blood, still hope and desire, we go to and fro and look up and down, but things that seemed remote are brought near, things that were inaccessible bow down, things that were insurmountable lie under the hollows of our hands."

"And you do not think your race nor, for the matter of that, ours, need ever perish?"

"Perish! We have hardly begun!"

The old man spoke very earnestly. Unconsciously he parodied Newton. "We are like little children who have been brought to the shores of a limitless ocean. All the knowledge we have gathered yet in the few score generations since first we began to gather knowledge, is like a small handful of pebbles gathered upon the shore of that limitless sea.

"Before us lies knowledge, endlessly, and we may take and take, and as we take, grow. We grow in power, we grow in courage. We renew our youth. For mark what I say, our worlds grow younger. The old generations of apes and sub-men before us had aged minds; their narrow reluctant wisdom was the meagre profit, hoarded and stale and sour, of innumerable lives. They dreaded new things; so bitterly did they value the bitterly won old. But to learn is, at length, to become young again, to be released, to begin afresh. Your world, compared with ours, is a world of unteachable encrusted souls,

of bent and droning traditions, of hates and injuries
and such-like unforgettable things. But some day
you too will become again like little children, and
it will be you who will find your way through to
us—to us, who will be waiting for you. Two universes will meet and embrace, to beget a yet greater
universe. . . . You Earthlings do not begin to
realize yet the significance of life. Nor we Utopians
—scarcely more. . . . Life is still only a promise,
still waits to be born, out of such poor stirrings in
the dust as we. . . .

"Some day here and everywhere, Life of which
you and I are but anticipatory atoms and eddies,
Life will awaken indeed, one and whole and marvellous, like a child awaking to conscious life. It will
open its drowsy eyes and stretch itself and smile,
looking the mystery of God in the face as one meets
the morning sun. We shall be there then, all that
matters of us, you and I. . . .

"And it will be no more than a beginning, no more
than a beginning. . . ."

CHAPTER THE FOURTH

THE RETURN OF THE EARTHLING

§ 1

Too soon the morning came when Mr. Barnstaple was to look his last upon the fair hills of Utopia and face the great experiment to which he had given himself. He had been loth to sleep and he had slept little that night, and in the early dawn he was abroad, wearing for the last time the sandals and the light white robe that had become his Utopian costume. Presently he would have to struggle into socks and boots and trousers and collar; the strangest gear. It would choke him he felt, and he stretched his bare arms to the sky and yawned and breathed his lungs full. The valley below still drowsed beneath a coverlet of fleecy mists; he turned his face uphill, the sooner to meet the sun.

Never before had he been out among the Utopian flowers at such an early hour; it was amusing to see how some of the great trumpets still drooped asleep and how many of the larger blossoms were furled and hung. Many of the leaves too were wrapped up, as limp as new-hatched moths. The gossamer spiders had been busy and everything was very wet with dew. A great tiger came upon him suddenly

out of a side path and stared hard at him for some
moments with round yellow eyes. Perhaps it was
trying to remember the forgotten instincts of its
breed.

Some way up the road he passed under a vermil-
ion archway and went up a flight of stone stairs
that promised to bring him earlier to the crest.

A number of friendly little birds, very gaily
coloured, flew about him for a time and one perched
impudently upon his shoulder, but when he put up
his hand to caress it it evaded him and flew away.
He was still ascending the staircase when the sun
rose. It was as if the hillside slipped off a veil of
grey and blue and bared the golden beauty of its
body.

Mr. Barnstaple came to a landing place upon the
staircase and stopped, and stood very still watching
the sunrise search and quicken the brooding deeps
of the valley below.

Far away, like an arrow shot from east to west,
appeared a line of dazzling brightness on the sea.

§ 2

"Serenity," he murmured. "Beauty. All the
works of men—in perfect harmony . . . minds
brought to harmony. . . ."

According to his journalistic habit he tried over
phrases. "An energetic peace . . . confusions dispersed. . . . A world of spirits, crystal clear. . . ."

What was the use of words?

For a time he stood quite still listening, for from
some slope above a lark had gone heavenward,

spraying sweet notes. He tried to see that little speck of song and was blinded by the brightening blue of the sky.

Presently the lark came down and ceased. Utopia was silent, except for a burst of childish laughter somewhere on the hillside below.

It dawned upon Mr. Barnstaple how peaceful was the Utopian air in comparison with the tormented atmosphere of Earth. Here was no yelping and howling of tired or irritated dogs, no braying, bellowing, squealing and distressful outcries of uneasy beasts, no farmyard clamour, no shouts of anger, no barking and coughing, no sounds of hammering, beating, sawing, grinding, mechanical hooting, whistling, screaming and the like, no clattering of distant trains, clanking of automobiles or other ill-contrived mechanisms; the tiresome and ugly noises of many an unpleasant creature were heard no more. In Utopia the ear like the eye was at peace. The air which had once been a mud of felted noises was now—a purified silence. Such sounds as one heard lay upon it like beautiful printing on a generous sheet of fine paper.

His eyes returned to the landscape below as the last fleecy vestiges of mist dissolved away. Water-tanks, roads, bridges, buildings, embankments, colonnades, groves, gardens, channels, cascades and fountains grew multitudinously clear, framed under a branch of dark foliage from a white-stemmed tree that gripped a hold among the rocks at his side.

"Three thousand years ago this was a world like ours. . . . Think of it—in a hundred generations. . . . In three thousand years we might make our

poor waste of an Earth, jungle and desert, slag-heap
and slum, into another such heaven of beauty and
power. . . .

"Worlds they are—similar, but not the same. . . .

"If I could tell them what I have seen! . . .

"Suppose all men could have this vision of
Utopia. . . .

"They would not believe it if I told them.
No. . . .

"They would bray like asses at me and bark like
dogs! . . . They will have no world but their own
world. It hurts them to think of any world but
their own. Nothing can be done that has not been
done already. To think otherwise would be humiliation. . . . Death, torture, futility—anything but
humiliation! So they must sit among their weeds
and excrement, scratching and nodding sagely at
one another, hoping for a good dog-fight and to gloat
upon pain and effort they do not share, sure that
mankind stank, stinks and must always stink, that
stinking is very pleasant indeed, and that there is
nothing new under the sun. . . ."

His thoughts were diverted by two young girls
who came running one after the other up the staircase. One was dark even to duskiness and her hands
were full of blue flowers; the other who pursued her
was a year or so younger and golden fair. They
were full of the limitless excitement of young
animals at play. The former one was so intent
upon the other that she discovered Mr. Barnstaple
with a squeak of surprise after she had got to his
landing. She stared at him with a quick glance
of inquiry, flashed into impudent roguery, flung

two blue flowers in his face and was off up the steps
above. Her companion, intent on capture, flew by.
They flickered up the staircase like two butterflies
of buff and pink; halted far above and came together
for a momentary consultation about the stranger,
waved hands to him and vanished.

Mr. Barnstaple returned their greeting and remained cheered.

§ 3

The view-point to which Lychnis had directed
Mr. Barnstaple stood out on the ridge between the
great valley in which he had spent the last few days
and a wild and steep glen down which ran a torrent
that was destined after some hundred miles of wind-
ings to reach the river of the plain. The view-point
was on the crest of a crag, it had been built out
upon great brackets so that it hung sheer over a
bend in the torrent below; on the one hand was
mountainous scenery and a rich and picturesque
foam of green vegetation in the depths, on the other
spread the broad garden spaces of a perfected landscape. For a time Mr. Barnstaple scrutinized this
glen into which he looked for the first time. Five
hundred feet or so below him, so that he felt that
he could have dropped a pebble upon its outstretched wings, a bustard was soaring.

Many of the trees below he thought must be fruit
trees, but they were too far off to see distinctly.
Here and there he could distinguish a footpath
winding up among the trees and rocks, and among

the green masses were little pavilions in which he knew the wayfarer might rest and make tea for himself and find biscuits and such-like refreshment and possibly a couch and a book. The whole world, he knew, was full of such summer-houses and kindly shelters. . . .

After a time he went back to the side of this view-place up which he had come, and regarded the great valley that went out towards the sea. The word Pisgah floated through his mind. For indeed below him was the Promised Land of human desires. Here at last, established and secure, were peace, power, health, happy activity, length of days and beauty. All that we seek was found here and every dream was realized.

How long would it be yet—how many centuries or thousands of years—before a man would be able to stand upon some high place on earth also and see mankind triumphant and wholly and for ever at peace? . . .

He folded his arms under him upon the parapet and mused profoundly.

There was no knowledge in this Utopia of which Earth had not the germs, there was no power used here that Earthlings might not use. Here, but for ignorance and darkness and the spites and malice they permit, was Earth to-day. . . .

Towards such a world as this Utopia Mr. Barnstaple had been striving weakly all his life. If the experiment before him succeeded, if presently he found himself alive again on Earth, it would still be towards Utopia that his life would be directed. And he would not be alone. On Earth there must

be thousands, tens of thousands, perhaps hundreds
of thousands, who were also struggling in their
minds and acts to find a way of escape for themselves and for their children from the disorders and
indignities of the Age of Confusion, hundreds of
thousands who wanted to put an end to wars and
waste, to heal and educate and restore, to set up
the banner of Utopia over the shams and divisions
that waste mankind.

"Yes, but we fail," said Mr. Barnstaple and
walked fretfully to and fro. "Tens and hundreds
of thousands of men and women! And we achieve
so little! Perhaps every young man and every
young woman has had some dream at least of serving
and bettering the world. And we are scattered and
wasted, and the old things and the foul things,
customs, delusions, habits, tolerated treasons, base
immediacies, triumph over us!"

He went to the parapet again and stood with his
foot on a seat, his elbow on his knee and his chin in
his hand, staring at the loveliness of this world he
was to leave so soon. . . .

"We could do it."

And suddenly it was borne in upon Mr. Barnstaple
that he belonged now soul and body to the Revolution, to the Great Revolution that is afoot on Earth;
that marches and will never desist nor rest again
until old Earth is one city and Utopia set up therein.
He knew clearly that this Revolution is life, and
that all other living is a trafficking of life with death.
And as this crystallized out in his mind he knew
instantly that so presently it would crystallize out
in the minds of countless others of those hundreds

of thousands of men and women on Earth whose
minds are set towards Utopia.

He stood up. He began walking to and fro.
"We shall do it," he said.

Earthly thought was barely awakened as yet to
the task and possibilities before mankind. All human history so far had been no more than the stir-
ring of a sleeper, a gathering discontent, a rebellion
against the limitations set upon life, the unintelligent protest of thwarted imaginations. All the
conflicts and insurrections and revolutions that had
ever been on Earth were but indistinct preludes
of the revolution that has still to come. When he
had started out upon this fantastic holiday Mr.
Barnstaple realized he had been in a mood of depression; earthly affairs had seemed utterly confused
and hopeless to him; but now from the view-point
of Utopia achieved, and with his health renewed,
he could see plainly enough how steadily men on
earth were feeling their way now, failure after
failure, towards the opening drive of the final revolution. He could see how men in his own lifetime
had been struggling out of such entanglements as
the lie of monarchy, the lies of dogmatic religion
and dogmatic morality towards public self-respect
and cleanness of mind and body. They struggled
now also towards international charity and the
liberation of their common economic life from a
network of pretences, dishonesties and impostures.
There is confusion in all struggles; retractions and
defeats; but the whole effect seen from the calm
height of Utopia was one of steadfast advance. . . .

There were blunders, there were set-backs, because the forces of revolution still worked in the twilight. The great effort and the great failure of the socialist movement to create a new state in the world had been contemporaneous with Mr. Barn-staple's life; socialism had been the gospel of his boyhood; he had participated in its hopes, its doubts, its bitter internal conflicts. He had seen the movement losing sweetness and gathering force in the narrowness of the Marxist formulæ. He had seen it sacrifice its constructive power for militant intensity. In Russia he had marked its ability to overthrow and its inability to plan or build. Like every liberal spirit in the world he had shared the chill of Bolshevik presumption and Bolshevik failure, and for a time it had seemed to him that this open bankruptcy of a great creative impulse was no less and no more than a victory for reaction, that it gave renewed life to all the shams, impostures, corruptions, traditional anarchies and ascendencies that restrain and cripple human life. . . . But now from this high view-point in Utopia he saw clearly that the Phœnix of Revolution flames down to ashes only to be born again. While the noose is fitted round the Teacher's neck the youths are reading his teaching; Revolutions arise and die; the Great Revolution comes—incessantly and inevitably.

The time was near—and in what life was left to him, he himself might help to bring it nearer—when the forces of that last and real revolution would work no longer in the twilight but in the dawn, and a thousand sorts of men and women now far apart and unorganized and mutually antagonistic would be drawn together by the growth of a common vision of the world desired. The Marxist had wasted the forces of revolution for fifty years; he had had no vision; he had had only a condemnation for established things. He had estranged all scientific and able men by his pompous affectation of the scientific; he had terrified them by his intolerant orthodoxy; his delusion that all ideas are begotten by material circumstances had made him negligent of education and criticism. He had attempted to build social unity on hate and rejected every other driving force for the bitterness of a class war. But now, in its days of doubt and exhaustion, vision was returning to Socialism, and the dreary spectacle of a proletarian dictatorship gave way once more to Utopia, to the demand for a world fairly and righteously at peace, its resources husbanded and exploited for the common good, its every citizen freed not only from servitude but from ignorance, and its surplus energies directed steadfastly to the increase of knowledge and beauty. The attainment of that vision by more and more minds was a thing now no longer to be prevented. Earth would tread the path Utopia had trod. She too would weave law, duty and education into a larger sanity than man has ever known. Men also would presently laugh at the things they had feared, and brush aside the impostures that had overawed them and the absurdities that had tormented and crippled their lives. And as this great revolution was achieved and earth wheeled into daylight, the burthen of human miseries would lift, and courage oust sorrow from the hearts of men. Earth, which was now no more

than a wilderness, sometimes horrible and at best
picturesque, a wilderness interspersed with weedy
scratchings for food and with hovels and slums and
slag-heaps, Earth too would grow rich with loveliness and fair as this great land was fair. The sons
of Earth also, purified from disease, sweet-minded
and strong and beautiful, would go proudly about
their conquered planet and lift their daring to the
stars.

"Given the will," said Mr. Barnstaple. "Given
only the will." . . .

§ 4

From some distant place came the sound of a
sweet-toned bell striking the hour.

The time for the service to which he was dedicated
was drawing near. He must descend, and be taken
to the place where the experiment was to be made.

He took one last look at the glen and then went
back to the broad prospect of the great valley, with
its lakes and tanks and terraces, its groves and
pavilions, its busy buildings and high viaducts, its
wide slopes of sunlit cultivation, its universal
gracious amenity. "Farewell, Utopia," he said, and
was astonished to discover how deeply his emotions
were stirred.

"Dear Dream of Hope and Loveliness, Farewell!"

He stood quite still in a mood of sorrowful
deprivation too deep for tears.

It seemed to him that the spirit of Utopia bent
down over him like a goddess, friendly, adorable—
and inaccessible.

His very mind stood still.

"Never," he whispered at last, "for me. . . . Except to serve. . . . No. . . ."

Presently he began to descend the steps that wound down from the view-point. For a time he noted little of the things immediately about him. Then the scent of roses invaded his attention, and he found himself walking down a slanting pergola covered with great white roses and very active with little green birds. He stopped short and stood looking up at the leaves, light-saturated, against the sky. He put up his hands and drew down one of the great blossoms until it touched his cheek.

§ 5

They took Mr. Barnstaple back by aeroplane to the point upon the glassy road where he had first come into Utopia. Lychnis came with him and Crystal, who was curious to see what would be done.

A group of twenty or thirty people, including Sungold, awaited him. The ruined laboratory of Arden and Greenlake had been replaced by fresh buildings, and there were additional erections on the further side of the road; but Mr. Barnstaple could recognize quite clearly the place where Mr. Catskill had faced the leopard and where Mr. Burleigh had accosted him. Several new kinds of flowers were now out, but the blue blossoms that had charmed him on arrival still prevailed. His old car, the Yellow Peril, looking now the clumsiest piece of ironmongery conceivable, stood in the road. He went and examined it. It seemed to be in per-

fect order; it had been carefully oiled and the petrol
tank was full.

In a little pavilion were his bag and all his earthly
clothes. They were very clean and they had been
folded and pressed, and he put them on. His shirt
seemed tight across his chest and his collar decidedly
tight, and his coat cut him a little under the arms.
Perhaps these garments had shrunken when they
were disinfected. He packed his bag and Crystal
put it in the car for him.

Sungold explained very simply all that Mr. Barnstaple had to do. Across the road, close by the
restored laboratory, stretched a line as thin as gossamer. "Steer your car to that and break it," he
said. "That is all you have to do. Then take this
red flower and put it down exactly where your wheel
tracks show you have entered your own world."

Mr. Barnstaple was left beside the car. The
Utopians went back twenty or thirty yards and
stood in a circle about him. For a few moments
everyone was still.

§ 6

Mr. Barnstaple got into his car, started his engine,
let it throb for a minute and then put in the clutch.
The yellow car began to move towards the line of
gossamer. He made a gesture with one hand which
Lychnis answered. Sungold and others of the Utopians also made friendly movements. But Crystal
was watching too intently for any gesture.

"Good-bye, Crystal!" cried Mr. Barnstaple, and
the boy responded with a start.

Mr. Barnstaple accelerated, set his teeth and, in spite of his will to keep them open, shut his eyes as he touched the gossamer line. Came that sense again of unendurable tension and that sound like the snapping of a bow-string. He had an irresistible impulse to stop—go back. He took his foot from the accelerator, and the car seemed to fall a foot or so and stopped so heavily and suddenly that he was jerked forward against the steering wheel. The oppression lifted. He opened his eyes and looked about him.

The car was standing in a field from which the hay had recently been carried. He was tilted on one side because of a roll in the ground. A hedge in which there was an open black gate separated this hay-field from the high road. Close at hand was a board advertisement of some Maidenhead hotel. On the far side of the road were level fields against a background of low wooded hills. Away to the left was a little inn. He turned his head and saw Windsor Castle in the remote distance rising above poplar-studded meadows. It was not, as his Utopians had promised him, the exact spot of his departure from our Earth, but it was certainly less than a hundred yards away.

He sat still for some moments, mentally rehearsing what he had to do. Then he started the Yellow Peril again and drove it close up to the black gate.

He got out and stood with the red flower in his hand. He had to go back to the exact spot at which he had re-entered this universe and put that flower down there. It would be quite easy to determine that point by the track the car had made in the stubble. But he felt an extraordinary reluctance to obey these instructions. He wanted to keep this flower. It was the last thing, the only thing, he had now from that golden world. That and the sweet savour on his hands.

It was extraordinary that he had brought no more than this with him. Why had he not brought a lot of flowers? Why had they given him nothing, no little thing, out of all their wealth of beauty? He wanted intensely to keep this flower. He was moved to substitute a spray of honeysuckle from the hedge close at hand. But then he remembered that that would be infected stuff for them. He must do as he was told. He walked back along the track of his car to its beginning, stood for a moment hesitating, tore a single petal from that glowing bloom, and then laid down the rest of the great flower carefully in the very centre of his track. The petal he put in his pocket. Then with a heavy heart he went back slowly to his car and stood beside it, watching that star of almost luminous red.

His grief and emotion were very great. He was bitterly sorrowful now at having left Utopia.

It was evident the great drought was still going on, for the field and the hedges were more parched and brown than he had ever seen an English field before. Along the road lay a thin cloud of dust that passing cars continually renewed. This old world seemed to him to be full of unlovely sights and sounds and odours already half forgotten. There was the honking of distant cars, the uproar of a train, a thirsty cow mourning its discomfort; there was the irritation of dust in his nostrils and

the smell of sweltering tar; there was barbed wire
in the hedge near by and along the top of the black
gate, and horse-dung and scraps of dirty paper at
his feet. The lovely world from which he had been
driven had shrunken now to a spot of shining scarlet.

Something happened very quickly. It was as if
a hand appeared for a moment and took the flower.
In a moment it had gone. A little eddy of dust
swirled and drifted and sank. . . .

It was the end.

At the thought of the traffic on the main road
Mr. Barnstaple stooped down so as to hide his face
from the passers-by. For some minutes he was
unable to regain his self-control. He stood with
his arm covering his face, leaning against the shabby
brown hood of his car. . . .

At last this gust of sorrow came to an end and he
could get in again, start up the engine and steer into
the main road.

He turned eastward haphazard. He left the black
gate open behind him. He went along very slowly
for as yet he had formed no idea of whither he was
going. He began to think that probably in this old
world of ours he was being sought for as a person
who had mysteriously disappeared. Someone might
discover him and he would become the focus of a
thousand impossible questions. That would be very
tiresome and disagreeable. He had not thought of
this in Utopia. In Utopia it had seemed quite possible that he could come back into Earth unob-
served. Now on earth that confidence seemed
foolish. He saw ahead of him the board of a
modest tea-room. It occurred that he might alight

there, see a newspaper, ask a discreet question or so, and find out what had been happening to the world and whether he had indeed been missed.

He found a table already laid for tea under the window. In the centre of the room a larger table bore an aspidistra in a big green pot and a selection of papers, chiefly out-of-date illustrated papers. But there was also a copy of the morning's *Daily Express*.

He seized upon this eagerly, fearful that he would find it full of the mysterious disappearance of Mr. Burleigh, Lord Barralonga, Mr. Rupert Catskill, Mr. Hunker, Father Amerton and Lady Stella, not to mention the lesser lights. . . . Gradually as he turned it over his fears vanished. There was not a word about any of them!

"But surely," he protested to himself, now clinging to his idea, "their friends must have missed them!"

He read through the whole paper. Of one only did he find mention and that was the last name he would have expected to find—Mr. Freddy Mush. The Princess de Modena-Frascati (*née* Higgisbottom) Prize for English literature had been given away to nobody in particular by Mr. Graceful Gloss owing to "the unavoidable absence of Mr. Freddy Mush abroad."

The problem of why there had been no hue and cry for the others opened a vast field of worldly speculation to Mr. Barnstaple in which he wandered for a time. His mind went back to that bright red blossom lying among the cut stems of the grass in the mown field and to the hand that had seemed to take it. With that the door that had opened so marvellously between that strange and beautiful world and our own had closed again.

Wonder took possession of Mr. Barnstaple's mind. That dear world of honesty and health was beyond the utmost boundaries of our space, utterly inaccessible to him now for evermore; and yet, as he had been told, it was but one of countless universes that move together in time, that lie against one another, endlessly like the leaves of a book. And all of them are as nothing in the endless multitudes of systems and dimensions that surround them. "Could I but rotate my arm out of the limits set to it," one of the Utopians had said to him; "I could thrust it into a thousand universes." . . .

A waitress with his teapot recalled him to mundane things.

The meal served to him seemed tasteless and unclean. He drank the queer brew of the tea because he was thirsty but he ate scarcely a mouthful.

Presently he chanced to put his hand in his pocket and touched something soft. He drew out the petal he had torn from the red flower. It had lost its glowing red, and as he held it out in the stuffy air of the room it seemed to writhe as it shrivelled and blackened; its delicate scent gave place to a mawkish odour.

"Manifestly," he said. "I should have expected this."

He dropped the lump of decay on his plate, then picked it up again and thrust it into the soil in the pot of the aspidistra.

He took up the *Daily Express* again and turned
it over, trying to recover his sense of this world's
affairs.

§ 7

For a long time Mr. Barnstaple meditated over
the *Daily Express* in the tea-room at Colnebrook.
His thoughts went far so that presently the newspaper slipped to the ground unheeded. He roused
himself with a sigh and called for his bill. Paying, he became aware of a pocket-book still full of
pound notes. "This will be the cheapest holiday
I have ever had," he thought. "I've spent no money
at all." He inquired for the post-office, because
he had a telegram to send.

Two hours later he stopped outside the gate of
his little villa at Sydenham. He set it open—the
customary bit of stick with which he did this was
in its usual place—and steered the Yellow Peril
with the dexterity of use and went past the curved
flower-bed to the door of his shed. Mrs. Barnstaple appeared in the porch.

"Alfred! You're back at last?"

"Yes, I'm back. You got my telegram?"

"Ten minutes ago. Where have you been all this
time? It's more than a month."

"Oh! just drifting about and dreaming. I've had
a wonderful time."

"You ought to have written. You really ought to
have written. . . . You *did*, Alfred. . . ."

"I didn't bother. The doctor said I wasn't to

bother. I told you. Is there any tea going? Where are the boys?"

"The boys are out. Let me make you some fresh tea." She did so and came and sat down in the cane chair in front of him and the tea-table. "I'm glad to have you back. Though I could scold you. . . .

"You're looking wonderfully well," she said. "I've never seen your skin so clear and brown."

"I've been in good air all the time."

"Did you get to the Lakes?"

"Not quite. But it's been good air everywhere. Healthy air."

"You never got lost?"

"Never."

"I had ideas of you getting lost—losing your memory. Such things happen. You didn't?"

"My memory's as bright as a jewel."

"But where did you go?"

"I just wandered and dreamt. Lost in a day-dream. Often I didn't ask the name of the place where I was staying. I stayed in one place and then in another. I never asked their names. I left my mind passive. Quite passive. I've had a tremendous rest—from everything. I've hardly given a thought to politics or money or social questions— at least, the sort of thing *we* call social questions— or any of these worries, since I started. . . . Is that this week's *Liberal?*"

He took it, turned it over, and at last tossed it on to the sofa. "Poor old Peeve," he said. "Of course I must leave that paper. He's like wall-paper on a damp wall. Just blotches and rustles and fails to stick. . . . Gives me mental rheumatics."

Mrs. Barnstaple stared at him doubtfully. "But I always thought that the *Liberal* was such a safe job."

"I don't want a safe job now. I can do better. There's other work before me. . . . Don't you worry. I can take hold of things surely enough after this rest. . . . How are the boys?"

"I'm a little anxious about Frankie."

Mr. Barnstaple had picked up the *Times*. An odd advertisement in the Agony column had caught his eye. It ran: "Cecil. Your absence exciting remark. Would like to know what you wish us to tell people. Write fully Scotch address. Di. ill with worry. All instructions will be followed."

"I beg your pardon, my dear?" he said putting the paper aside.

"I was saying that he doesn't seem to be settling down to business. He doesn't like it. I wish you could have a good talk to him. He's fretting because he doesn't *know* enough. He says he wants to be a science student at the Polytechnic and go on learning things."

"Well, he can. Sensible boy! I didn't think he had it in him. I meant to have a talk to him. But this meets me half-way. Certainly he shall study science."

"But the boy has to earn a living."

"That will come. If he wants to study science he shall."

Mr. Barnstaple spoke in a tone that was altogether new to Mrs. Barnstaple, a tone of immediate, quiet,

and assured determination. It surprised her still
more that he should use this tone without seeming
to be aware that he had used it.

He bit his slice of bread-and-butter, and she could
see that something in the taste surprised and dis-
pleased him. He glanced doubtfully at the remnant of the slice in his hand. "Of course," he said.
"London butter. Three days' wear. Left about.
Funny how quickly one's taste alters."

He picked up the *Times* again and ran his eye
over its columns.

"This world is really very childish," he said.
"Very. I had forgotten. Imaginary Bolshevik
plots. Sinn Fein proclamations. The Prince. Po-
land. Obvious lies about the Chinese. Obvious
lies about Egypt. People pulling Wickham Steed's
leg. Sham-pious article about Trinity-Sunday. The
Hitchin murder. . . . H'm!—rather a nasty one.
. . . The Pomfort Rembrandt. . . . Insurance.
. . . Letter from indignant peer about Death
Duties. . . . Dreary Sport. Boating, Tennis,
Schoolboy cricket. Collapse of Harrow! As though
such things were of the slightest importance! . . .
How silly it is—all of it! It's like coming back to
the quarrels of servants and the chatter of children."

He found Mrs. Barnstaple regarding him intently.
"I haven't seen a paper from the day I started until
this morning," he explained.

He put down the paper and stood up. For some
minutes Mrs. Barnstaple had been doubting whether
she was not the victim of an absurd hallucination.
Now she realized that she was in the presence of the
most amazing fact she had ever observed.

"Yes," she said. "It is so. Don't move! Keep
like that. I know it sounds ridiculous, William, but
you have grown taller. It's not simply that your
stoop has gone. You have grown oh!—two or
three inches."

Mr. Barnstaple stared at her, and then held out
his arm. Certainly he was showing an unusual
length of wrist. He tried to judge whether his
trousers had also the same grown-out-of look.

Mrs. Barnstaple came up to him almost respect-
fully. She stood beside him and put her shoulder
against his arm. "Your shoulder used to be exactly
level with mine," she said. "See where we are
now!"

She looked up into his eyes. As though she was
very glad indeed to have him back with her.

But Mr. Barnstaple remained lost in thought.
"It must be the extreme freshness of the air. I have
been in some wonderful air. . . . Wonderful!
. . . But at my age! To have grown! And I
feel as though I'd grown, inside and out, mind and
body."

Mrs. Barnstaple presently began to put the tea-
things together for removal.

"You seem to have avoided the big towns."

"I did."

"And kept to the country roads and lanes."

"Practically. . . . It was all new country to
me. . . . Beautiful. . . . Wonderful. . . ."

His wife still watched him.

"You must take *me* there some day," she said.
"I can see that it has done you a world of good."